HIGH PRAISE FOR ANNA DESTEFANO!

"This new urban fantasy has an attention-grabbing plot and interesting characters that provide excitement and suspense. And the psychological tension provides a satisfying head trip.... The story line satisfies and leads to a cliff-hanger conclusion."

—*RT Book Reviews* on *Dark Legacy*

"*Dark Legacy* combines Gothic overtones, secret government technology, a psychic heroine, a brilliant and charming hero and a lightning-fast plot to create a sure winner."

—*New York Times* Bestselling Author
Lori Handeland

"Anna DeStefano's remarkable stories of the healing power of love touch the heart with hope. One of the genre's rising stars ..."

—Gayle Wilson, Two-time RITA
Award–winning Author

"DeStefano's chilling, mesmerizing tale draws readers through a horrifying mental nightmare and brings them safely, if not unscathed, to the other side. Fans of psychological suspense—especially the clinical kind—may find this especially fascinating."

—*Library Journal* on *Dark Legacy*

"*Dark Legacy* is a spine-tingling blend of dark suspense and a paranormal romance that explores the deep powers of the human mind and heart.... Anna DeStefano keeps the reader poised on the very edge until the last page as danger upon danger arises, as image upon image builds to the final confrontation and shocking revelation ..."

—Merrimon Book Reviews

Secret Legacy

ANNA DESTEFANO

Dorchester
Publishing

DORCHESTER PUBLISHING

May 2011

Published by

Dorchester Publishing Co., Inc.
200 Madison Avenue
New York, NY 10016

ISBN 13: 978-1-4285-1111-8
E-ISBN: 978-1-4285-0962-7

Visit us online at www.dorchesterpub.com.

To Leah and Michelle.
Your vision thrives in the dreams you nurture.

To Andrew and Jimmy.
Fantasy and imagination are only possible
because you remind me to play.

To Anna Adams,
for the memories that knowing you
has gifted back to me.

To Nina Bruhns and
the Low Country Romance Writers.
Secret Legacy was conceived in
the footprints I've left on your unforgettable shore.

To everyone who believes in
just a little more than we should.
Faith opens doors and worlds and futures,
promising a tomorrow to heal each yesterday.

Secret Legacy

Amanda,
Sweet Dreams,

Twins will be born to the line. And with them, great good to commence. Or great evil, should darkness descend. Through them, another will come, to spread light far and wide. Or to cast the ultimate shadow on a lost mankind.

—The Temple Legacy

Specto. Tego. Asservo.

—The Watcher's Creed

CHAPTER ONE

There was a magnificence to the ocean's embrace, violet blue perfection hinting at secrets below. Cool channels wrapped Sarah Temple in velvet, promising her redemption. Luring her deeper. Dream currents caressed as they charmed, beguiled, seduced her into believing that tonight her search would end.

She'd agreed not to come. She'd made them believe she couldn't. Dreaming alone was reckless. But what she had to do was too important, too dangerous, to let them follow. They would have stopped this to keep her safe.

But there was no "safe" for Sarah. There was only the truth, and setting it free. And freedom wouldn't come until she faced the insanity of her nightmares.

As she rushed through the welcoming sea, deeper than they'd ever let her go, acceptance wrapped around her. She drank it down, drowning the doubt that whispered through her dream. She wasn't crazy. She was terrified of her mind's darkness. But conquering the nightmare was the only way to stop the pain. And to make them believe her. To find the proof that would protect everyone. She wouldn't allow another innocent to suffer because she was too weak to face the truth.

Richard would be furious. He'd never fail her again, he'd said. He was determined to guide her through this. As if Sarah could trust him after what he'd done. As if there were another path for her besides this one.

Streaks of color pulled from every direction. Ribbons of red and pink bleeding into crimson. It was a beautiful display. Terrifying and tempting and drawing her closer to the soul-deep cry that needed her here.

Then the colors became a voice.

And the voice was calling to her.

"Help me . . ." it whispered.

Loneliness ripped at Sarah, dragging, shoving, pushing her toward the nightmare's hidden heart. It was a baby's cry, she realized. It was a whimper. A little girl's pain. It was the shriek of a woman full grown, betrayed by every indecent thing that had been done to her. Demanding that Sarah hear. That she keep swimming.

She'd gone too deep to breathe or see clearly. The colors had lost their vivid hues, abandoning her to a watery tomb.

"Help me . . ." she cried.

Then the water, too, was gone.

Sarah's head spun as she staggered down a twisting tunnel that echoed with taunting pleas that no one believed were real. There was nowhere to stop. No place to rest. The light she needed to guide her wasn't there. Nothing was revealed by the dream's next turn, or the next, except her growing fear that she would fail.

She looked back before she could stop herself. Her gaze lifted to the surface where Richard's raven had always waited, poised to protect her if she'd let him. There was no shadow there tonight anticipating her call. No warrior in the world beyond the dream, fighting to protect her. Sarah had made sure of it . . .

CHAPTER TWO

Colonel Richard Metting stood in the control center of the Watchers' underground bunker, studying a wall of monitors and hiding the fact that he could feel Sarah's sanity splintering. The cries that she heard in her nightmares were screaming through his mind now, too. Along with flashes of his dream symbol—a raven—circling above an angry sea.

She was dreaming.

Alone.

If her recklessness was discovered, the council of elders presiding over the Brotherhood would command that her legacy be neutralized. Richard's job would be to execute the order. She'd be exiled to an irreversible coma.

"We've observed only routine activity due to shift change," Mike Donovan reported from the surveillance team monitoring the Trinity Psychiatric Research Center. "Only vetted staff entering and exiting the building. There are no doctors or medical personnel on-site except those assigned to existing cases. Hourly sweeps detect no psychic activity, no dream projections."

In other words, the center continued to function as what it had always portrayed itself to be: a state-of-the-art asylum for those in need of long-term care. It had been Sarah's home for ten years, while she'd languished in a coma. It had become her prison when the covert government agency funding the place decided her and her twin's gifts would become the foundation for an unstoppable psychic weapon.

Richard's brotherhood of Watchers had shut down the center's Dream Weaver program. But Sarah's mind was still in crisis. Her dreams grew more out of control every day that she resisted his help. Now Watcher teams assigned to two other family lines whose legacies were Brotherhood priorities had detected psychic surveillance of their activities. Someone—presumably the center—had pinpointed their locations. The security of key Watcher activities had been compromised just a month after bringing the Temples under Brotherhood protection.

Another shriek from Sarah's nightmare seared through Richard's mind. He shielded the psychic energy from the others in the bunker. She shouldn't have been capable of projecting a dream. Sarah shouldn't have been able to independently connect with his or anyone else's consciousness.

"Awaiting orders," Donovan relayed.

Richard pressed a button on the device wrapped around his ear, accessing the transmission. "Continue surveillance."

He closed the link and unhooked the receiver. He tossed it aside and braced his hands on the edge of his workstation, forcing down Sarah's panic and pain so he could think.

He was the Temples' Watcher, but he also held a top command position within the Brotherhood. His job was to analyze, strategize, then carry out whatever action was best for all the gifted families the Watchers protected, and for the psychic realm at large. A single legacy was sometimes required to pay an unfair price in order to protect the whole. It was a brutal paradigm Richard had become intimately familiar with as a young boy, when his own legacy had been in play. A reality he'd had no difficulty guiding other lives through during the two decades he'd risen up the Brotherhood's chain of command. Then his mind had felt the first brush of Sarah's complex, vulnerable energy.

There'd been something special, powerful, there that he and the Watchers hadn't been ready to silence, no matter how risky preserving the Temple Legacy continued to be. But tonight's activities might force the council's hand, if the work of a man who'd been dead for over a month was still a threat through Sarah's mind.

"There's no evidence that Tad Ruebens has been replaced," Jeff Coleridge said, his thoughts in tune with Richard's. Richard's second-in-command had killed the center director who'd led the push to control the Temples' powers. "Nothing to suggest that Dream Weaver research is now focused on the child Sarah says she's hearing. This voice is merely another symptom of her psychosis. And now her mind may be bleeding key Brotherhood information to our enemy."

"Or the center could be continuing its dream work on her behind psychic shielding we haven't penetrated. The way they've been tracking other legacy families without our detection."

"You're wasting time and resources exploring Sarah's fantasies. We need to shut down the center's access to us through the twins' minds, or wherever else it's coming from."

The exposed Watcher teams had regrouped, relocated, and their psychic shielding had been reinforced, effectively masking their activities. The status of both surveillance ops had been escalated to "observe and protect." The legacies involved were once more off the grid. But Jeff was right. It was a short-term fix at best. The Brotherhood had to know how the families had been targeted in the first place.

"Our intel shows no evidence of continued dream testing at the center," Richard reasoned out loud. "No reason to believe they're still interested in the twins' ability to control others through shared dreaming."

"Zero whispers on the government side, too." Jeff scrolled through the latest report. "No elevated psychic activity at any known testing sites since we brought the twins within the bunker's shields. But Sarah's emotional stability is degrading to dangerous levels, while our security has become compromised."

"Ruebens's work damaged her mind far worse than her sister's."

"Damage you haven't been able to reverse, even after we ended the hold he and his wolf image had on her."

Richard braced himself so Jeff wouldn't sense the fear and confusion flooding his mind from Sarah. He reined in the impulse to run to her quarters. To somehow stop the agony his brotherhood was thrusting into her life.

His eyes narrowed.

He should have alerted his elders the moment he sensed her dreaming consciousness. Even without the threat of an intelligence leak, Sarah projecting a dream matrix beyond their control was a disturbing development. If the center was making a new play for her legacy, every minute Richard delayed notifying the council put everyone the Brotherhood protected at risk. But he couldn't give her up yet. He refused to accept that her mind was beyond his ability to save.

"Take the control center." He headed for the elevator bank built into the back wall.

He'd failed to protect Sarah from Dream Weaver, but he'd done everything he could for her since Ruebens's death, including working with the twins in his dream lab while maintaining the emotional distance Sarah had demanded. Distance that was no longer an option.

"Orders?" Jeff slipped on Richard's earpiece and took over reading the psychic activity reports streaming to them from teams across the globe. He shot Richard a questioning glance.

Like many of the Watchers who'd sworn to prevent control of powerful gifts like the Temples' from falling into the wrong hands, Jeff saw the twins as ongoing threats. The Brotherhood's near-disastrous resolution of Richard's mission to derail Dream Weaver, then Richard's insistence that Sarah and Madeline be brought to the command bunker, had created an unfriendly environment toward the women, even within their council of elders.

No one could know about Sarah's rogue dream until Richard brought her mind back under his control.

"Up the alert on center activity and the search for possible satellite testing locations," he said.

"And when there's still nothing to report?" Jeff asked.

Richard punched the button to take him deeper into

the bunker—to Sarah's sleeping quarters just off his dream lab. "Then I'm sending you out on the next sweep. No one's more motivated to prove me wrong about this legacy than you are, right?"

CHAPTER THREE

The dream shifted, sensing that Sarah was weakening. Water rushed back, dragging her through the tunnel that had become a maze of endless corridors. Each turn was the beginning. Never the end. Never the way forward.

There was no air to breathe. Her fear fed the sea's hold. There was no mind to steady hers in the darkening surge. There were only screams, growing louder but never leading her to the light. Until the cries were suddenly coming from Sarah herself. Until they'd always been hers.

Sarah covered her ears. She surrendered to the next turn, to the madness. She'd come for this, to let the dream take over. She might be lost here forever, but she wasn't stopping. Not until she reached the little girl calling to her with both beauty and exquisite pain.

"Trinity . . ." Sarah said into the sea. "Where are you?"

Her voice tumbled through murky water, joining with the never-ending cries and building until the sound was pushing, lifting, driving Sarah toward a door covered in the vibrant colors from before. They were melting into one another now, creating a mottled, grotesque stain the tint of dried blood.

The sea slammed her against the door's surface. Her nails

dug into its battered wood. Her heart thundered, straining for oxygen. Her lungs burned, refusing to expand.

"Open it," a child insisted. "Help me . . . See what we've become."

Sarah clawed at the latch's gnarled loops. There was light waiting on the other side, like morning's new promise sprinkling hope across a diamond-kissed shore. Trinity would be there. A magical child no one else could hear. A fantasy born from a promise of redemption. A dream that Sarah had come to make reality.

Except her mind had been trained for death, not dreams. Her fantasies bred deception, not promises fulfilled. Her nightmares had destroyed too much for her to be anyone's savior now.

What if the darkest part of her lurked just beyond her grasp—shadows waiting to use her for evil, instead of the light she needed to set free?

Screams swallowed more of the dream.

"Trinity . . ." Sarah begged.

The water, the cries, the impassible door . . . Her dream ocean had become a soulless, empty place waiting for her to fail. She fought the latch. She yanked and twisted and pulled until there was nothing left. Ribbons of blood swirled into the sea's eager embrace.

"This is where you belong," the ocean chanted, soothing her panic. "This is why you came alone. Let the light go. You don't want to hurt anymore."

But there was suddenly another energy fighting to be heard, infusing the frigid water with vitality and warmth. A raven flew above the sea. His strength and logic filtered into Sarah's mind, demanding that she resist the sea's embrace. That she release the water and the latch and the door and her failure to reach Trinity. He wanted her to come back—to him.

"Wake up," he projected from the other side of sleep.

His voice was every good thing that had once tempted Sarah. Then trusting him had been her greatest failure.

"Damn it, Temple," he said, "you're in v-tach. Break the dream link before your heart gives out."

His psychic strength battered at the mental shields she'd secretly strengthened. The hidden place inside her still connected to him yanked her through the tunnel, away from the truth she'd risked so much to reach, until she was struggling with the calmer currents near the surface.

"Help me . . ." Trinity begged from below.

"Wake up . . ." the raven called.

But his concern wasn't real, Sarah reminded herself. His job was to control her legacy. He didn't care about Trinity. He'd never cared about Sarah. Not enough.

She dove deeper, looking for the door again. There was no gentle seduction now. The ocean grabbed her with greedy claws. She welcomed the brutality, as long as it took her back to Trinity. The raven flew above the ocean's surface, tracking her descent. When she found the girl, he would see. He'd believe. He'd come back for the child even if Sarah couldn't save her. He'd have no choice. Trinity would be too important for the Brotherhood to leave behind.

"Release the dream." Hands gripped her shoulders in her sleeping quarters.

Fingers bit into her skin, shaking her. The powerful consciousness she'd once given her heart to layered storm sounds, wind and rain and lightning, over the roar of her sea-swept currents. Their familiar vision of a misty summer forest tempted Sarah. He knew exactly where she was weakest.

But she clung to her nightmare, free-falling with no end in sight. There was no more tunnel for her to run through. No maze leading to the truth.

"*Trinity,*" *Sarah called into the icy water.*

"*Come closer,*" *the ocean chanted.*

"*Help me,*" *a lonely child begged.*

"*Wake up,*" *demanded the voice that had saved Sarah from the darkness before, only to feed her to a monster that had destroyed her mind.* "*Release the dream,*" *he demanded.* "*Come back to me before it's too late.*"

CHAPTER FOUR

"Wake up!"

Richard braced his hands on each side of Sarah's body. He wasn't sure which he wanted to do more—crawl onto the bed and hold the woman whose mind was shredding itself or shake her senseless.

"Why did you wait so long to call me?"

His muscles clenched against the compulsion to force Sarah's mind back to her sleeping quarters. He'd have risked it if they'd been dream linked. But interfering in whatever was happening behind her flickering eyelids when he wasn't fully integrated into her dreaming reality would risk splitting her consciousness. He might permanently strand her identity in whatever vision controlled her mind.

His fingers wrapped around her delicate wrist to track her racing pulse.

He winced.

He'd become Dream Weaver's lead researcher to block the center's attempt to harness the twins' gifts. The center's goal: to develop a weapon that allowed psychics to embed undetected dream programming into an innocent's mind, then to control waking behavior by triggering daydreams the subject was powerless to stop. He'd coordinated years of psychic projection research for the Brotherhood before he'd been chosen for the mission. Now, thanks to his Dream Weaver study, the Watchers knew more than ever about how Maddie and Sarah's gifts worked. Knowledge that wouldn't do Sarah a damn bit of good if she kept self-destructing.

She refused to regress her consciousness back to the past, to the memories of when her gifts had first begun to unravel. She refused to work on healing what was broken inside her—the damage the center had preyed on. She insisted on pushing further into the dream instead, and her dreaming mind was destroying itself.

A REM state could turn lethal. If the mind lost control to a dream, the body's reaction to the stress could stop the heart. Blood pressure could escalate beyond the circulatory system's tolerance. Injuries inside a dream's matrix wouldn't correspond to identical damage in the real world, but the brain could literally attack itself if a vision was intense enough, causing bleeds and scarring visible only through ultrasounds and scans.

"Sarah . . ." he whispered. "Let me in. Let me see what's going on."

Her arm twitched. Her mind flashed the image of his raven soaring above a seething ocean. He caught a glimpse of the murky depths Sarah was sinking to while the nightmare hounded her, wanting to subdue, control, consume her mind. He sensed nothing connected with the Brotherhood's security breach. Instead, he could feel a malevolent impulse within the dream itself, driving Sarah's growing obsession to find a child she insisted was six years old. A little girl she called Trinity.

Sarah was drowning in her nightmare, and help from him or any Watcher was the last thing she wanted. Which left Richard only one option to reach her besides alerting his elders. He fumbled with the communications unit installed beside the bed. The line opened, intercom on. He speed-dialed a two-digit number. The connection rattled to life.

"What . . . Sarah?" a female voice stuttered, ragged with sleep. "It's one in the morning. Why—"

"Get down to your sister's quarters." Richard felt Sarah's lungs starving for oxygen, straining to inhale, failing. "Your sister's dreaming."

He disconnected. Madeline had been unaware of her sister's crisis. Sarah was blocking wherever her mind had gone from her twin, too.

The council's orders had been clear. Sarah either gained control of her gifts, or the danger posed by the twins' ability to project emotion and behavior into others' reality would be silenced. The Brotherhood's role in monitoring the line between a psychic's potential benefit to society and the harm that could be caused had evolved into a policing presence over the last decade. The time when their activities were limited to surveillance and guidance was fast disappearing. Entities like the center were maneuvering the Watchers into a war, and the Temples' legacy was a prime target.

"What are you doing?" Richard curled his fingers around Sarah's. It was an inappropriate gesture between an objective Watcher and his principal, but he couldn't let go. "Let someone help you before it's too late."

A child's desperate pleas echoed through their minds.

"Move!" A rush of dark hair, a wave of fury, announced

Madeline's presence. She shoved herself between Richard and her twin. "What have you done to her?"

"The dream reached me all the way in the control room." Richard staggered from losing his physical connection with Sarah. He fought to maintain their psychic link. "We have to get her mind under control, or I'll need to alert the Brotherhood."

Madeline took the hand he'd dropped. He sensed her attempting to send her mind into her sister's. When the twins were linked in a projection, Madeline's control balanced Sarah's more impulsive gifts.

"She won't let me in." Madeline glared over her shoulder. "What is she doing dreaming outside the lab?"

Richard had no answers. Sarah's daily drug regimen shouldn't have allowed a dream state without his intervention. And without his monitors and specialized equipment, he had no way to buffer Sarah's mind from the dream matrix's pull.

"Tell me what you hear," he demanded. "The screams from her ocean sequence. I felt them—"

"Luring her to her death . . ." Madeline's and Sarah's coloring was identical. Their toned bodies. The classic curves of their beautiful faces. It was almost as if Sarah were standing before him, dressed in rumpled pajamas, strong and safe and spitting mad.

Madeline's forehead wrinkled.

He realized he was staring.

She turned back to Sarah.

"I . . . I think the cries are the same," she said. During the twins' dream work, Madeline had reported hearing faint sounds that could have come from Sarah's phantom child. "A little girl needing help. But . . . something else is moving through the ocean, trapping Sarah in the nightmare. Or maybe she doesn't want to let the water go this time. I don't know . . ."

Richard rounded the bed to Sarah's other side. "In the last twenty-four hours, we've had two untraceable intelligence breaches. Your sister's mind is being seen as the most likely source of a leak to the center, even before the council hears that her dreams have broken from our control."

"And she's guilty until proven innocent, because of how badly your *brotherhood* mishandled protecting us from Tad Ruebens?"

"Unfortunately, yes."

Sarah's head jerked. Her eyes darted side to side behind their closed lids. Her breathing grew choppier.

Her physical responses to dream stimuli should have been suppressed by her REM rhythms. But whatever was happening in the nightmare was breaking through. Richard took her wrist in his fingers, needing to feel her pulse. Needing her touch again, period. Her heart was beating too faintly. Too fast. It wouldn't absorb much more abuse. Her head jerked again.

Maddie cupped Sarah's face between her hands, deepening their connection. She gasped and staggered backward. Sarah shuddered.

"Stop . . ." Madeline pressed her fists to her own temples. "Make the screaming stop. I can't breathe. Sarah . . . she can't breathe."

"Take her hand again." Richard forced his own lungs to expand.

He'd seen a stronger flash of Sarah's nightmare, felt her more clearly, when he and Madeline were both touching her. Breathing deeply, he narrowed his focus to Madeline's terrified gaze and downshifted to the mission tactics that had saved his life countless times since he'd left behind the reckless teenager he'd once been and became a Watcher.

Nothing existed except completing the mission before him. His breath came in on the thought. He exhaled as the next took hold. There was no moment but now. *Inhale.* No feelings except determination. *Exhale.* Confidence. Acceptance. *Inhale.* No resistance. No regret.

"We have to get into the dream together." He kept his voice calm, his mind and his body functioning in perfect harmony now. "Don't let her pain distract you. Don't let the nightmare control you. Separate what's real from what isn't, just like in the lab. We have to help Sarah regain control of her mind. To do that we have to understand the parameters of the matrix she's lost in."

Madeline shook her head.

Distrust glazed her eyes.

Shock.

"It's phantom pain," he reminded her. "You're feeling Sarah's confusion, nothing more. Take her hand. Let your energy mingle with hers. She's hunting for Trinity. Focus on her search. Merge your emotions with the dream. Emotions are the link that brought you back to your twin after ten years apart. Give us something to work with now. Be Sarah's connection to this reality and accept my help the way she can't. I promise, I'll bring you both out of this."

Madeline swallowed.

She blinked.

Hatred flared in a gaze that was identical to Sarah's,

except Madeline's eyes were a mossy green to her twin's deep gray.

She returned to the edge of the bed.

"Damage my sister further—" Her fingers curled around Sarah's. She jerked as their minds connected, firing fresh dream images to Richard. "Let one more piece of her be lost to the mess you've made of our legacy, and you'll never dream again without wondering when I'll show up to make you pay."

He nodded, accepting both Madeline's terms and her ability to follow through on her threat.

Sarah's ability to read and affect others' psychic energy was escalating. The backlash of not being able to control her powers was damaging her untrained psyche. While Madeline's intuitive skills at redirecting emotions and conflict had eased Sarah's confusion, she had also grown to be as offensively powerful as her sister, when properly motivated.

Through her and Sarah's link, he could feel new warmth flowing into Sarah's mind. Powerful healing. Clear purpose. Unconditional love. The admirable traits Madeline had somehow retained, despite the darkness the center had inflicted on their lives.

"Sarah?" Madeline merged more fully with her sister's dreaming mind. "Where are you?"

"Focus first on where she's been."

It was a familiar pattern. Madeline linked with Sarah while Richard listened and directed and tried to draw meaning from the symbols and emotional patterns the sisters experienced within the ocean Sarah's mind kept returning to.

"She's resisting leaving the dream," he said. "She's

swimming closer to danger. We have to reach her before I call more Watchers down here. Where was she when her survival instinct kicked in, and she reached out to me?"

"There was darker water . . ." Madeline's gaze grew vague, but her eyes never closed. Never blinked. Then they glittered with new awareness and the strength of the twins' minds when they were fully joined. "She was terrified of the ocean's heart. Afraid she'd fail, that she'd never get the truth out. Then you were there, and she won't leave now until she proves it to you . . ."

"Proves what?"

"Trinity . . ."

The thought, in Sarah's voice, whispered through their minds. The child's cries grew even louder. Madeline's expression clouded with fear as she absorbed Sarah's desperation to save a terrified little girl, a haunting echo of Sarah's Dream Weaver programming that Richard had yet to clear.

"There were beautiful colors waiting for her in the water," Madeline said. "They led her to . . . a door that hurt her. She was bleeding when she let go. But she can't . . . I can't . . ."

The cool green of Madeline's irises darkened, deepening to her twin's smoky gray.

"I can't leave her there," Sarah's voice said through her sister. *"You have to see that she's real. You can't let them destroy her, too."*

The skin on Richard's arms prickled as Madeline—Sarah—begged for his help.

Jarred Keith stumbled into the room, his eyes heavy

with sleep. But his body and his mind were alert and focused.

"Can't let who destroy whom?" The former psychiatrist pulled Madeline into his arms, careful not to disturb her connection with Sarah.

He caressed Madeline's face with steady fingers. He stared into her eyes, silent communication rippling the air between them.

"The . . ." Madeline's voice returned to its own timbre. Tears streamed down her face. She turned toward Richard. "There's a voice calling her from the deeper water, telling her to give up. The center's already put her through so much. What if they're taking her mind back?"

Madeline leaned into Jarred. Richard didn't push for details. Jarred would balance Madeline's mind and, through Madeline, the twins' link. Richard forced himself to stay the hell out of the way. He checked his watch.

He had to call in a Watcher team.

Sarah's mind was too powerful to leave spiraling.

"I'm here," Jarred said to Sarah's twin. His voice was firm. Confident. Demanding, without imposing itself, the way Richard had taught him to focus his own newly discovered psychic talent when Madeline needed help. "I'm here, sweetheart. You're not alone."

"From now on, we're not in this alone . . ." Madeline's mind whispered.

The promise she'd made Sarah the night they'd defeated Ruebens reached out to both Richard and Jarred, absorbing them into her deepening connection with her sister. She squeezed Sarah's hand.

"We'll find Trinity together," she promised her twin.

"Let me help you. Show me what's happened so I can look for her, too."

Sarah's consciousness shifted closer . . .

Through Madeline's unshielded mind, Richard saw a rush of color. A swirl of dark confusion. The ocean's jumbled demands were luring Sarah to a truth that was too deeply hidden, maybe not even real at all. And she was too far in to turn back, to survive alone, or to heed the call of a raven circling so high above the water's surface that only his shadow was visible . . .

"Oh, God." Madeline stared up at Jarred. "I can feel her. She's dying."

"Sarah?" Jarred's attention shifted to Richard, then back to the woman shaking in his arms.

"No. Trinity. Sarah thinks she can feel Trinity dying in the ocean, but she can't reach her."

Madeline collapsed against Jarred. Her eyes returned to the color of Sarah's deepest gray. She stared at Richard.

"You have to believe me . . ." she said in Sarah's voice. *"None of you want to believe me. Your precious council doesn't want her to be found, any more than you want me or Maddie to grow strong enough to live beyond your control. But they can't let the center have Trinity. Once they know she's real, they'll help me. The council will have to take her away from the center. You'll see . . . I'm not leaving until you—"*

"Let go." Richard grabbed Sarah's shoulders, the last of his objectivity gone. "Release the dream and the cries for help and whatever you thought you'd accomplish without us. Let your sister bring you back to the surface. I can hear Trinity now. So can Madeline. Once we know what we're dealing with, we'll find a way to help her."

It was a promise he had no business making. Worse, it was one Sarah wouldn't believe. He'd hidden too much from her for too long for her to believe anything he said.

"It's . . ." Madeline's eyes rolled back. Her eyelids closed. "The screaming . . . It's killing her."

"I need her and Sarah back here," Richard said to Jarred, "before they give the council even more reason to silence their minds."

Jarred's flat stare promised retribution. He looked seconds away from dragging the woman he loved from Sarah's side. But he covered Madeline's hands with his, then wrapped her fingers tighter around her twin's. Madeline shivered as his consciousness centered her. Strengthened her. From the start, Jarred's devotion had helped Madeline believe, whenever it was too painful, too impossible, for her to keep going on her own.

Sarah's agitation eased with her sister's. Her tremors stopped, but her system was still in distress, her pulse racing, her blood pressure no doubt off the charts.

"I've about had enough of this," Jarred bit out.

He knew firsthand the price the Temples had paid for Richard's tactical victory over the center: Madeline and Sarah's nonexistent freedom, their fragile sanity, their mother's death, now this.

Richard ignored the other man's frustration and reined in his own fear. He was Sarah's Watcher. He had to stay focused on tactics. On his mission. Letting emotion distract him would damage this family even more than he already had. He covered Jarred's and Madeline's hands with his, pressing them against Sarah's body.

"Find her." He closed his eyes and sent his mind

deeper, praying his presence could guide Madeline's without driving Sarah's even further away. "Don't let your sister search any deeper for the child. Tell her we need her back here, so we can convince the elders to engage the Brotherhood. Tell her that if she doesn't come back, there's no hope of saving Trinity or your legacy."

CHAPTER FIVE

Fury burned through Maddie as her mind and Metting's merged. Sarah was in danger. Again. And Maddie needed her sister's raven to help them. Again.

She didn't trust the man or anyone in his brotherhood. But she couldn't stop Sarah's destructive obsession with Trinity alone, and Metting was light-years ahead in understanding how her and Sarah's minds had been manipulated using dream science and psychic programming.

Metting's head was lowered over where his hand covered hers and Jarred's and Sarah's. The psychic energy surrounding him was as cool and nonthreatening as ever. Then he looked up, and the desperation shimmering in the dark black of his irises had deepened with the predatory intent of a bird of prey protecting his lair.

A knot of foreboding grew in Madeline's chest.

This wasn't just about Metting covering his ass with the elders. Or the Brotherhood's lead Watcher tracing a child's haunting cries back to whoever or whatever was damaging Sarah's control. Metting may have used Sarah to score a Brotherhood win over Dream Weaver, but there was more firing behind his warrior-scientist pose than honor and code and duty to his cause. Too much more. And wading through another round of emotional muck with this man was the last thing Sarah could handle.

"You don't have to do this," Jarred's mind said. The degree of his hostility toward Metting came in second only to Maddie's. *"You don't have to keep trusting him while he lets shit like this happen."*

"There's no one else in the godforsaken place even pretending to be on our side," Maddie projected back, shielding their conversation from Metting.

Sarah hadn't been able to tolerate Richard's thoughts in her mind while she deprogrammed the behavioral and psychic triggers left from Ruebens's work. Maddie had taken Richard's place, trying to break down her twin's ocean dream. But Richard was the expert with the equipment and medication, and it was his experience that kept pulling them back from the brink every time Sarah's mind began to fray.

"We're losing her to something we don't understand, and I'm not strong enough to help her without him."

Jarred's fingers made soothing sweeps over Maddie's hand. In the place in their linked minds where they'd forged an intimacy she hadn't believed possible for her, his presence was as solid as ever.

"Whatever you have to do," he said. *"I'll be right beside you."*

And he would be. If Maddie fought. If she ran. If she fell apart again under the responsibility of protecting her twin and the dark legacy their psychic abilities had become. Jarred would never leave her. Never judge her. He'd die for her, and she for him. It was an unshakable union she suspected Sarah had once wanted to build with Metting—before he'd betrayed her.

"*Let's go get your sister,*" Jarred said. "*I'll anchor you here. I'll make sure Metting brings you both back. I won't let another dream rip you away from me.*"

Maddie let her mind linger for a moment longer, wanting Jarred to feel her need to stay. Then she looked down at Sarah's sleeping form. She closed her eyes, reached deeper into the connection they'd rebuilt. She opened her thoughts more fully to Metting's chilling determination, wrapped her consciousness in it, and sent her mind back into Sarah's nightmare ocean . . .

She could feel her twin identifying with the nightmare's darkness. She could sense Sarah's willingness to be absorbed in it, even to die in it, for the sake of a mystery child she insisted was in danger. Maddie could feel her sister's mind slipping further away. And a part of her wanted to disappear into the dream's darkness with Sarah. To fall away from the reality of how little chance their legacy had to be the healing, positive force Maddie had fought to make of her life.

Embraced by the shifting currents of Sarah's mind, it was easy to imagine a life of aimless drifting. They could both be free of the responsibility and the disappointment and fear and failure.

"*Careful, sweetheart.*" Jarred drew closer, both physically and mentally. His arms and mind wrapped tighter around Maddie, enveloping her with the love she could never leave behind. "*You're not going anywhere.*"

His presence centered her, enabling her to safely connect with more of Sarah's emotions.

"You're feeling the pull that's bound Sarah to wherever

her mind has gone," Richard said. "Follow it, but stay focused on your connection to Jarred outside the dream. Join with Sarah's mind, but be separate. Retain control of your own identity, just like our work in the lab."

"You'd better know what you're doing," Maddie said to the shadow image of a menacing bird flickering beyond the dream ocean's surface. *"Sarah doesn't trust herself or me or, God knows, you. She just might prefer staying in this awful place to believing in anyone's promises again."*

CHAPTER SIX

"Sarah?" the voices called. *Minds she couldn't belong to and still follow Trinity. Voices insisting that she* "Come back to us . . ."

Sarah could feel her twin's desperation. *Maddie's anger for how the Watchers had manipulated their lives until this madness was all they had left. Jarred's energy was there, too. Calming. Soothing. Centering. Richard was closer than before. Stronger than all of them. Determined to keep Sarah's mind under control.*

They were all refusing to—

"Let me go!" *She drifted deeper into the ocean.*

"Never . . ." *their combined thoughts pushed back.*

"I'm not leaving until I find her," *she insisted.*

But the sea swirling around Sarah had grown more frigid. And the numbness made searching harder. It had been so long since she'd felt warm.

"The light is here," *she reminded herself.* "It's on the other side of the door. I'm not quitting until—"

"Whose light?" *Maddie asked.* "The ocean's? The water's trying to destroy you. Don't trust it."

Sarah collapsed onto what felt like rocks covered in broken glass. The sea's floor. There was no door in sight. There was nowhere left to look. She'd been waiting for weeks for this moment. She'd lied to everyone, convinced she could find Trinity here on her own. Now she'd failed.

"I was right there," she said. "But I couldn't . . ."

"I saw the door." Maddie's face became a reflection in the murky water. "We'll get you back to the door, Sarah. We'll find whatever is on the other side."

"You know what's there." The dream choked Sarah with cries that might as well be silence, because she couldn't reach them. "You've always known. But all you care about is keeping us safe. Just like Mom. We'll never be safe, not while the center has Trinity."

"We'll stop them together." Richard's mind moved closer. "You'll help us figure out the dream's purpose. You'll tell us everything we need to know about Trinity. Then we'll—"

"I won't leave her."

"Leave who?" her twin asked. "Look around you, Sarah. You're alone. No one else is here."

"She never stops crying." Sarah pressed her fists to her ears. She drank down more of the sea, letting it wash away the horrible sound.

"I can hear her now." There were tears in Maddie's voice. "Come back. You don't have to prove anything anymore, but we need your help. We won't find her door again without your memories."

Sarah watched her sister's reflection grow more solid within the deadly vision. Brighter colors returned with Maddie, a rainbow of amethyst splendor trailing toward the surface, where a raven circled. But the hues were already fading.

"Go away," Sarah yelled. "You'll die here."

"If you stay, I stay." Maddie grabbed her arm. Her nose began to bleed. The sea washed the stain clear, but more blood followed.

Maddie pulled, her strength overwhelming Sarah's resistance. She fought the rising current and somehow got them both moving. Terrified for her sister and the beating Maddie's mind was taking, Sarah stopped fighting as they neared shallower water, where it should be easier to breathe. Only it wasn't. Maddie's image flickered. Faded out, then back in.

"Help me . . ." *cried a defenseless child Sarah was certain was being tested and programmed by center scientists.*

Maddie made a weak attempt to kick through to the surface, only to sink back to Sarah. Both of them drifted lower.

"Let me go," *Sarah begged.* "You're dying."

"When are you going to get it?" *Maddie's image held tight to Sarah's hand.* "Hide from me, and I'll find you. Try to get yourself killed following some guilty compulsion to make up for your past, and I'll drag your ass back to life. We're sisters, Sarah. You're not staying here alone. We're in this together."

"Break the link," *Jarred demanded, his presence stronger near the surface.*

"We're losing them both," *Richard said. His raven's shadow circled closer to the water. His mind beat away at the dream's reality.*

Sarah grabbed her twin as Maddie collapsed. She glared up at her raven's reflection. She tried to open her eyes in her sleeping quarters in the Brotherhood's bunker. To fight her way back. But she was too weak. The water growled in excitement—a predatory animal circling its prey.

"Help me," *Sarah begged Richard's dream image, terrified of inviting him even deeper into her thoughts, but even more afraid now for her twin and Trinity. Too many people had already suffered because Sarah couldn't control the power she'd never wanted.* "Please, don't let them die, too."

The raven's reflection circled higher. For a second, she was certain he'd abandon them. Then his image dove beneath the dream's surface, finally free to unleash the unworldly psychic power that had secured his position leading the Brotherhood in its mission to tame Sarah's legacy.

He hurtled toward Maddie and Sarah, slicing through the water. He grabbed them in his talons, capturing but not hurting. Dry, warm wings surrounded them, creating a pocket of life-giving oxygen. Sarah felt her sister's heart falter, weakened from battling Sarah's sleeping mind for too long. Her own body began to convulse.

With a menacing shriek, the raven soared toward the surface.

"I've got you," he said.

It felt like a new dream, having his voice back in her mind, even though she was certain trusting him again would destroy her.

"You have to wake up from here," he said. "Madeline's unconscious. Your link to her is stronger than mine. Bring your sister back. Wake up, so you can bring her over."

"Promise you'll protect Maddie when the Watchers find out what I've done."

Sarah longed to close her eyes and let the ocean take her again. To quit, just as Maddie had said, so she didn't have to face the reality of the commitment she'd just asked Richard to make. But that would mean sacrificing her sister and Trinity, and protecting her family was all Sarah had left.

"Promise," she said, "that you'll bring us back to find Trinity."

"You have my word." Richard's raven panted as he fought the ocean's pull. "Break your links with the dream, and we'll figure out the next step together."

But she could no longer feel the safety of his strong wings wrapped around her, or the comfort of Maddie's heart beating close by. Trinity's cries were softer, too. Even farther away. It was becoming harder to hear anything at all, even her raven's voice in her mind.

"Let go," the ocean chanted. "This is where you belong."

"Stay with me, Sarah," Richard called.

Her dreaming reality dissolved to darkness . . .

CHAPTER SEVEN

"Sarah!" Richard shouted inside the dream.

She was unconscious. Without her awareness feeding their link, sustaining his identity, the ocean vision was rapidly draining his psychic reserves. The matrix began to waver. He closed his raven's wings even tighter around the twins.

The second she'd welcomed him into her nightmare, he'd felt another mind scanning his from somewhere in the sea. Something beyond Sarah's awareness, most likely whoever was projecting the nightmare to her from the center. A consciousness he'd have to identify, for him to have any shot at protecting both Sarah and his brotherhood.

He blinked her sleeping quarters into focus. Her head lolled beneath his chin, her body convulsing. Madeline still clung to her sister's hand, but she'd collapsed, unconscious, against Jarred. The doctor was wiping at the blood trickling from her nose.

"What the hell is going on?" Jarred demanded. "Why are they still dreaming?"

"Maddie's too weak to disengage. They're both unconscious inside the dream."

"Then pull them out."

"I can't risk it."

Richard told himself to reach for the comm unit beside the bed, but his arms wouldn't obey. He couldn't make himself let Sarah go.

"I need at least one of them lucid," he said. "The nightmare's already disintegrating. If I force a break now, both twins' minds could be lost."

"Maddie's brought Sarah back before."

"The nightmare's in control this time."

Richard stared at Sarah's slack features. She was dying in his arms.

"Disengage from the dream, Alpha," he ordered. *Alpha* had been her clinical designation at the center. She hated the name. She'd be furious with him for using it now. He was banking on it.

"Jarred." He could barely force the words out. "Call for backup. I won't be able to hold on to their minds much longer."

There was an angry pause.

"Metting needs a dream-recovery team in Sarah Temple's quarters," Jarred finally shouted into the comm unit to an operator who wouldn't miss the fear in the psychiatrist's voice.

Richard felt Sarah's chest above the collar of her cotton nightgown. Delicate skin. Racing pulse. Too-weak heartbeat. He sent his consciousness deeper into her sleeping mind. There was nothing now where her thoughts had been.

"Stay with me, damn it," he projected.

The sisters were so close to the surface, lying limp and unresponsive, encircled by his raven's wings. He'd only need a flicker of consciousness, one of them awake and willing, to bring them both back.

"Do something to get through to Madeline," he growled to Jarred, "before my team arrives and the situation is removed from my control."

"Maddie?" Jarred shook Madeline. "Sarah's still in danger. She's not free of the ocean. Save your sister, sweetheart. Open your eyes in the dream. Wake up!"

There was a feminine moan, followed by a flash of lavender light streaming through the dream link—Madeline's consciousness reengaging. Her mind, weak but determined, wrapped around Richard's. In the dream's ocean, her image and the raven's faltered, then held. She stirred and reached for her sister's hand. In Sarah's quarters, Madeline's fingers tightened around her twin's.

"Sarah . . ." her mind called. "We're almost there. Let the dream go. Please . . . You have to—"

A streak of anger shot through their minds, a flash of furious gray from beyond the ocean's pull. A second later, the doors to Sarah's quarters slid open. Jeff Coleridge and a Watcher team filled the tiny room, prepared to neutralize whatever new threat the Temple Legacy posed to the Brotherhood.

"Step aside," Jeff demanded, his presence displacing the last of the healing energy Madeline had helped Richard create.

Richard fought to stay grounded to the scene in Sarah's quarters. His vision blurred as he sustained his presence in the nightmare, too. Jarred was blocking Jeff from advancing on Madeline.

"Don't touch her," Jarred said. "They're—"

"They're dreaming beyond Metting's control, or you

wouldn't have called us." Jeff grabbed Madeline's arm. He tried to pull her away.

Madeline shuddered, Jeff's aggressive energy swamping her hold on the dream. Richard sensed her mind surfacing.

"Don't . . ." Her eyelids fluttered but didn't open. Her identity straddled reality and the nightmare. Her body began to tremble. "Sarah?" she called out.

"You're hurting her." Jarred grasped a fistful of Jeff's black shirt. "Let her go. Give her and Metting a chance to—"

"Step back." Jeff's voice was cool steel.

The recovery team stood waiting with a portable defibrillator and a crash cart that held the pharmaceuticals Richard had designed to enhance the dreaming mind's reintegration into its body. Each Watcher's psychic talent would prove invaluable, too, as the dream's damage to the twins' minds was triaged and treated.

"The less you resist," Jeff warned, "the easier ending this will go for everyone."

"Ending it how?" Jarred demanded.

"However it takes."

"Lieutenant . . ." Richard warned. He couldn't finish the sentence. He could feel Madeline's distress beginning to stir Sarah's mind. He only needed a few more seconds. One more push to wake Sarah up.

He and Jeff shared a tension-filled stare. Richard nodded his consent to his second's unspoken plan. Jeff's methods wouldn't win him points with Jarred, but his instincts were as on the mark as ever.

He pulled Madeline away from the psychiatrist. The twins' hands and minds lost contact.

"Sarah!" Madeline screamed. She collapsed to the floor.

"Let her go." Jarred fought his way to her side. "You're—"

"Hurting her," said the woman in Richard's arms. Sarah's consciousness surged back to her quarters. But her eyes didn't open. The nightmare still owned too much of her. "Let go of my sister," she demanded.

"That's it," Richard whispered into her ear, hating the pain and the mess and the hopelessness he couldn't seem to banish from her life. "Wake up and kick the crap out of all of us for hurting Madeline."

In the dream, his raven's wings folded her closer.

"Battle your way back, Sarah," his mind demanded. *"Fight me. Hate me forever, but come back. Trust me just one more time . . ."*

He heard himself begging and accepted what it meant. Right or wrong, the emotional distance he'd forced between them was gone, and there was no going back. Not for him. Not after this.

"She's coding," someone reported as his men worked over Madeline.

"Damn it, Maddie," Jarred demanded, "don't do this."

The zap of the defibrillator sizzled through Sarah and Madeline's link into Richard.

"Maddie!" Sarah's image cried in the dream.

Her eyes jerked open in her quarters.

Her mind jolted fully back to reality.

"Maddie?" She strained against Richard's hold.

"Let them work with her." Richard held Sarah down while he clung to the shadow of her mind that was still joined with his. "Madeline was unprotected in your dream. No shields in place. No recovery plan. And I'm in no shape to help her. Let my men stabilize her."

Richard's ability to move between psychic states was far stronger than the twins', and he was barely staying on his feet without the aid of the metabolic stabilizers he'd developed to lessen a dream link's toll on a dreamer's body.

He wouldn't let Sarah roll off the table to get to her twin. "Madeline's system is in crisis," he said. "My people know the transition protocol. They'll—"

"They'll kill her . . ." Sarah blinked back tears. Then her gaze hardened. Madness transformed her expression. "Just like Tad Ruebens wants them to."

"Ruebens is dead."

"Just like *you* want them to!"

"I want to—"

"All you want is to get rid of us. You think I don't know, that I can't hear what your men are thinking? They want to let us go. To shut our minds down. Your elders want to. I won't let you. You can't send me back to the darkness, where I can't help Trinity."

She dragged Richard to her bunk with startling strength and flipped him, pinning him to the mattress, straddling his waist, her knee pressed to his groin. She should have been too weak to move. The nightmare's psychic backlash should have been incapacitating her the way it had Madeline. But Sarah's fingers bit into the pressure points on either side of Richard's throat exactly the way he'd taught her, first in dream sequences while her coma had imprisoned her, then in the center's gymnasiums.

From the start, Sarah had been a prodigy, mastering every physical challenge he placed before her. She was a natural at the combat skills that Watchers honed to stay mission ready. And she was at the moment in a killing rage, her mania focused on eliminating what she saw as her greatest threat—him.

"Release, Alpha," he rasped.

"Don't call me that." Her grip tightened.

Lack of oxygen would lead to blackout in under a minute. Ignoring the gray crowding his vision, Richard threaded his fingers through the dark hair cascading down Sarah's neck. He pushed up until their faces were close, their gazes locked.

"Do this—"

His world narrowed until it was just her. Just them. Just as it had been at the very beginning, when recognition had fired inside him with the first brush of her mind.

"—and Trinity will be lost. Madeline, too, because the Brotherhood will be done risking the security of our other legacies to foster yours. Kill me, and my men will take you out. Whatever we could learn from your ocean dream will be lost along with you. No one will be there to protect the child you've risked all this to reach."

"Get your hands off him." Jeff stood at the foot of the bed, leaving the recovery team and Jarred to their frantic work on Madeline. His sidearm was poised for a kill shot.

Sarah's hand clamped tighter around Richard's trachea.

Richard ran his fingers through her hair. He wouldn't stop her. He wouldn't hurt her again.

"Let her go, Richard," Jeff instructed. "She's clearly

still being manipulated by the center. She's beyond even your mind's reach."

Richard ignored him.

"I'll protect you and your legacy, no matter what it takes," his mind whispered through his link to Sarah. *"Believe that. Stop being a threat the Brotherhood has to silence. Be the warrior your sister and Trinity need."*

"Drop your hands, Ms. Temple." Jeff's determination to stop her legacy flooded their minds. "Get your claws off Colonel Metting's throat and out of his fucking mind, or I'll drop you. Last warning."

Sarah flinched.

Trembled.

Her hate-filled gaze held Richard's, then dimmed to a resigned emptiness that devastated him. Her hands slid from his neck. Her rage faded from their connection. As one, they fell to her bunk. Richard cradled her to his body, too weak to do more as she began to seize.

"Get the recovery meds over here," he ordered over the shock of feeling her mind slipping away.

Chapter Eight

"We're getting closer with every projection," the raspy voice said over the scrambled connection. "Her mind is becoming even more unstable. That's worth whatever risks today's episode presented."

"Not if the Temples self-destruct before you get what you want," he said.

"They won't. Keep reporting on schedule, and we'll take care of the rest from our end."

"Metting's been absorbed into the dream," he said. "The Brotherhood's on alert because of the leaks." Developments that he had no doubt were connected.

"Degrading Alpha's condition to allow the dream to take control is the only matter you need be concerned with," the voice said. "Dr. Metting's interference is a variable we've already anticipated. His involvement tonight preserved Alpha for the next simulation. One more ocean projection will be all we need. Your job is to make sure that next dream happens, and then give us the details to control it."

"The elders know she's capable of projection beyond Metting's control. You won't get another chance."

"Of course we will," the voice insisted. "The dream

patterns are in place. Her psychic strength is growing. Metting will champion her legacy. The council will be greedy enough to want more power at their command. Alpha is primed to reach for Trinity without Madeline to stabilize her. Once she does, the direction of the Temple Legacy will return to the center for good."

"Control will return to the child, you mean."

A circumstance he couldn't allow to happen. Nor could he permit the Temples' abilities to grow any further beyond Watcher safeguards.

"The child's actions are under our guidance," the voice assured him. "Her devotion to the work she's begun is unshakable. Her motivation is strong, if a bit immature. She'll handle Alpha's impending psychic break as skillfully as she's caused it. Trinity will be ready to take advantage when Sarah herself initiates their next dream contact."

"'The hand that rocks the cradle is the hand that rules the world . . . ,'" he quoted.

He swallowed his disgust at his own part in using a six-year-old girl to wage psychic battle.

But Metting had lost his perspective. He'd left the Brotherhood irreparably vulnerable. If that meant staging a center victory in order to draw the Brotherhood into a battle they'd already have won if Metting had allowed the twins to be terminated along with Tad Ruebens—then so be it.

"We're making the world a safer place for all children," insisted his center contact.

This was the same shortsighted idiot who'd believed a Watcher could be lured into betraying his brothers with promises of fortune and a position of power within the government's psychic testing program. For now, he'd play along. But he had his own agenda, no matter the sacrifice.

"Realigning the twins with Trinity's maturing abilities," his contact said, "creates the capacity to protect all the world's innocents from whatever evil strikes. The Temple Legacy's promise can't be allowed to languish because your council is too timid to take advantage of their potential."

The Temple Legacy had foretold of the arrival of psychic twins whose gifts would preclude the arrival of an even more powerful mind—Trinity's. Augmenting the twins' psychic abilities with Trinity's mastery of Dream Weaver technology would allow the center to implant lucid daydreams into any subject's mind. Those untraceable commands could then be remotely triggered, inducing behavior—from forcing someone to wear a color they hated to compelling her to bring a gun into a crowded mall and open fire. The subject would be completely powerless to stop her programming and would have no memory of its source.

His contact's rhetoric about protecting innocents was a cover for the center's real objective—long-range weaponry, where any mind, anywhere, could become a government-targeted time bomb. And with the Temples fully under center control, the government would have secured an unstoppable mechanism for breaching other legacies like theirs. Other legacies that had just been exposed.

For the safety of humanity, Sarah's and Madeline's and Trinity's minds had to be silenced for good.

"Just make sure," his contact instructed, "your council allows Sarah Temple to continue her dream work. It's time for you to earn your keep. Make it happen."

"Then my advice is to solidify the link between Sarah's consciousness and Trinity's as soon as possible. Metting's going to be on a short leash. Even if the elders agree to risk another episode like today, their patience will be at the breaking point."

"As I said," the voice agreed, "everything is proceeding exactly as planned."

CHAPTER NINE

"I felt something in Sarah's dream," Richard said to his second-in-command. He and Jeff had just arrived at the Brotherhood's secure surveillance location in the woods surrounding the center's main complex. It was less than an hour since Sarah's dream, and Richard's system was still battling the toxic aftereffects of the projection. "Something organized. Planned. It was the same consciousness that was trying to trap her in the dream. Whatever it was, it's not here."

A mile to their left, a stretch of Massachusetts highway was a daily conduit for suburban commuters who spent a quarter of their waking life driving to and from Boston. But the center's ten-year-old facility had been constructed at the heart of a thousand acres of government-owned property that was kept under constant surveillance.

Jeff's finger went to the communicator clipped around his ear, adjusting his reception of the intel streaming from the bunker's command center.

"Are you saying you sensed the source of our leak in the nightmare?" he asked.

"It wasn't looking for Brotherhood intel," Richard

answered. "It wanted Sarah, and it wasn't happy when Madeline and I showed up to get her out."

"You completely sure?"

Richard sighed. Being completely sure of anything could get a warrior killed.

"You should have let me deal with her," Jeff said. "Seeing Sarah's hands around your neck was enough to convince me that she's a risk we can't continue to take."

"How would that have benefited the Brotherhood? Her mind is our only connection to whatever the center may be using Dream Weaver to do." Richard stared at the complex through the leafless oaks, silently willing the building he'd infiltrated a year ago to reveal its secrets.

"You didn't win yourself any points with the council. You should have alerted them as soon as her rogue dream started."

Richard kept his mind tuned to the forest's energy and to his faint connection to Sarah. "I've given them even more reason to question my loyalty to my oath."

"Should they question it?"

"No."

He'd proven his allegiance to his Brotherhood long ago. When he'd had to choose between following his parents' misguided use of his gifts or helping stop them. His fight for Sarah's chance to embrace her legacy didn't change his commitment to the path he'd chosen on that fateful night.

"You have our reports." Mike Donovan, the surveillance team's lead, approached from Richard's other side. "Nothing's been missed here."

"Your intel is in order." Richard refocused on the task at hand.

Donovan's team had detected no traces of psychic activity at the center, either while Sarah was dreaming or when the Brotherhood's two satellite teams were exposed. Meanwhile, an energy spike had registered off the charts at an unmanned surveillance site on the other side of the state. A deserted but strategically significant location the Brotherhood couldn't afford not to investigate.

Every Watcher team not currently entrenched in a level-one mission had been recalled pending further orders, all but the recon team the council was staffing to fly out within the hour. A team Richard had yet to be placed in charge of. Instead, he'd been directed to make a final, hands-on determination about the need for further observation at the center, to return to the bunker to debrief Sarah about her nightmare, then to advise the council on how to deal with the chaos his continuing dream work with the Temples was causing.

He turned toward a child's distant cry making its way to him on the late-night breeze.

"You want a read from the inside?" Jeff asked.

Richard had helped vet a center infiltration plan the Brotherhood had yet to execute. After his time within the complex posing as Dream Weaver's project lead, he knew every access point to the facility. How to disarm every sensor. There were hidden passageways and unmarked entrances to labs and storage rooms that he alone was aware of.

"They'd know we're coming," he said.

"What?"

"I can feel it."

"And you're sure of this how?" Jeff asked.

Richard wasn't ready to admit that Sarah's mind,

though momentarily sedated, was still speaking to him. That through their link, he somehow knew that making a move on the center tonight would be a mistake.

"Call it gut instinct," he said. "We're not going to find any answers here, not now. And they're waiting for us to try. That gives them the victory before we step one foot inside."

"You can't go to the elders with nothing but your gut," Jeff warned. "The council wants answers that will end this mess with the lowest possible body count, while keeping our other legacies intact."

"Messes have a way of ending bloody whenever they damn well please." Richard closed his eyes and listened to the sound of a lost child crying and an angry ocean laughing in victory. "We need the twins' minds functioning and open to cooperating with us so we can understand what's threatening the Brotherhood through them."

"Are you ready to explain to the council exactly how you're planning to guarantee Sarah and Madeline's cooperation?"

"No."

He'd promised Sarah they'd save Trinity. Following through on that pledge would garner her further cooperation with the Brotherhood, but the answers they needed to get the job done were still trapped inside her mind, memories that she refused to analyze. And she still didn't trust Richard. Not enough to let him guide her back to her past, or forward into another pass through her ocean dream.

He headed toward their Jeep, leaving tracks in the damp ground that would be covered in frost come sunrise.

"Pack it up," Jeff said when Donovan fell in step beside them.

"Is the council sending in a new surveillance team?" the younger lieutenant asked. Questioning his superiors was a breach of protocol, but Richard approved of his enthusiasm to understand tactical command strategy.

"No." Jeff's unfriendly stare discouraged additional questions as he and Richard opened their doors.

Donovan's hands snapped behind his back. He silently awaited further instruction.

"Manned surveillance at this site is shut down," Jeff said. "Leave your equipment here, battle shields in place."

"Battle?" Donovan blurted. He checked himself this time, his "at ease" posture becoming more rigid. His gaze dropped to the ground.

"We're to assume we're under psychic attack until further notice," Richard answered, cutting the kid some slack. "Monitoring the center's stronghold won't buy us anything until we know how they're projecting center programming into Sarah Temple's mind."

"We have to assume they aren't doing it from here," Jeff added. "And we can't send in a team to confirm until we can weaken the complex's strategic advantage."

Donovan nodded, his eyes narrowing as he absorbed the information. "Identify plans, alliances, weapons," the newly trained Watcher recited, "before attacking an adversary."

It was the progression of tactical warfare all Watcher recruits were taught. Battles could be lost along the way without conceding defeat, as long as an army's priorities were clearly defined and set and implemented, regardless of the enemy's progress toward their own goals. It was the same logical path Richard had tried to follow while he worked with Sarah. Except she'd never been his opponent, and logic had never been all she really needed from him.

"Report back to the bunker once you're done here." Richard slid behind the wheel, leaving Donovan to disengage his team and eradicate the evidence that anything besides woodland creatures had set foot on the surveillance site. "The council needs you for a new objective."

Jeff's door shut soundlessly. After Donovan moved on, he pinned Richard with a hard stare.

"They would know we're coming tonight?" he asked.

"Yes." Richard started the Jeep and reversed into the path that in less than an hour would be erased as if it had never existed.

"And who are 'they' exactly?"

Richard accelerated. "A wolf, a child, and a homicidal ocean," he said, wincing at the ludicrous sound of the only answer he had to give.

"You believe the child Sarah is hearing is real now?" Jeff asked when they'd reached the main road.

"The Temple prophecy predicted another psychic force emerging from their line."

"Only vaguely. A prophecy can be twisted to mean damn near anything." Jeff shook his head. "The damage the center's done to Sarah's mind is basic battle tactics—whittling away at a target's resistance until they cultivate the means to attack an opponent's operations from within."

"What if it really is a child, not the center, calling for Sarah?"

"Does it matter? Her mind's clearly been programmed to project a new Dream Weaver matrix, whoever she's dreaming about. If that's allowing someone to keep tabs on our activities, all of it undetectable to any of our sensors, we're fucked. You're going to have to come up with something more before you face the council."

"It's as if the presence I sensed was deliberately trying to drive Sarah over the edge. If she's their link to us, what would they gain by unraveling her consciousness?"

He kept his speed to five miles beyond the limit instead of rushing back to Sarah, who was still sleeping off the effects of the nightmare and the drugs that had finally secured her and Madeline's recovery. But the sounds and sensations and shadows he'd touched in Sarah's mind were still calling to him.

"What if the person pulling all our strings is Sarah herself?" Jeff asked.

"There was another consciousness there. Someone pushing her toward the instability we've assumed was merely a breakdown."

"A wolf, a child, or an ocean?" Jeff snorted. "That should be easy enough to sell to the council."

"Sarah's mind is still our best resource for unearthing the government's plans."

And it remained their greatest threat, because she refused to access the memories that would help them understand what had been done to her mind.

Richard had to get himself tasked to lead the ad hoc recon team the council was sending to the small mountain town where the Temple twins had grown up—even though the exercise felt like even more of a trap than assaulting the center's complex would be. He'd need leverage to convince the elders that his and Sarah's presence was essential to the mission's success. That taking her back home was the key to unlocking the past's hold on her mind. He'd need Jeff's help getting the team in and out intact, once they had boots on the ground.

The Jeep's tires ate up the miles between them and the bunker, speeding Richard closer to a confrontation with Sarah he couldn't put off any longer. He checked his rearview for signs of life in the night's darkness. Satisfied that they were alone, he killed the Jeep's lights and slowed to take the rural highway's next turn. Without braking further, he guided the Jeep to the right of the guardrail that had been erected to protect motorists from the steep drop into the icy river yawning two hundred feet below. Skill and familiarity and extrasensory awareness enabled him to navigate the path down the ravine. Jeff braced a hand on his roll bar, trust implicit in his otherwise-relaxed posture.

"You really think Sarah's going to open up to you now?" Jeff asked as they reached the riverbank and headed for one of two concealed bunker entrances that accommodated motor vehicles. Two others existed, catering to different modes of transportation. "I nearly had to shoot her to get her talons out of you."

"I'll convince her." Richard's eyes narrowed as he relived the feel of her hands closed around his neck and the rush of betrayal that had screamed from her mind. "The only way for me to protect Sarah and the Brotherhood is to finally push deeper into her mind."

"God help us all." Richard's top lieutenant sounded genuinely nervous for the first time.

CHAPTER TEN

In the magical, unguarded place that revealed itself just before waking, Sarah drifted within a dream she'd tried to banish forever. A fantasy that had begun inside her coma. It had tempted her to hold on. To want more. To believe that even someone like her could deserve a second chance.

It was a dream of being held. Being accepted. Being wanted and cherished and needed for nothing more than who she was. All that she was, even the parts that would always be broken. It had meant everything—the promise of someone clinging to the good she couldn't feel inside herself.

The illusion had bloomed to life with his first touch. She'd let herself crave the perfection of it, even though she'd known it couldn't last. In her fantasy, her failures melted away and she finally stopped running. She'd been drawn to the light he'd promised. Light that was beyond her closed lids now, demanding that she see, as reality took a stronger hold.

Panic shook her as the present returned. Rage. Loneliness. Until the fading dream taught her how to hate once more. How to hate *him*—Richard—for continuing to ask her to believe. For saving her with promises that he'd abandon again when she needed him most.

He was holding her, just beyond waking, with his muscled arms wrapped around her and his powerful mind coaxing her from the darkness. She could feel his heart beating. She could sense his determination to bring her back to a world where dreaming had never been more dangerous. Sensitive hands rubbed warmth into her body—warrior's hands that could soothe as easily as they could maim or kill.

The recovery drugs released more of their hold. Sarah told herself to push away. But he was already easing off the bed. When she realized her hands were clinging, she made herself let go.

Memories attacked as he moved out of reach. The sound of his voice telling her to hate him, fight him, to do whatever she had to, to come back to him. She found herself sitting on an exam table in the bunker lab he'd built to contain and repel psychic energy. It was a near replica of the room the center had kept her in. He'd no doubt assured his council that the lab's precautions would protect them from whatever was still wrong with her. And for a while he'd been right. For a while, she hadn't been able to connect to other minds beyond the lab's walls.

A child's cries shrieked to her from somewhere beyond her nightmare. Beyond the bunker. Beyond the woods that cloaked their location. Evil was building within Sarah, no matter what anyone did to stop it. And she could sense Richard's awareness of it. His acceptance. His determination to fix her all over again.

"Nothing about you is inherently evil." He walked

across the dream lab, dressed in the dark fatigues the Watchers wore inside the bunker and on night missions. "Stop punishing yourself for your past."

There was a lethal edge to him when he shed his lab coat. A predatory alertness, a ruthless drive to protect, always crowding Sarah no matter how much distance she kept between them.

"Is that why your council has me locked in here again?" she asked. "Because they trust the goodness in my soul?"

"Your ocean dream was being driven by a consciousness beyond yours. Until we know by whom and why, you'll either be in here behind the lab's shields or accompanied by someone who can help you control your response."

"Namely you." Her voice stumbled over the words, her stomach knotting.

He handed Sarah a sports bottle filled with one of the electrolytic concoctions she choked down after every dream she and Maddie explored. She began to drink, making herself ignore the way his short military haircut accented the strong lines of his face even better than the longer style he'd worn while masquerading as an eccentric scientist.

"Tonight was an out-of-control projection someone else triggered." He gave a quick nod of approval as she continued to drink. "I suspect by using the programming Tad Ruebens embedded in your mind before his death. Until we can tell the council more, that's the best I've come up with."

Sarah took several more swallows. She concentrated on keeping down the mint-flavored liquid as she fought a psychic and adrenaline overload worse than she'd ever experienced. Her straw hit bottom. Richard handed over a new bottle. When half of the orange goo inside was gone, he made eye contact. His latest potion rumbled in her stomach.

She caught him inhaling slowly and releasing his breath in time with hers. His energy flowed with unnerving ease through their restored telepathic connection, enhancing her recovery without overpowering her thoughts. The tightness in her diaphragm eased with his help, mocking her weak attempt to settle her nerves on her own.

She held his stare through it all.

He blinked first and looked away.

"Your elders must be thrilled that the center's influence over me isn't quite as finished as you've insisted it is," she said. "Are your men planning a lynching for Maddie and me, or will a symbolic burning at the stake suffice?"

"If the council decides to neutralize your legacy, placing you in a chemically induced vegetative state will be effective enough."

Sarah shuddered. She stared at his jaw, at the late-night shadow of his dark beard, anywhere but into his understanding, unyielding gaze.

"I've met with them briefly," he said. "A full report is scheduled for tomorrow. You disengaged from the vision when you realized your sister's life was in danger. Your control over your presence in a dream matrix has grown strong enough for you to manipulate your dreaming identity on your own. That's progress I've been able to spin to our advantage for now, because it leaves us a chance to turn your programming against the center in the future. Whether or not we have anything more to bargain with depends on you and what we manage to accomplish next."

"I almost killed you when I broke the dream link." She turned until her legs were hanging over the side of the bed. The room danced around her. "I've killed before because a voice in a dream told me to. Is more of that what you're hoping to accomplish?"

The screams in Sarah's mind grew louder. She set the empty bottle aside. She tunneled her fingers into the snowy white blanket wrapped around her, clinging to the moment instead of falling back into the nightmare still calling to her.

"Ruebens's programming is clearly still driving your dreams." Richard was beside her, yet still keeping his emotional distance. "But you fought him at the center in every nightmare. You ran from him, then from me, when you thought I was part of his plan for Dream Weaver. You fought his programming again tonight, and this time you succeeded. You pulled yourself back on your own. Understanding how you did that, re-creating the phenomenon, will go a long way toward convincing the council to continue our work here in the lab."

Succeeded?

Re-creating the phenomenon?

She scooted farther away, rejecting the impulse to lean into Richard's warmth. She wanted to laugh like the loon she was until she couldn't stop. Until she couldn't breathe. Until she found the release, the silence, her dream ocean's desolate floor had offered.

"My mother's dead because of my legacy," she said. "My father, too, even though a slippery road and an eighteen-wheel semi took care of him as much as the mess my powers had made of our lives. Everything evil that's happened to my family began with me. My sister was hurt again tonight, because of me. And let's not forget the innocent hosts the center experimented on because you let them use me. How many people have suffered because there's no way to stop what I'm becoming? And none of it would have happened, if—"

"If I hadn't infiltrated the center and pulled your mind back from your coma," Richard finished for her. "You had no choice but to play out the hand you were dealt, Sarah."

"And when exactly do I get a choice? When do I start living on my own terms, instead of being forced to answer your endless questions, and to wait for your council to decide to 'neutralize' me and Maddie?"

His raven black eyes concealed secrets he'd never share. He'd once again buried the haunting tenderness she'd sensed when she first woke in his arms. Only duty remained. Honor. And whatever version of the truth suited his purposes.

"You have no choice tonight," he said. "You won't, until your mind is fully under your own control. And the only way to do that is to face the memories you're avoiding, so we can safely trigger more of the Dream Weaver programming driving your visions."

Sarah glanced at the bruises her fingers had left on his neck.

"How's that plan working out for you so far?" she asked.

"We'd have a better shot at averting another disaster if you'd let yourself trust me."

It was an unforgivable suggestion. She didn't dignify it with a response. Richard was suddenly looming over her, his hands clenched in the blanket beside hers.

"You've refused for a month to commit to our work together. But you called out to me when you were out of options in the dream." He sounded as shocked as she'd been when she realized what she'd done. "Then you nearly died. Because a part of you wanted to believe the voice telling you to give up more than you'd let yourself believe in me."

The tremor of fear in his voice didn't make it to his expression. He was too disciplined for that. Logical scientist and brutally trained warrior, the last thing Colonel Richard Metting would let dictate his behavior was honest-to-God emotion. But Sarah was more than terrified enough for both of them.

She *had* wanted to die. Anything was better than failing again. Anything was preferable to the soundless, emotionless nothing of another coma, and giving Richard's elders the satisfaction of banishing her there.

"My mind's disintegrating and there's nothing anyone can do about it, regardless of what happened in my past." Her voice was paper thin. "That's the price I paid for trusting you the last time."

"I infiltrated the center to protect you."

"I was a pit stop on your crusade to protect the world, and your council's mission to control the psychic realm before groups like the center can stake their claim."

"The center would have continued to develop Dream Weaver with or without me. The Brotherhood had to stop their weapons testing. I protected you as best I could. I'm doing everything I can to help you now."

The hollowness of his argument twisted between them. "But you don't want help, do you? In fact, you're so gun-shy you're willing to do whatever it takes to keep all of us away. Your stubbornness will be a death sentence if you don't get over the Brotherhood's involvement in what the center did to you. Keep hating me if it gets you through what we have to do next. But wake up and stop fighting by yourself, Sarah. Work with me. Trust my experience. Let me in."

Sparks snapped in his dark gaze.

"I need Maddie, not you." She needed anything but feeling Richard's thoughts reaching for hers while she fought the nightmare's call. "I'll work through my memories with her. We'll come up with something to tell the council tomorrow. Some way to prove Trinity's real and worth letting the dream take me under again."

She'd debriefed with her twin after every dream link they'd shared since coming to the Watcher's bunker. Only this time, Maddie hadn't been there when Sarah woke. This time, it was Richard and his unrelenting Watcher's logic bearing down on her.

"Why didn't you tell me?" he demanded.

"That the dream's been in control from the start?" She shuddered. "And if I had?"

"I would have—"

"You would have told your precious council, who were already looking for a reason to put my sister and me out of our misery."

"I would have helped you process the dream's pull and found a way to stop it from coming for you."

"Who said I wanted it to stop? There's a child out there, and the center is using her. What if we're too late already? I couldn't live with myself if I ignored her the way the rest of you are."

"Without my corroboration, the council has no reason to believe anything you're seeing in your dream. And you haven't given me the chance to uncover the proof they need. As it stands, your psychological instability is their only concern. You wouldn't be allowed to reengage with the nightmare now, no matter what you and Madeline uncover."

Sarah knew she'd crossed an unforgivable line, dreaming on her own when her mind had already caused so much destruction. The reckless path she'd chosen hit home for the first time as she absorbed Richard's intimidating stare.

"An innocent little girl is being ripped apart, the same way Maddie and I were," she tried to explain, hating him for being her only chance to get back to Trinity. "I wouldn't . . . I couldn't let them hurt her, too."

Sarah closed her eyes against the unwanted memories of her own mind at Tad Ruebens's mercy, invading others' thoughts, programming them, hurting strangers the way she was being hurt. Her will had slowly eroded, dying, until there'd been no light left to cling to.

The gentleness of Richard's finger caressed her cheek, ripping her back to the present. She could handle intimidating and angry from him. But not gentle. Gentle could never happen between them again.

Except she was leaning into his touch before she could stop herself. Then into the flicker of his consciousness—into the part of him she still remembered as *Rick*. The voice from the darkness of her coma that had promised intimacy. Closeness. Belonging. The perfection of what she'd thought she'd found called to her from their shared memories, rushing her deeper into the emotional dependency on him she'd forced herself to abandon. Everything she'd believed she and Richard could be together was still waiting for her in his touch. Everything he'd destroyed, when he sacrificed her to fulfill his duty to his Watchers.

A tear streaked down her cheek.

"Stop blaming yourself," he said, "for what the center's done through you." His thumb wiped the corner of her eye. "Stop running from the wealth of information we could pull from your memories of Ruebens's programming and from your life before you came to the center. You have to trust me enough to tell me—"

"I have told you, but you won't listen." Sarah steeled herself against his compassion. "Trinity's all that matters now. I can't go back and change the rest, but I can reach her in my dreams. We have a real lead to finding her now. Let Maddie and me work through the nightmare's memories and figure out what they mean. If you want me to trust you, get out of my head. Stop pushing me. Focus on convincing your council that another dream projection has to happen. Go get my sister so she can help me."

His pupils narrowed to pinpricks of emotion. She felt his struggle for control. He dropped his hand from her face.

"You always were a smart woman," he said. "So why are you so determined to rush back into danger? You were lured into that ocean, Sarah. Your nightmare's intent was to control your mind, not help you find the truth. I felt it, just like I finally felt how real Trinity's cries sound to you. I watched Madeline's mind crumble under the dream's control. What makes you think that won't happen again? Does your sister have to die before you accept my help?"

Sarah slapped his face. His hands snapped to her arms. His frustration fired through their deepening connection.

"I love Maddie," she insisted. "I tried to protect her from what I had to do."

His biting grip softened, his thumbs rubbing soothing circles. His consciousness wrapped around Sarah's with a gentleness that made her dizzy.

"You were protecting yourself," he said. "You were looking for a way out of doing the real work you have to do, and disguising it as some reckless mission to dig for the truth. The truth is that the two of you still don't know enough about what you're doing to control something as powerful as this projection. Blame me for doing my job, but don't take your hatred for me out on Madeline. Or Trinity, assuming she turns out to be real after we analyze your nightmare."

"She's real."

Sarah struggled against his hold. She gave up when it became clear he wasn't letting go.

"Then so is the danger she's in if you don't let me take the lead from now on." Richard released her and watched her wrap her arms around her body. "Without my help, you won't find the proof you want that something's calling to you from the nightmare."

"It was Trinity."

"Was it? Did you see her?"

Sarah didn't answer. She didn't have to. Because Richard was there now, sensing her memories and her doubts.

"The only thing we know for certain that's waiting in your nightmare is death," he said. "Yours and too many others, if we aren't careful. Other legacies are in play because of this mess. Developments I don't have time to explain. Things are about to get even uglier, and I can't give you a choice of whether to cooperate. My mind anchoring yours, understanding all of you, is your only shot to prove what, if anything, is real about Trinity."

"You said you heard her."

"I sensed you needing to find something, someone, who kept moving away the further you fell into the dream. And there was fear holding you back. Weakening you. Tell me what you were afraid of."

"I . . . I don't know." She couldn't remember anything clearly with Richard so close, except for his dream raven's demand that she come back to him. And the growing connection between them that had once felt as effortless as breathing.

"There was no little girl. Not the way you described Trinity in the dreams you and Madeline shared when Ruebens first drew your minds together. There was a dark presence. Voices. Power and purpose. Who knows what the programming he embedded is doing now. It's possible none of this is about the missing piece to your legacy."

"She's real . . ." Sarah saw the door again, deep within an unforgiving ocean, the memory growing stronger as more of Richard's energy merged with hers.

She felt his focus narrow. Hazy images took shape in her mind, blooming to life . . .

A scarred door. Light shining just beyond it while Sarah allowed herself to be dragged away, her hands torn and bleeding, the ocean taking her to an empty, painful place that felt too familiar. Too right. Too much like the near death of her coma. Except there was more than emptiness there now. There was the shadow of a crumbling house that hadn't existed in the nightmare. And a shadowy room waited for her within, where a mind called to her, demanding that she come back and—

"Help me," Trinity cried from inside the dilapidated structure while Sarah ran away, just as she had in the nightmare's ocean. Only now she was running through the woods, desperate not to see . . .

She shoved the vision away, along with Richard's centering presence.

"I can't remember any more." She opened eyes she hadn't realized she'd closed and found Richard's face inches away, his cheek reddening from where she'd struck him.

"Can't or won't?" The intensity of his focus told her he'd seen everything she had. "Tell me about the house, Sarah."

"That . . . that didn't happen in the dream. That place, it wasn't part of the ocean matrix. It was—"

"That place? You mean your nightmare's reflection of the house you grew up in?"

"What?" That's exactly what it had been, she realized. And Trinity was waiting for her there. Sarah was suddenly certain of it.

"I heard her, too," Richard said. "Something broke through your memories from the ocean nightmare just now. A new matrix overpowered them. It felt like the same presence I sensed when I dove into your projection."

Sarah's stomach surged. The liquid she'd swallowed threatened to force its way up. "There's never been anything from my past in the dream's matrix. My parents' house isn't part of the projection."

"It is now. Your mind's telling you that's where you'll find Trinity."

"But that makes no sense. She can't be there."

"Most likely not." Richard's features hardened into a warrior's mask, everything except the worry in his dark eyes. "But something else is, and it's affecting your control. Which means we have to get to the bottom of it."

"What? No—Maddie and I have to get back into my nightmare." Dredging up the past would only make that more difficult, if not impossible. Sarah was barely clinging to her sanity now.

"You're not dreaming again without me," he said. "Every time you project, every memory you have from now on, I'll be there. Accept that, and the council will give you another chance to search your ocean. But this new projection is too important to dismiss. So is the surge of psychic energy near your family's original home in Lenox that occurred at the exact moment that your dream took over your sleeping mind. A Watcher recon team is deploying in less than an hour to check it out, and you and I are going to be on it."

"Recon? But Maddie—"

"Can't help you. She almost died tonight trying to drag you back. The dream almost absorbed both of you. I have to convince the elders that won't happen again and that it's worth the risk of going back into your ocean to figure out what the dream wants. Something in Lenox is linked to you beyond the nightmare's hold. That will be enough for me to secure us both a place on the mission."

"You . . . you want me to go home? I haven't been there for—"

"Ten years. Since your father died and your own injuries from the accident led to a psychotic break that left you in a coma."

Sarah shivered. "I can't—"

"You either go back with me now and help me sell the elders on your willing participation, or you won't get another chance to find Trinity. Your questionable control and your growing psychic abilities have become too much of a wild card. We have to prove you're an asset the council can't afford to marginalize."

"I . . ." She was leaning closer to Richard, hating herself for needing him. "Promise me that if I do this, you'll get me back to my dream. Make me believe you'll protect my legacy no matter what happens in Lenox."

She was begging for a reason to trust a man who'd taken a blood oath to protect the world from freaks like her. A man who was holding her again, as if he couldn't make himself stop. Richard's fingers brushed at the fear leaving watery trails down her face.

He shook his head and turned to go.

"We're wheels up in forty-five minutes," he said. "Find a way to talk yourself into working with me and my team instead of fighting us."

"I want my sister," Sarah said over the sound of his raven's wings rustling through her mind. Their minds.

He keyed the lab's door open.

"Get some rest," he said. "You're going to need it."

He left without looking back. The lab's electronic locks clicked into place. The distant crying of a lost child Sarah shouldn't be able to hear grew louder. Cries she hadn't realized Richard had been shielding her from the entire time he'd been by her side.

Chapter Eleven

"You'll have ten minutes from touchdown to takeoff," Richard said to Sarah. He'd positioned himself between where she was huddling in the corner of the transport helicopter and the remainder of the six-man team he was leading. "The team will secure the perimeter while you lead me to the source of the consciousness calling to you. It's vital that the council understand how whatever's here is linked to your dream."

At the moment, what was vital was that Sarah didn't hurl in front of the Watchers as their covert helicopter descended swiftly and silently toward her past. The shadows of her abandoned childhood were only seconds away, while a little girl's cries grew stronger in her mind.

She could feel Richard's strength augmenting her barriers, shielding her from her dream's echoes and the thoughts of the other Watchers. Not that any of them had spared so much as a glance her way since he buckled her into her seat. Jeff Coleridge seemed particularly determined to pretend she wasn't sitting there, dressed in Watcher blackout fatigues and ignoring her right back.

"What if whatever your sensors detected here has nothing to do with me?" she asked.

The whisper-soft whoosh of the helicopter's blades slowed as the pilot touched them down in the clearing just beyond the house her father had purchased the month before Sarah and Maddie were born. Across the secluded lot where she'd played as a child, the two-story Colonial's appearance shimmered in the moon's pale gray reflection. Its shattered windows and peeling paint and drooping shutters accused her of neglect. Of running. Of forgetting everything so she could survive, only to end up feeling just as empty and broken and irreparable as the home she'd once loved.

"This is all about you." Richard stood, bending enough to keep his head from smacking the transport's low roof. He helped her to her feet. "My men are trained to track psychic threats. They'll have your back while you lead us to whatever's connected to you here. Something spiked when you were lost in your dream. We have to know what."

"Do we?" Sarah let him lift her to the ground. Her fingers clenched in the smooth fabric of his shirt while he adjusted the Kevlar vest he'd strapped on her when they arrived at the bunker's flight bay. "This place feels like a grave. Digging around here is only going to make things worse."

She'd never been more certain of anything in her life.

"Sometimes things have to get worse before they can get better." Richard wrapped his arm around her, his mind, too, and led her toward the rusted-out screen door at the top of the back porch. "Something's calling to you here. Something real I can sense. That gives us leverage with the council. It's time to prove to the

Brotherhood that you can be trusted to align your personal search for Trinity with our strategic needs. Let's get this done and get out of here."

He nodded to Jeff, whose hand gesture sent the team fanning around the house's perimeter. Sarah sensed more was being communicated among the men. But Richard was shielding her from the Watchers' telepathic communications while he blocked the team from picking up on the growing sense of dread consuming her.

He led her up the rickety steps, guiding her around loose, splintering floorboards until they were at the dilapidated door. The frayed edges of the torn screen were razor sharp. Sarah's fingers twitched, feeling again how the latch to her ocean dream's door had sliced into her tender flesh.

"This is wrong," she said.

"Yes." Richard pulled against the weather-roughened frame. The door opened, its hinges protesting with an unholy screech of metal against metal. "But I'm going to help you see it through."

It was a living nightmare, stepping back into what had been a sunny kitchen, seeing the cobwebs and layers of dust and rodent droppings covering everything. It was as if the darkness that had consumed her and Maddie's legacy had cloaked this place, too.

"How did this happen?" She didn't resist as Richard led her through the kitchen to the equally empty dining room, the tattered curtains there no match for the moon. Its light sought out each speck of decay. "My parents sold this house to another family after they moved. They had a little boy, Mom said. Lenox is the perfect place to raise children. How could those people have abandoned everything like this?"

"Our research turned up police reports," Richard said. "Five years ago, the family began reporting strange sounds. Unexplained damage and accidents. Voices racing through the house at all hours of the night. No perpetrators were ever caught. The father finally fell down the stairs one night after hearing a commotion below. He said he'd been pushed. There was no evidence of a break-in. The family moved away but has been unable to sell the property. It's developed the reputation of being—"

"Haunted." Sarah could feel a malevolent energy seeping through the place. It was the same consciousness that had been calling to her for a month. Richard could buffer his team's thoughts from her mind, but there was a presence here stronger than even his powers to block, and it was glad she'd come.

"Help me . . ." a child's voice called from Sarah's memories, and from—

"Upstairs." She raced through what had been her family's sitting room. She couldn't stop herself, no matter how badly she wanted to run back to the helicopter instead.

Her foot caught on uneven floorboards that had warped from years of disuse. She lurched toward the ground, her balance still compromised from the dream's aftereffects. Strong arms caught her, pulled her close, and wrapped her in the present, while the past screamed for her to give it control.

"I'm with you, remember?" Richard said into her

ear. It wasn't a whisper, but she could barely hear him.
"Every dream. Every memory. We're doing this together."

Sarah struggled to get away from him. She had to get
away from him. The house was insisting. Her nails bit
into the intimidating muscles of his arms. He calmly set
her on her feet as something inside her, beyond her,
kept building, hating, demanding that she make him
pay. That she make all of them pay.

"Pay for what?" Richard's grip tightened. "Why
would she want to make us pay for anything?"

"She, who?" Sarah pressed her hand against the pressure throbbing behind her right temple and focused on
his voice alone. It wasn't real, she reminded herself—
the other mind reaching for her wasn't really here.

"Trinity," Richard said.

Sarah's knees buckled.

He caught her closer. "Whatever's plugged into your
dream of her wants you here, upstairs, remembering
your fears of this place. It wants you fighting me and the
team of men outside who are protecting you."

"No." She refused to be losing control again. "It's
just being back in the house. This became a horrible
place for me. No matter how perfect it looked or how
hard my parents tried to make us into a happy Ameri-
can family, this place was a nightmare. I was their worst
nightmare here, and I can't go back to being that person. Don't let me go upstairs. I told you not to bring me
here. Something horrible is going to happen."

Richard's grip propelled her toward the steps instead.
"We're getting to the bottom of this."

"I'm—" She stumbled on the bottom step, only
righting herself because Richard's mind and physical

strength were augmenting hers. "I'm not in control. I'm losing myself, I can feel it. Worse than in the dream ocean. I can't stay in control here."

"Exactly." He all but dragged her to the top of the landing. "Someone wants you losing it. They wanted the other family long gone. They wanted this place looking like the raw end of a nuclear meltdown, so it would make coming back hurt you even more. Why is that? What would they hope to gain?"

"I . . ."

It wasn't a "they." Richard had been right. It was just one voice this time. One mind.

"Help me . . ." Trinity called down the dark hallway that led to where Sarah and Maddie's bedrooms had been. *"I'm here. I've been waiting for you."*

Sarah stumbled toward the lost child. Her bedroom door was closed. Its paint and condition had somehow remained pristine, the perfection of it a grotesque parody of the wasteland surrounding it.

"Is it real?" Her mind flashed to the image of the horrible door in her dream.

"It's a mess," Richard said, clearly not seeing the same thing she did. "But it's real enough."

He reached for the doorknob. Turned it so he could push the door inward.

"No!" She grabbed his arm, their psychic connection firing deeper until she could see the scarred, mottled reality of the door he was touching. "I can't go in there. I won't be able to stop whatever's on the other side."

"I'll be with you." He shook off her hold.

"No, you won't." She felt her identity slip even further away.

The door swung open . . .

. . . to a vision of the bedroom of her childhood.

Richard's grip disappeared from her arm. He was no longer standing beside her. The rest of the Watcher team was no longer circling the house and investigating the shadows and cobwebs downstairs. Sarah's senses narrowed to her daydream of standing in the doorway of her little-girl room, staring at an image of herself sitting cross-legged in the center of her bed, facing the empty wall above her headboard.

The child looked over her shoulder toward the door, her eyes a crystalline blue instead of Sarah's gray.

"You can't stay." Her voice was soft, drawing Sarah across her pink carpet toward the bed and its bright pink spread. "They don't want you here. But I had to . . . I've been waiting for so long. I knew you couldn't stay away forever. And I had to see if you were really real."

The childlike sentiment "really real" was something Sarah and her twin had said to each other during the dark nights they shared their hopes and dreams and the bizarre things that kept happening to them. Things their parents refused to accept.

"The Watchers only gave me ten minutes." Sarah reached her hand toward the child's soft hair. She pulled back before touching, afraid to break the spell.

"They made you come." The child glanced over Sarah's shoulder. "He made you."

"I . . . I was afraid."

"Of me."

"No, sweetie." Sarah closed her eyes against the sentiment. She had to remember that whatever consciousness was driving this vision was dangerous. But it felt so real. She'd been searching for Trinity for so long. It was impossible not to believe just a little. "I've been fighting to find you."

"They don't want you here." The child turned back to the wall she'd been staring at. *"They'll find out, and they'll come for me."*

"The Watchers brought me." Sarah inched closer, sensing the little girl's growing distress and the resentment simmering beneath her soft words. *"They want to help you."*

"Not them . . ." Images began to form on the wall. Black-and-white, hazy reflections of an unforgiving ocean. *"Them. The people telling me to dream."*

"The . . . The center doesn't know you're here? They didn't send you?"

"I had to know. For me."

"Know what?"

"If it was true, what he said. How much you'd hate me."

Cries began to call to Sarah from the pictures on the wall. There was no color there, no clear form to the images. But something about them, something about the whole vision, seemed alarmingly familiar.

"Who said I'd hate you?" she asked. The scene on the wall began to shimmer. The bed and floor beneath her began to quake.

"He told me you wouldn't ever believe," the child said. The distorted image of a wolf appeared in the picture's corner nearest her. *"That you'd never want to."*

"Sarah?" Richard called from the other side of the daydream. *"What are you seeing? Who are you talking to? The room's empty."*

"He said you'd want them more." The little girl pouted. The wolf in her picture snarled. *"He said if you found me, all you'd do is run. From me. And he was right. You're finally here, but you hate me just like he said."*

"Ruebens?" Sarah's heart kicked against her ribs as the beast in the image grew clearer.

She did want to run.

She didn't want to believe any of this.

"Ruebens is dead," she insisted to the child on the bed.

"So are you," the little girl responded in a deeper voice. It was the ocean's voice from Sarah's nightmare. "All of you are dead if I want you to be."

Pain seared through Sarah's body. She dropped her knees, her head screaming.

"Stop!" She could feel Richard's agony beyond her vision.

He was stumbling closer, hitting his knees beside where she'd collapsed in the dilapidated bedroom.

"So easy," the wolf hissed from the wall scene in the ocean nightmare's voice. "Your fear makes it so easy."

"Stop it." Sarah's lungs were filling with water. She fought to be free of the daydream she'd been sucked into, to find her way back. Every muscle in her body clenched in spasms of pain.

"Break the dream's hold." Richard gripped her arm. "The team's on its way up. They'll stop you if you don't end the attack on your own."

"They're coming," said the little girl on the bed. The angelic-looking, psychotic child Sarah refused to believe was Trinity. "They'll take you away from me forever, just like he said. And you'll let them. You'll do anything not to believe in me."

There was pain, fear, hatred in the words. And it made no sense. None of it. Why the hell couldn't anything make sense anymore?

Sarah slammed her hands to the floor, feeling the last of her control shred. "You're not real, little girl. None of this is real. Why am I here? What the hell to do you want from me? All of you, why won't you leave me alone?"

They weren't her words, she realized. The dream's demands

were flowing through her, owning her, directing her to make the world pay for her loneliness and pain as the child and the bed disappeared, replaced by a menacing raven standing beside Sarah in her otherwise-empty bedroom, reaching for her, poised to destroy her . . .

Richard felt Sarah's mind return from wherever she'd gone, but her consciousness hadn't come back alone. The presence he'd sensed in the ocean dream, then again when she'd stared transfixed at the empty room they'd walked into, was still controlling Sarah and blocking him from getting through to her consciousness.

"Come back to me." He knelt beside where she'd crumpled to the ground, shaking off the pain that had sizzled through both of them. He was holding her, clutching her close. "Release whatever you saw."

She'd been talking into thin air, experiencing an altered reality he couldn't see.

"Get off me." Her anger surged through them.

"Not a chance. You're having a lucid dream. You have to break the projection's hold."

The door to the room slammed shut as she trembled. It flew open again. A demented wind howled down the hallway, funneling into the room, around them, then out the shattered window, blowing out even more glass.

Tuning into his team's psychic link, Richard sensed them advancing from the stairs, drawn by Sarah's screams when her vision had attacked both herself and Richard.

"*Stay back,*" he ordered through the team's link. "*Sarah's not stable.*"

"*We've got to move,*" Jeff replied. "*The bunker's detected multiple telepathic energy surges. We're on someone's radar.*"

"The center's. Sarah was sucked into a vision as soon as she entered the house."

"Shut up!" She beat against his chest. Her mind battered against the shields he'd been using to keep the others from detecting her meltdown. "I won't let you destroy us. You can't—"

"Stop it." He shook her. "Wake up, Sarah. We have to go."

"I'm not going anywhere with you." Her voice rose with each word, softening as it grew more brittle, sounding almost childlike. "All of you, why won't you leave me alone!"

Richard flew backward, propelled by the force of her hands pushing against his chest and her possessed mind shoving against his. He crashed against the already-crumbling wall beside the door, his head making contact with a sickening crack. His ears rang. Plaster rained down.

Jeff and Donovan rushed into the room.

"Stay back," he warned, but the other men were already airborne, landing in a heap in the hallway.

The door slammed behind them.

"Everyone stand down," Richard projected, sensing the remainder of the team preparing to storm the room.

He pushed himself to his feet. He ran his hand over the back of his skull. He wiped blood-smeared fingers on his pants and approached Sarah. His mind cautiously tried to reach the essence of the woman whose memories had somehow triggered this.

"This isn't you, Sarah. Something here is controlling your mind, and you're still lost to whatever you saw. We have what we need for the council. You're finally remembering and that gives us something to work with. Now we have to get back to the transport."

His meds would subdue her if need be. Her power to project others' realities had been growing so rapidly, he always carried a complete series of his dream protocol whenever he worked with Sarah. But adding the burden of another round of psychotropic stabilizers to her body's taxed stamina would further delay her full recovery. And the Brotherhood needed her mind whole. Richard needed her back in his lab by morning, remembering even more before the elders called them to the mat.

"You hate me," she whimpered in a child's rasp, her dark eyes lightening until they became a crystal clear blue. "You all want to use me. I don't want to do this anymore."

"Then wake up."

Sarah's mind was growing even more distant, becoming even less her. The bitterness of whoever was controlling her was seething to full life. And it was someone psychically strong enough to toss him and his men around, and to block his search of Sarah's mind for their identity. Debris lifted off the floor. Leaves and dirt and bits of trash swirled around them.

"You don't want me to wake up," Sarah spoke for whoever was controlling her mind.

"You're right." Richard swallowed his panic. He protected his eyes against the maelstrom of grit stinging his face. "Whoever you are, you can go straight to hell for all I care. But you can't take Sarah with you. Alpha?" he called. "Release the link. Target release, and reset to zero. Reset, Alpha. Now!"

It was the override command he'd embedded into

Sarah's Dream Weaver programming when they'd first worked together at the center. It was his back door into her dreaming mind, one he hadn't needed to use since bringing her to the command bunker. Now it wasn't making a dent. Nothing was reaching her.

He felt for the pouch of meds snapped to his belt and withdrew a vial. He brushed Sarah's cheek with his lips.

"I'm sorry," he said.

He jammed the hypodermic into the most accessible vein, given his awkward hold—in her neck—and pushed the plunger home. Her body seized instantly. Her beautiful eyes grew opaque, then warmed to their natural gray before her lids dropped. The flotsam racing around them fell to the floor like puppets whose strings had been cut. The room's door creaked open, scraping as its top hinge gave way, clinking to the ground. The world grew silent in the same instant that Sarah's rigid muscles fell slack. All of them, including her heart.

Richard fumbled for his belt and the shot of adrenaline that would counteract his recovery protocol's effect.

His team stormed the room.

"We have company," Jeff said.

Blood trickled from a gash along the man's cheekbone, but his hands were steady on his assault rifle. He reached for the night goggles resting on his forehead and slipped them into place. Donovan and the rest of the team followed his lead.

"The helo had to bug out," he added. "Transport's waiting at the alternate location."

Richard slipped his own goggles into place, then rose without administering the adrenaline, staggering to his feet as he brought Sarah with him. His team took position around them, three in front with Jeff leading, two guarding Richard's rear.

"*Sit rep?*" he asked with his mind as he carried Sarah down the hallway, then the stairs, his consciousness digging for hers.

"*Minor injuries,*" Jeff reported.

Richard could feel his second's mind scouting ahead for attackers as the team moved through the house to the kitchen. They paused as a unit at every corner. At each critical point of exposure, Jeff scanned their escape route while the rest of the team remained alert, their rifles at the ready, anticipating possible attack from every vantage point.

"*The bunker detected a six-person assault team before their position was cloaked.*" Jeff glanced back to Richard before continuing through the kitchen, his unspoken evaluation of the situation clear.

As Richard had suspected, someone at the center had known their team would be there. They'd known long enough to not only deploy a response while someone screwed with Sarah's mind, but to utilize psychic cloaking, a rare telepathic talent. One Richard had mastered as a child.

"Break contact with command," Richard verbally ordered. "No psychic communication until we're in the air. We're going black."

They heard the deafening report of automatic gunfire a second before what was left of the kitchen windows exploded inward. Shards of glass flew around them as they dropped to the floor. Gritting his teeth, exhaustion dragging at the last of his power reserves, Richard covered Sarah's lifeless body with his own, closed his eyes, and envisioned the dark cloak of anonymity that was now the team's best chance to rendezvous with their helicopter in a secluded clearing three-quarters of a mile away, an alternate location Richard had selected, anticipating a trap. One they had to assume the opposition knew about as well.

"They're driving us," he said over the blast of another round of automatic gunfire.

He drew his Beretta from his holster, shouldering off his rifle and handing it to Donovan, where it might do some good if the team needed backup ammunition. His free hand shifted to his med kit. Cursing, he made himself not remove the adrenaline. He curled Sarah's body closer instead. Oxygen deprivation wouldn't take a toll for several minutes, and the team couldn't afford the distraction of Sarah recovering consciousness while they were under siege, her mind most likely out of control.

"I want the strike team down in two minutes," he commanded. "Understood?"

"Let's get it on," Jeff responded for the team.

"Take point," Richard ordered. "Simms and Jackson, flank. Donovan, Reese, and Walker, you're with me. Protect the package."

Each man silently regained his footing, crouching low and out of the range of the bullets still flying in through the windows. So far, the house's solidly built walls were holding. As a unit, they checked the positioning of the Kevlar suiting that protected their vital organs. The rest of their shielding would come from their unity as a team and their trust in Richard to hide their movements while they countered the opposing team's assault.

They approached the kitchen door from the right, shielded from the screen's nonexistent protection. Richard closed his eyes and moved with his men, his instinct tracking their progress, his intuition feeling out the field of operation beyond the house. His mind pushed through the psychic resistance of the center's soldiers, arrowing straight to the information he needed and leaving no trace of his presence.

"Four securing the yard," he said. He could see their opponents in his mind. They were confident that their positions were secure. "Two moving to the right: automatics. One to the left: sniper rifle. One on the roof. Three are waiting beyond their team's assault position, holding back in the woods between here and the alternate rendezvous. Counterattack," he ordered. "We breach their assault, prevent further communication of our position back to the center, and carve a path to the helo. We'll take them all in under sixty. Move!"

Jeff challenged the door first, firing cover rounds. Reese and Walker advanced, followed by Donovan, then Richard, who slipped Sarah over his shoulder so his right arm was free. Reese and Walker covered next, firing continuous rounds through the screen. Jeff pushed past them, rolling and coming to his feet as the rest of the team exited the house behind Reese and Walker, who opened fire to the right and left.

While the men took out the attackers on either side, Jeff pivoted and downed the sniper on the roof. A bullet slammed into his thigh, dropping him.

"Son of a bitch!" he said as Donovan helped him

back to his feet, the younger lieutenant still firing. He and Reese and Walker took care of the last man securing the yard. Simms and Walker secured the rear as the team kept moving, their rifles and gazes in constant, coordinated motion.

The immediate threat eliminated, they made it to the woods, gaining on the remaining center operatives who were now advancing from their concealed positions. Richard continued to cloak the team's movements while he breached the opposition's shields and thoughts.

"Five seconds until they're in range," he told his men. "Two in flanking positions. Donovan, you and Jeff fall back. Reese and Simms, take the point. I have the trees."

Advancing his team into the assault, using their momentum to their advantage, Richard counted down.

"Three," he said. "Two. One."

His men opened fire before they could physically see their marks. Richard trusted them to hit their targets, while he kept his attention, his mind, his Beretta, trained on the threat he sensed lurking somewhere in the winter-stripped branches above them.

He closed his eyes.

He shifted once again to instinct alone.

Fear made its way to him on the wind, a spark of it that was quickly covered. But not quickly enough. Richard kept walking, shifting Sarah's weight to achieve better balance. He lifted his shooting arm, opened his eyes, and fired at the shadowy figure perched a hundred yards away, twenty feet up.

The body fell to the ground, the man dead before he landed.

Richard knelt, laying Sarah onto the blanket of leaves

that covered the frozen ground. He ripped off his night goggles and removed the adrenaline from the pouch at his hip. It only took a glance to verify the medication and its dosage. He plunged the syringe into Sarah's heart, then tilted her head back, cleared her airway, and began to breathe life into her deflated lungs.

"We need to get to the helo." Jeff's voice was thin with pain. His thoughts clouded Richard's with a wave of anger. "We're exposed here because of whatever connection the center still has to her. We have to move."

"I need another minute." Richard linked his hands, his fingers locked, and pumped Sarah's chest.

He needed to feel her heart beating beneath his touch, or he'd lose his mind. He needed her consciousness connected with his again. Mission or no mission, a growing part of Richard needed Sarah, period, and that piece was in control now. He touched his lips to hers. Forced air into her body.

"Transport is a minute away, Colonel." Jeff's use of Richard's title held a biting edge. "Two, tops. There's a defibrillator. We'll get her back once we're airborne. We'll secure her mind for the council's debriefing, but we need to get out of here."

Richard glared up to where his second was leaning against Donovan, Jeff's leg a bloody mess from the bullet he'd taken fulfilling the same duty to their Watcher's Creed that he was now demanding Richard honor.

"Thirty seconds." Richard lurched to his feet, cradling Sarah's insubstantial weight to his chest. "I want us in the air in thirty seconds."

He moved toward the alternate rendezvous, stumbling, his body screaming at the nonstop psychic load he'd been shouldering since racing from the control center to Sarah's quarters. His men fell in step around him. As a team, they pushed to reach their ride in time to revive the dangerous mind likely responsible for the attempt the center had just made on their lives.

CHAPTER TWELVE

Agony arced through Sarah, clenching every muscle in her body. Air was forced down her throat, while thoughts, feelings, minds battered her consciousness. Somehow, from somewhere, she found the energy to struggle up from the darkness. Dazed, she turned her head away from the face hovering over hers. She batted at the hands pumping her chest.

"Sarah . . ." Richard's swell of relief was immediately followed by the silencing of every mind intruding on her own, except for his.

"Take it slow," he projected.

"Leave me . . ." She curled into a ball. She realized she was on the floor of the helicopter. She tried to take a breath, to clear the haze keeping her from thinking. Her chest throbbed in retaliation for whatever they'd done to her. "Leave me alone."

Richard's hand cupped her cheek. His mind pressed closer instead of away. Relief. Worry. Fury. His thoughts consumed her with raw emotion.

"I almost lost you," his mind whispered.

"What . . ." She licked her lips. They were dry. Cracked. "What happened?"

Instead of answering, Richard shut his mind away again and reached for something clipped to his belt. "This will help you rest." He pressed the needle into her arm.

"You bastard." She turned her head to find Jeff Coleridge sitting near her, on one of the helicopter's benches. His cheek was bleeding. A wound in his leg had been tied off with rubber tubing. "Tell me what . . ."

Snippets of memory descended before she could finish. The mission. Her parents' house. Her ruined bedroom. The unreal confrontation with herself as a child, only it had been someone else. Someone who—

"It wasn't Trinity." She grabbed for Richard's hand, her gaze locking on to Jeff's hate-filled expression as he stared directly in front of him.

She glanced to the rest of the team, none of whom would make eye contact. There were huge holes in what she could recall, just like her unreliable memory of her ocean dream. But she could remember her mind being controlled by a power beyond her understanding. Her mind, linked with another, had shoved Jeff and a second Watcher back. She'd forced Richard away with more power than he could control. She'd wanted, needed, to kill.

"It wasn't me." But she had felt a connection. Another consciousness dragging her deeper into the parts of her own mind that terrified her. Her grip tightened on Richard's hand. She looked back to him. "It wasn't Trinity. Tell me you believe that."

"We'll figure it out" was all he'd say, while he kept his own thoughts and feelings locked away now. "Rest until we get back to the lab."

She didn't want to rest. She didn't want to close her eyes. What if the council decided it was best that she never woke up, because of what he'd forced her to face here? What if she'd just proven that she was as crazy and unstable as they'd assumed.

"It wasn't me . . ." Her eyes closed, Richard's meds taking over. "Please. I'm not crazy. Don't let them . . . don't let them take my mind away. Not before we can find . . ."

Her ability to speak failed before she could beg for the chance he'd promised she'd have to reach Trinity—the real little girl she'd heard in her ocean, not the demon she'd found in her shattered past.

"Please," she projected. More than ever, Richard's help was her only hope. *"I'll do whatever you want to figure this out. Just make them let me wake up . . ."*

CHAPTER THIRTEEN

Richard fought to keep his mind on his dream database despite Jeff's agitated stare from the other side of his desk.

Jarred was monitoring Madeline's recovery. Sarah was still unconscious, in isolation in the lab. And Richard's consolation prize for the night's insanity was a killer psychic hangover, analyzing his data for some clue that would protect the Temple Legacy for another day, and enduring his sleep-deprived second-in-command's hair-trigger temper.

"Sarah Temple never should have been allowed to initiate a dream sequence on her own." Jeff, mobile with the help of crutches, had tracked Richard down in his quarters after the recon team had debriefed and their report had been transmitted to the council. "Let alone accompany us on a mission. If she'd have been restricted to the lab and stayed hooked up to your monitors—"

"Moving her to private sleeping quarters was a calculated gamble. So was her participation in the trip to Lenox."

Richard reread what he'd recorded from his recollection of Sarah's nightmare and his observation at her parents' home. He erased the records, just as he had twice before. He kept typing gibberish, his mind refusing to process anything but the memory of Sarah lying lifeless in his arms before he'd revived her.

"Building a working relationship with the twins is essential," he said. "That wouldn't have happened, keeping Sarah caged in the lab around the clock."

"Are you calling what happened tonight Sarah working *with* us? We've been attacked twice because of her, three times, if you count the other legacy teams."

"I got into her nightmare. She joined the recon team and started facing her memories."

"I don't expect the council's terribly impressed with your results," Jeff said.

"Not yet."

Richard studied the man he'd come the closest to trusting of anyone in his adult life, weighing how much was safe to share of what he'd discovered when he confronted Sarah. But if he was going to keep his mind focused on his job when he returned to the lab, he needed to war-game what he knew. Something he and Jeff had done countless times before.

"The ocean dream came looking for Sarah," Richard finally admitted. "Exactly how I felt something, someone, controlling her behavior during her vision in the house. She didn't initiate either link."

Jeff unclipped the portable comm unit from his belt and slapped it to the desk's steel surface, waiting for Richard to spit out the rest.

"It was like . . . feeling her being seduced," Richard said.

"It has to be the center. Clearly, Ruebens embedded the need to find a fictional child into Sarah's mind. Her obsession with Trinity is the government's link to our operations. Tonight, they pulled the trigger on two other legacies and nearly took her twin, you, and our entire recon team down protecting her."

"Except Trinity didn't feel like a figment of Sarah's imagination. Or a fantasy that Ruebens planted. Or even a child, not in the ocean nightmare when I was joined with Sarah's consciousness. The presence that possessed her in her bedroom was too strong to be an untrained child's. The council has to approve another ocean-dream projection, so we can get to the bottom of what's going on. When I debrief Sarah, uncovering the details the elders need to make that decision will be—"

"You're going to debrief her?" Jeff shifted in his chair, easing the pressure on his leg. "Alone. That's Madeline's job, isn't it? You know, in your foolproof process for reclaiming control of their legacy for the Brotherhood."

"Not anymore."

"Would that be because you're no longer sure you can reclaim Sarah's mind? Or because you suspect she's a willing accomplice to what the center's doing? Or maybe you're just covering your ass."

Richard pushed back from his computer and stood. His friend's stillness deepened, as if Jeff were bracing for a blow Richard had no intention of delivering. He needed the debate. He had to be sure, if he was going to convince the council to allow him to work with Sarah once she woke.

"Those are the wrong questions." Richard's stride ate up the carpet from one side of the office to the other. Then he planted his butt back in his chair.

"What's the right question?" Jeff relaxed.

"If this is the center making its move to reclaim Sarah for Dream Weaver, but Sarah's not leaking information to them, how did they know the precise time to retarget her mind? Hearing the little girl she says is Trinity, feeling this connection to the child that her twin doesn't, all of it grew organically from a month of recovery work."

"Or from someone at the center gradually feeding her imagery that they waited to trigger until she grew strong enough to do serious damage," Jeff suggested.

"Someone who would have needed intel to track Sarah's ability to process the complexity of tonight's visions." Richard welcomed the violence growing inside him. Its toxic bite renewed his determination to do damage to whoever was orchestrating this.

Jeff's frown formed a trench on either side of his mouth. "You're saying she wouldn't have been strong enough to project the nightmare or the lucid daydream in Lenox before now, and someone knew that."

"But they weren't counting on her reaching out to me when she got in over her head, or that our connection would be strong enough to pull her back both times."

"She tried to kill you, Richard."

"Because you were hurting her sister, and then I was threatening her connection with the child she thought she was seeing at the house."

"Or were we threatening the projection's plans? Either way, she's the wild card here—her dreaming mind, and whoever's controlling it. The council wants to shut this circus down. How can you rationalize talking them out of it?"

Richard saw again Sarah's heartbreaking desperation

in the chopper, when she begged him for the second chance he'd promised if she endured the recon mission. He shoved down the compulsion to spare her from how much worse things had to become if they were going to identify what or who was driving her breakdown.

"Maybe hearing Trinity in the dream is a premonition." Richard rolled the possibility over and over in his mind, needing more than mere logic to lead him to the right conclusion. "When she was on the run from the center, Sarah saw the rendezvous point for her showdown with Ruebens long before the confrontation occurred. Madeline decoded the dream's symbolism and we terminated Ruebens and his team."

"Barely." Jeff's skepticism was a reminder of how close Richard had come to watching his men take out Sarah and Madeline along with the center's director.

"We can't discount the possibility that Sarah's mind is projecting the child's image to warn us," Richard said.

"About what? That she's dream-sharing with someone besides her sister? Someone pulling the same strings as Ruebens?"

"If I don't explore the nightmare that started this"— Richard was listening to his instincts now more than to Jeff—"we'll never know what the center is gunning for."

"They want the twins under their control."

"Actually, the center wants the Temple Legacy, and I'm no longer convinced Sarah and Madeline are the only players in their sights."

Richard ran another search through the database that tracked every detail he'd gleaned from the twins' accounts of their dreams. His second-in-command used his crutches to round the desk and watch him sift through observations that could be sorted by date, time, symbol, and theme.

"You keep circling back to the child," Jeff said.

"We can't afford to rule out the possibility that Ruebens set Sarah's latest breakdown into motion before his death to secure the center's advantage in controlling a piece of the legacy we haven't found yet. Which means shutting down Sarah's mind would eliminate our only link to reaching Trinity, if she truly exists, for the Brotherhood."

Richard's fingers flew over his keyboard. A grid formed on the oversized touch screen, contrasting date-specific entries against the most common symbols in each dream and their frequency of appearance. He manipulated the image with his fingers, overlaying the report onto his sparse entries from tonight's dreams. He tweaked the display, focusing on instances of voices speaking from Sarah's ocean.

The frequency of occurrence had increased at a marked pace, while other repeated incidents and symbols had come and gone from Sarah's dreams with little or no pattern. Almost as if the voices and the cries calling to Sarah had been driving toward tonight's episode. He closed his eyes and felt for the answers, trusting the data. He had to be sure, at the precise moment that he'd never been less confident that his instincts could remain impartial.

As Sarah had become stronger and more stable, her results in the dream lab had grown more splintered. Her dream work became less predictable and produced fewer successful results as her primary focus became getting out of the lab and away from his probing questions. Richard had wanted to see her need for independence as a good sign. He'd agreed to her private sleeping quarters in return for her improved cooperation in their lab work. All of which had been documented in his daily reports to the elders, which were distributed to every Watcher in his chain of command. His weakening hold on Sarah's mind would have been an easy extrapolation for anyone to make.

The suspicion growing inside Richard knotted like a fist in his diaphragm.

"Someone with access to the details of my work with Sarah is acting as a pipeline to the center," he said. "They're using my reports to track the appearance of the exact symbols they'd need to manipulate Sarah's mind."

"A Watcher?" A wave of disgust shot from Jeff's mind to Richard's. "You don't think Sarah is our leak, even though someone's possessing her mind. But you believe a Watcher is helping the center?"

"Someone who could relay the locations of other Watcher teams and even tonight's mission details."

"Someone on *our* team?"

One of the trusted comrades they'd served with for years, some of whom Richard and Jeff had personally trained and handpicked for command positions.

Richard didn't want to believe it either. But there was a bone-deep truth to his suspicion. And he'd long ago learned to trust his ability to knit seemingly unconnected facts into unshakable reality before others could see the patterns. This wasn't the time to second-guess his own gifts.

It was how, when he was just a boy, he'd known to

trust the Brotherhood when his own legacy began spiraling out of control. It was how he'd known over a year ago that Sarah Temple's mind was in play, based only on a routine Brotherhood status sweep of the family lines they'd tracked for generations. His reputation for alerting the elders when it was time to engage before a legacy's principals were in play was unparalleled. So he'd been given unprecedented latitude to initiate, monitor, and control the dream testing performed on Sarah.

"You're going to sell the council on one of our own working with the center?" Jeff asked. "That's your reasoning for continuing to empower the Temple Legacy, instead of neutralizing it the way most Watchers think you should have a year ago?"

Richard swept his fingers across the touch screen, sending his data scattering. He pushed away from his desk and his feelings for Sarah—and his own growing suspicion that if he had to choose between protecting her and honoring the calling he'd sacrificed everything to follow, he'd save Sarah.

He forced objectivity into his memories of her nightmare and her lucid dream in Lenox. He analyzed and weighed possible alternatives and saw only what had been there. Felt only what the ocean's murky depths had allowed Sarah to feel. He embraced only the facts that would help him save her and defend the psychic realm.

"Someone's feeding information to the enemy," he said, "and I've sensed nothing from Sarah that tells me she's responsible. We have a mole positioned deeply within our order, and the clues to who that is and what the center's planning are locked in Sarah's mind. The

Brotherhood has to get back into her nightmare, not just to understand the consciousness Sarah's labeled as Trinity. We have to identify who's helping the center target our operations."

He sensed his friend searching his thoughts for conflicting motives. Hidden agendas.

Jeff tapped his fingers across the screen, returning order to the chaos Richard had created. "The council may have already decided that you're the weakness the center's exploiting within the Brotherhood. And that the safest course of action is to return Sarah's mind to a vegetative state, where she and your attachment to her are no longer a threat or a potential asset to anyone."

"Then my job is to convince them that they're being premature." To honor his Watcher's Creed while somehow protecting Sarah and her legacy at the same time.

"It's going to be okay." Maddie's head lay cushioned on Jarred's bare chest. "Once Metting lets me work with Sarah again, it will be okay."

She wanted to lose herself in the soothing rhythm of Jarred's breathing. He was alive. She and Sarah were alive. They were free of the center, even though Sarah had agreed to participate in an insane mission to their childhood home that had resulted in more than one of the Watcher team members returning injured. Even though Maddie still couldn't feel her sister's mind because Sarah had once again been whisked behind Metting's dream-lab barriers, for tonight they were all safe. And each day they stayed that way was a miracle Maddie hadn't believed possible just a month ago.

Jarred's arms tightened around her. The magic of

his mind stroked away at her confusion and doubt. She'd never needed to believe in him—in them—more.

"I felt your heart stop beating tonight." Her fiancé's pulse raced beneath her ear.

Her fiancé.

He'd proposed the night they'd moved into the Brotherhood's state-of-the-art headquarters, just hours after her mother's death. Maddie had agreed without hesitation. Then she'd refused to plan a ceremony until they were free of the Watchers. Not that she and Jarred needed others to validate their bond. They were already joined as completely as two people could be.

"You brought me back." Maddie nuzzled her cheek against the ridges of muscle a month of physical conditioning had added to Jarred's chest. "You always bring me back."

His memories returned her to Sarah's nightmare, to the moment that the ocean's negative energy had overcome Maddie. His love and commitment and protection hadn't been enough to hold her.

"Metting's people got my heart started again," she said. "They know what they're doing."

"Until Sarah drags you into the next dream neither one of you can control."

"It was worth it." Maddie forced her hand to relax its grip on Jarred's arm. "Once Richard deals with the council and gets me back in the lab, he'll help us figure out how to keep Sarah safe."

"A part of me hopes the elders shut down that damn lab."

Maddie pushed against Jarred's chest and sat beside him.

"Without the lab's shields, Sarah will be vulnerable to her dream's call. Look at what happened in Lenox."

"Then let Metting handle her like he did there, now that he's back in her mind."

"I can't. I—"

"I felt your heart stop beating." Jarred kissed her cheek. His lips feathered over hers, then he pulled her back to their warm sheets and tucked her beneath him. "I won't let them take you away from me, Maddie."

His promise spread through their minds. He stroked strong, callused hands down her body. His fingers spread beneath her nightshirt, seeking, finding, making her crave his touch even more. It would be so easy to forget the madness. The danger. The threat to everything they'd become.

But darkness was lurking, waiting to strike the next time her twin's mind was undefended. Just like—

"It's been waiting all along . . ." Jarred said, his thoughts flowing with hers.

Memories from the nightmare reached for them. A rising sense of desperation and pain and fear and . . . hopelessness. Sarah's dream had been a sea of hopelessness.

"Oh, God," Maddie gasped.

"Let it go for the rest of the night," he said.

"I . . . I can't. I just got my sister back from her coma. From what the center's deranged testing did to her. Now something's lurking in Sarah's ocean, trying to take her away from me. Something that's—"

"Been waiting all along," Jarred repeated.

Heat burst through them, sparking and building and consuming them with thoughts and feelings and emotions that weren't theirs. Maddie felt Jarred's mind fine-tuning images that had been hovering just beyond her reach for hours, begging to be understood.

"I heard the screaming while you were there." His next kiss was soft, gentle, coaxing. "The cries for help. I felt Sarah's fear that she couldn't stop them. Why was she willing to face such a terrible place alone?"

Maddie gazed into the clear blue of Jarred's eyes. Her twin's memories had become hers the instant Sarah allowed Maddie into the matrix. Now they were his, too.

"She was drowning . . ." Maddie said as a lifetime of pain rushed through her. "Trinity's screams were killing her, and Sarah couldn't make it stop. She never could. The screams, the voices . . . Sarah's heard them before." It was so clear now, with Jarred's insight leading Maddie through her twin's memories. "She's tried to stop the cries and failed over and over again."

"In the dream lab?"

"From the very beginning. That's part of what she's been afraid to remember."

Madness had been slowly consuming Sarah's mind forever, stripping away her control. The call of her demons must have been even worse back at their old house.

"Sarah's been dreaming of drowning in her mind's madness since—"

"Since you were children." Jarred laid his forehead against Maddie's. His body nestled beside her. His arms pulled her closer.

"When we were just little girls, Sarah used to talk about the strange things she heard in her mind. Things and people and places that would come to her when she was asleep or awake. Things that weren't real. Our mother told her to forget them. Not to believe them. So Sarah forgot. She's refused to remember it ever since. But the voices were so real this time, Jarred."

"It's going to be okay." Jarred kissed Maddie's cheek.

"No, it's not." Fresh tears flooded her eyes. Her heart. "Sarah's been running from this her whole life. Now she's seeing a dark ocean trying to kill a little girl . . . It's madness. The same insanity that locked her into her coma before. It's coming back. And I swear, Jarred, I don't think she can escape it this time."

Chapter Fourteen

Sarah sensed her twin's fall into troubled sleep. The dream lab's technology should have been blocking Maddie's psychic energy. But Sarah had known the exact moment when Maddie was informed about what happened on the Watcher mission to Lenox. She'd felt her sister accept just how dangerous Sarah's instability had become.

Maddie was now wrapped securely in the arms of a man who would do anything to help her. Sarah felt herself smile, when not too long ago she'd hated her twin for having that kind of honest connection to cling to. But you didn't hate family for having what you never would. At least Sarah didn't. Not anymore. Not the Sarah she wanted to be.

She allowed herself a twinge of jealousy as she thought back to her naive belief that she'd found the same kindred spirit for herself in Richard. Then she remembered his ultimatum from before the recon mission—that she had no choice but to work with him, remember with him, or her battle to regain her sanity was over.

She didn't know how to belong to either her past or her present, not the way Maddie did. From the very start Sarah had been too messed up to make relationships work, even within her own family. Now, if she didn't find a way to accept Richard's help when he came back for her, she'd lose all that was left—her twin and Trinity—for good.

Sleep promised a blissful reprieve. Her mind and body were clamoring for rest. But losing consciousness risked inviting the voices and images in her mind closer, even with an IV in her arm that should render her chemically incapable of achieving REM state. She would dream again. And the cries for help reaching her through the lab's psychic safeguards made dreaming alone too dangerous.

She closed her eyes instead and relaxed into the mental exercises Richard had taught her. Routines that had balanced her mind during the secret hours they'd worked together inside the center. Using them, linking their energy, he'd strengthened her ability to read and project emotions. Through dream-sharing, while she was still too weak to move from bed, he'd helped her retrain her body to walk and then run. Once she recovered enough to work with him in the center's gyms, his routines and ability to focus psychic power had augmented the speed with which she learned to execute an array of skills and disciplines.

The memory cut deep. He'd still been "Rick" then. She'd still wanted the partnership, the unity, that she'd have to force herself to accept now. She hadn't known yet how addictive and dangerous trusting Richard would be. Or that he'd turn out to be no different than the other scientists. Except he'd lied, when the others hadn't, which had made him the worst of the bunch. He'd made her believe. He'd saved her from her coma, only to make her his Dream Weaver guinea pig. He'd planned to betray her from the very first touch of his mind.

Shaking off the anger that always came with thinking of the past, she released the pointless memories, imagining them as insubstantial as a gust of wind blowing past her. She sat, legs crossed, on her bunk. Her arms rested against her knees and the loose black sweats the Watchers wore off duty. She normally wore scrubs in the lab, but tonight Richard had left her sweats.

Breathing in, she focused on the smooth feel of fleece against her skin. Breathing out, she felt the T-shirt's matching texture. The featherlight fabric's softness registered with each breath. The cloth's loose folds allowed for unrestricted movement. Uncomplicated ease. Sarah closed her eyes, picturing the sensation of clouds sweeping across her skin. Clouds that she'd first discovered in her coma's nothingness.

She directed her mind to reclaim the images that had tempted her back from that darkness: A summer storm blowing on a misty day, shot through with sparkling streaks of sunshine. Tendrils of light reaching into darkness. Illumination that had first been Richard's voice, then his thoughts, and finally his touch, as his mind taught her how to find him in the beautiful imagery, then to trust him, and then to follow him out of the silence that had consumed her.

She kept a flicker of her awareness grounded in the bunker's dream lab while she used the cloud imagery to soothe away the last of the fear and panic and guilt that had taken hold in the nightmare, then at her parents' house. She was floating, not sitting. Breathing, not grasping. She was searching for balance and clarity and purpose, instead of returning to the chaos of her visions.

Richard had taught her to let go of *then* and *now*. That there was no *before*. No *next*. There was only the silvery texture of moving freely. The silky feel of floating in a cloud's embrace and letting everything else go.

Then it was time to fly free, through sparkling light and wisps of color and the flickers of cloud shadow and sunbeams dancing across the sky. The vision became Sarah. Flying became breathing. Breathing became her path. Inhaling the clouds and the light. Exhaling as she soared higher.

But the darkness followed, no matter how fast she moved or how high the light took her. There was no escaping it. Dread competed with the vision's brightness. An ocean's murky depths called for her to return to where she really belonged.

Her breath faltered.

Her meditation's silvery promise began to fade.

She needed . . .

She needed to—

"—absorb the clouds' freedom into your mind," Richard's voice said. "You have to find a way to feel them despite all the rest. Become them. Let their freedom fill you until there's no room for conflict."

Sarah opened her eyes, not surprised to find the main source of her conflict standing in the doorway. Trinity's cries and the nightmare's call had lessened as soon as Richard arrived.

A quick sweep of their telepathic link told her he'd disabled the sensors that would have alerted his team to the lab's sealed entrance being breached. The cameras recording every move she made would see nothing of what happened next. He was a wizard with electronics, as much as he was at harnessing psychic energy. He'd personally designed most of the bunker's safeguards.

They'd be alone for as long as Richard wanted them to be.

Sarah knew little about the extrasensory gifts he'd inherited from his own family's legacy, beyond the rumor that his had been one of the most powerful lines the Watchers had dealt with until they'd involved themselves with Sarah's. He could sense, persuade, and neutralize minds, manipulate his environment without anyone knowing, leaving no trace of his presence when he was done. He could anticipate unseen danger and formulate an instant, brutally logical strategic response. He'd mastered psychic and emotional control that had once made her feel safe.

Tonight his level stare felt like an ambush.

"How's your breathing?" The familiar cadence of his voice had the power to transport her all the way back to the beginning if she let it, to when she'd waited anxiously for him to arrive each night at the center so their secret work together could begin.

"Not good." There was no point in lying. He was already in her mind, searching out the truth for himself.

"Shall we?" He motioned toward the gym that was connected to the dream lab. He'd changed out of his fatigues into sweats identical to hers.

Sarah worked out in the gym alone or sometimes with her twin after dream simulations, or whenever the surging energy in her mind became too much. Physical activity was another of Richard's methods for sorting through the illusive, half-formed thoughts she frequently couldn't tame after a projection.

"You want to pick my mind apart in the gym?" she asked the man her subconscious kept trying to kill.

A man who could no doubt sense the violence blooming back to life inside her again. But that was evidently too damn bad. There was work to be done, and he was just the loyal soldier to produce the results his council demanded. The last of her meditative clouds evaporated. Hatred collided with her instinctive need for his calming presence. Richard inhaled deeply, breathing through the pain she hadn't meant for her mind to thrust at him.

God, she really was a monster.

"It's just fear and confusion," he said.

He freed her from the monitor leads and IV tubing that had restricted her to the bed, as if being the target of her psychic assault meant nothing.

"It's an instinctive response to tonight's upheaval and the memories you faced," he said, "and being forced to grow your skills too quickly. You should have been trained since birth to control the emotional component to your telepathic abilities. Your parents' denial of what you would become eventually led to their deaths. Now that job falls to me, even if it means taking a few stray blows along the way. That's why we're going to work in the gym. Your nightmare and lucid daydream were stronger than anything you've experienced since leaving the center. You can't meditate their aftershocks away with gentle, rolling clouds. You need to vent."

Sarah froze in the middle of pushing herself off the table.

"I need control." She sounded weak. She felt weak. Incapable of facing what was about to happen. She felt trapped because she had no choice but to endure this man's methods if she wanted Trinity and Maddie and their legacy to survive.

Debriefing memories she couldn't safely access on her own would require projecting them into a new vision. The alternate reality would have to be controlled, the same as if what she was remembering was happening all over again, or she could cause even more damage. Focusing and suppressing a vision's impulses was difficult enough with Maddie's help. Adding the strain of a workout with Richard to the mix was unnecessarily reckless.

"The nightmare will come for me again when I start to remember," she said. "Or the anger in my insane daydream will take over. And—"

"I'll be there from the start this time." He sounded so sure, even after her disastrous results in Lenox. "But we need to get your body moving. We need to bypass whatever's keeping your mind from opening fully to mine. I have to relive what you saw with you. No holding back. You're going to work through your resistance and find a way to trust me."

"Trust you to push me into another psychotic break?"

Richard's eyes narrowed. "Whatever it takes to get to the truth."

Sarah's feet hit the floor.

She dropped the last of her mental barriers.

Her rage swamped them both.

"I just might kill you." She walked past him on shaking legs. "Is that the truth you're looking for?"

"It's as good a place to start as any." He followed her

into the gym. "Anything's better than you continuing to run from the work we should have begun together a month ago."

They hadn't sparred since the center, back when he'd promised to take care of her and guide her through the Dream Weaver programming and protect her from the other scientists. She hadn't wanted him and his insight anywhere near her since.

The gym's door whooshed shut behind them and locked securely, sealing off the outside world. They walked to the center of the workout mat. The darkness Richard said he wasn't concerned about seethed inside her, and there was no one to vent it on but the man she hated.

Sarah attacked without warning, leveling a roundhouse kick that Richard deflected with ease. Her stamina was surprisingly intact after the beating her mind and body had taken. Or maybe it was the rush of satisfaction feeding her, driving her to pound away at the bastard blocking every strike she made.

He was a master of every Eastern discipline on the books, and some techniques known only to warriors who were called to sacrifice more than should be expected of mortal man. She was a novice in comparison. But from the beginning, she'd embraced his lessons and his promises that their work would move her closer to freedom. The skills he'd taught her became an extension of her betrayal now, while echoes of the ocean's demands rolled off her, vibrating, bleeding, screaming into the night.

And there her raven was, accepting her the way no one else could. Encouraging her loss of control while malevolent memories of nearly dying, nearly losing Maddie, and failing to reach Trinity crept closer.

"Stop thinking of me as your dream raven." He blocked a series of body blows from her arms and legs, combinations that she wouldn't have been strong enough to execute without his energy feeding hers. "Leave what happened at the center outside our work, outside this room. Stop making me the enemy or I can't help you."

"When I think of you as anything but a lying bastard—"

She executed a round of compact chops with her left arm, then her right. Circling, she attacked, then deflected his response. *Once.* Reverse. *Twice.* Regaining her balance. *Again.*

"—it makes me want to destroy us both. You love the truth so much, let's focus on yours."

She kept advancing. When Richard didn't retaliate, she kept attacking.

"I trusted you at the center, when you made me believe you cared about something beyond your Watcher's oath," she said. "Stupid. I'm too weak to do what needs to be done now without endangering my sister, so you're forcing me to work with you again no matter how much I hate you. Even more stupid. You can convince yourself that what you did to me to control Dream Weaver wasn't just as warped as Ruebens's plans. But you and I both know the truth—you were my enemy then, and you always will be. Which makes the two of us locked in here together the stupidest thing you've done yet."

Chapter Fifteen

Richard swept his leg to drop Sarah. She sidestepped, then paused on the balls of her feet, waiting, hoping he wasn't through. She sure as hell wasn't.

He'd wanted her out of control.

Unguarded.

Be careful what you wish for, Colonel.

He used her defensive posture to advance and push her to the gym's padded wall. Moving too fast for her eyes to track, he pressed his forearm against her throat. The pressure threatened to cut off her oxygen, a reminder of her attempt to strangle him earlier.

"It might be advisable before we're called in front of the council—" His hold was firm but not lethal. His smile was easy, while her chest rose and fell with each restricted breath. "—to find a way to downplay just how intent you are on making me pay for everything that's happened to you."

"You're a master at hiding the truth. Maybe you can give me some pointers."

The pain that streaked through them tasted of her betrayal and Trinity's cries. Sarah let the emotions build, channeling them. She allowed tears to shimmer in her eyes. She relaxed into Richard's hold. Settled deeper against the wall. Created distance, while tempting him to follow.

When he leaned another breath closer, his gaze softening with regret, she slammed her forehead into his face.

Blood gushed from his nose.

She escaped to the other side of the gym.

"You're doing just fine without my help." He wiped beneath his nose. His dark gaze simmered with admiration. "But you're still holding back. Pummeling me to bits might make you feel better, but it's not going to get us past your compulsion to put yourself at risk to avoid working with me. It's not going to tell us why your mind's so obsessed with Trinity, or how your dreams are controlling you with the sound of a child's voice. Stop wasting both our time, Alpha."

"Don't call me that."

Her moniker at the center had been his idea, intended to depersonalize their connection in public. It was a reminder now that she'd been merely a means to an end. That she'd trusted a man named Rick whose loyalty had been a lie from the very start.

She advanced, thinking only of hurting him as badly as he'd hurt her. He stepped into her momentum and clamped his hand around her throat. Without breaking stride, he propelled her to the floor. He'd been toying with her until then. She could feel it through his touch, their telepathic link deepening. Her emotional free-for-all was allowing him freer access to her mind, exactly as he'd planned.

"Tell me about the voices in your projections." He

knelt, his knee near her shoulder, in position to make an easy pin if she chose to struggle. "Focus on the dream ocean in your nightmare first. I have to understand who we're fighting."

Sarah wanted to yell that *they* weren't fighting anyone. But an ocean's demented current was lapping at the edges of her consciousness. Certain death waited in her memories, and her mind was suddenly clinging to Richard's strength. Her eyes fluttered closed as she fought to hold on to reality.

The nightmare would be waiting, the moment she dropped her psychic shields, and she was suddenly terrified to go back.

"I can hear it calling you." Richard's concern drew closer. "You said you wanted the nightmare to find you tonight. How long have you been waiting for it?"

"I . . . I don't know."

But she did, and his mind was returning her to the dream's cool, clean welcome. To the ocean's currents and the darkness beyond. Sarah had prepared for it. She'd made sure she was alone when it came. That way she wouldn't hurt anyone else, and her raven wouldn't be able to stop her.

"Open your eyes." Richard's hand cupped her chin, his grip tightening until she complied.

"Let me go."

"I'm your guide in your memories." He controlled her attempt to jerk away. "Tell me you understand that."

"You're—"

"Not your enemy. Not in this vision. Get your emotions under control and stop hiding from me. I'm your

Watcher. You have nothing to fear from showing me the truth."

Except that he was also the man she'd dreamed might one day love her. Then he'd methodically, deliberately, destroyed her ability to tolerate the caress of his hand on her face, or his mind steering her thoughts.

Richard's focus homed in on her unguarded thoughts. His gaze widened.

"Sarah . . ."

He was sensing the loneliness welling inside her. Through their link, she felt his mind form the answering apology she couldn't bear.

"I'm—" he began.

"Don't you dare say you're sorry."

Sorry for ever touching her? Sorry for not anticipating her desperation to hold on to the first genuine connection she'd found with anyone besides her twin? Sorry that he now had to deal with her missing what they'd had, long after his complete emotional withdrawal?

"Get out of my mind," she begged. "Stop digging up things that don't matter anymore."

"Of course they matter." Understanding battled with the regret in his voice.

Something else was there, too. Something deeper brewing beneath Richard's control that he wasn't allowing Sarah to feel. Or maybe she didn't trust herself to. Because a weak part of her wanted to crawl into his lap and spill every last secret she'd never trusted to anyone, not even Maddie.

But giving him her trust again would kill Sarah the

next time she became an asset he had to sacrifice in his psychic war.

"I won't let you hurt me anymore." She lifted her chin, daring him to defend what he'd done. "I don't know you. I never really knew you. No one does. You don't let anyone see the truth. You show people whatever you need them to see, to get what you want. How do I trust that again?"

"This can't be about us." His mental barriers slammed down, and he was once again an objective scientist. Her Watcher, nothing more, just as he'd said. "It can't be about past mistakes that can't be undone. If we don't process your nightmare and understand how you were lured there, it will control you again. Then everything we could learn from your dream will be lost."

Trinity's helpless cries were still calling to Sarah. Richard was no longer shielding them. And he was hearing every single plea while he tried to help Sarah invite them closer and believe that she could control her addiction to stopping them. Until the truth was suddenly there, blooming in both their minds, unfolding as vividly as if it were happening all over again.

Sarah startling awake. A child's cry for help echoing in her quarters, not just in her mind. The promise of a dream tempting her to let the pleas consume the night. Sarah shaking while she fought their power . . .

"How long ago did you decide to let the dream have you?" Richard asked. The deep timbre of his voice grounded her consciousness to him and the gym, as well as the vision.

"When I realized that the ocean was my way out.

Controlling it was how I'd be free from this, from you, for good."

"Free? That's why you're so determined to go back? You and Madeline almost died in the nightmare's matrix."

"My sister following me was your doing, not mine. And if I hadn't come back, at least . . . at least it would have finally been over."

Her last admission came as a sob.

Hearing it out loud, Sarah accepted how close she'd come to giving up.

"What would have been over?" Richard's fingers aligned with the pressure points near her temples, deepening their link. "The connection I never should have allowed to grow between us at the center? Is that why you turned to the dream for help, instead of me?"

"I can't talk about this." Sarah tried to sit up, roll away. "You won't understand. You never understood."

"Then listen instead." He kept her pinned beside him, his body warm and his strength feeling like a perfect dream of protection and acceptance. "I was feeling the same things you were, Sarah, when I found you in your coma. I've never had that kind of connection with anyone." The bedrock honesty in his voice tempted her to believe each lie. "I shouldn't have acted on it, but I was too selfish to keep my distance. It felt too good, discovering something so perfect after a lifetime of not believing it would happen for me."

Tempting?

Perfect?

He'd wanted her, too. Was that supposed to make what he'd done okay?

"I can't . . ." She winced as a little girl's cries for help screamed through her. The same little girl who'd tried to kill them in Lenox.

Twice now, she'd failed to find Trinity. And the pain of it was too close, everything hurt too much, with Richard's arms wrapped around her, protecting her, while he kept his emotions shut away and denied her the sense of belonging that had once felt like home every time he touched her.

"I can't handle this," she said.

"How long?" he insisted. "How long have you been fighting the nightmare's call alone?"

"Since the night Ruebens died," she admitted, her voice breaking along with her control.

The night she'd insisted that the name Trinity be given to the cries that had begun with Ruebens's revelation of a third, secret piece to her legacy. That night, a little girl's voice had bloomed to life in Sarah's mind along with her nightmare's pull, sounding stronger and clearer than anything Sarah's mind had conjured as a child.

"Satisfied now?" she demanded.

Richard's presence searched deeper into her thoughts. "Not until you show me everything. Let me in completely, Sarah, the way you did when you first woke from your coma."

"But you—"

"I hurt you, I know. Badly. Everything I let happen between us was a mistake. I became too emotionally attached to protect you properly. I lost my objectivity. And I'm sorry. You have no idea how much. But you have to let me back into your dreams. Completely. We're running out of time to save you and Madeline and—"

"Trinity . . ."

The shared thought flashed another memory through their developing vision.

This time, she was seeing Richard racing into her sleeping quarters and finding her mind lost to him.

He was leaning over her unconscious body and begging her to come back to him. He was panicked at the thought of losing her forever . . .

Back in the gym, his face was only inches away while Sarah absorbed his desperation to bring her back—his out-of-control emotions flooding an unguarded moment he'd meant for no one else to share. The honesty of it pierced the emotional distance between them until suddenly she was feeling the pieces of him, the real Richard, that he kept so carefully locked away.

"I . . ." She closed her eyes. "I . . . I can't do this again."

"I won't let the attachment between us became a problem," he promised, already pulling his essence back.

"What attachment?" There was no attachment. "I can't—"

"I'll make this right, Sarah."

"How?"

She'd survived a month of working with Maddie under Richard's supervision by convincing herself that he'd never felt anything real. They'd never even kissed. She'd told herself that the answering need she'd thought she sensed in him had existed only in her head.

How did she keep believing that now?

"We'll keep our emotions separate from our projections this time," he said. "It's what's worked for me with every other legacy. It's a key skill we teach all our

Watchers. When I found you, I let myself forget the damage that losing control can do to a mission. Work with me instead of against me until we get through this, Sarah. We'll find the answers we need. Then I promise, you won't have to have anything more to do with me."

Hearing the sadness in his voice as he vowed to let her go for good, feeling it, was the final straw.

"And what exactly happens when working with you turns into you messing with my mind all over again, in the name of doing your duty and stopping the center?" It was the only truth she could let matter in the no-emotion, no-attachment working relationship he was suggesting. "What if the darkness that Ruebens grew inside me turns out to be all that I was ever meant to belong to? What if the damage Dream Weaver caused, that horrible thing that we found in my bedroom, is all that I am now, and I trust you with it again, and your council orders you to stop me for good?"

"I'm not going to let that happen."

Richard's callused fingers soothed healing circles against her temples. His conviction that he could protect both her and his oath to his fellow Watchers filled her.

"Show me where you're afraid you belong," he said. "What were you so afraid we'd see in your nightmare that you were willing to die to keep it hidden? The center is using your fears against you, Sarah. Don't let working with me be one of them. Trust me to take away the secrets."

Exhausted, off-balance, and confused beyond bearing, Sarah felt the last of her resistance melt beneath the pressure of his mind . . .

They were both seeing her father dying in a fiery car crash while she stood and watched. Maddie's fight to save Jarred's life flashed next, after Sarah's damaged mind had nearly killed him, too. Then they were reliving Sarah's mother's death at Tad Ruebens's hand, another nightmare Sarah had been too out of control to prevent.

"You couldn't have stopped any of it." Richard stood beside her in the vision, absorbing each memory without judgment. "Your mother didn't prepare you or your sister for your legacy. I didn't protect you from Tad Ruebens's assault. But I'll be here from now on."

"I don't want you here." She tried to open her eyes, but she couldn't break free of the vision's momentum, building as her connection with Richard deepened. The sickening montage kept playing, showing her the things Ruebens had forced her mind to do through Dream Weaver. "I don't want you here ever again."

"Yes you do, so you can let these memories go." Richard's image grabbed her hand, sending more of his psychic power coursing through her mind. "Some part of you still wants more than the guilt that the nightmare's darkness feeds on, and the isolation you've convinced yourself will keep you safe. If not, coming here with me wouldn't have been possible. Where else do you need to return to?"

The dream jumped to a memory of ribbons of color leading them through the nightmare's sea. There was more light than before, she realized, as the ocean channeled them through an endless maze that felt more like a trap than she remembered. With Richard beside her she could breathe better. She could see more as his dream image cradled her closer. They accelerated through the twisting tunnel. He turned his back only a second before they crashed into the door, shielding her from the collision's impact.

It was still Sarah's hands that bled as she struggled with the latch. Her lungs were burning now despite his calming presence. But he was there this time, when her mind let go of the compulsion to reach the truth on the other side of the door. She felt him stiffen behind her as she accepted that the cries for help were as much hers as Trinity's. She didn't dare turn back to see his reaction. But his arm circled her waist, his understanding touch comforting her whether she wanted to believe in it or not.

Seething water took them deeper. When they reached the ocean's floor, there was no panic this time. No fight to escape.

"What drew you to this place?" he asked.

Sarah turned to him finally. And in her vision's reality the man beside her was once again her patient teacher. The hero who'd saved her mind. The kindred spirit she'd trusted to bring her back to life.

"Rick?"

It was Rick that she'd secretly needed when there was no place else to fall and the ocean was closing in.

"Focus on the memories," he said, "not me. There's another voice besides Trinity's here. We have to know what it's saying. How it convinced you to stay. You'd already given up when Madeline entered the dream. Why aren't you fighting your way back to the surface or the door?"

The sea's currents shifted around them.

Angry.

Closing in.

Richard fought to keep the vision and Sarah focused.

"The water wanted me here," she said, seeing and hearing through his experience now, not just hers.

"Yes." A rush of current obscured his image, then he came back into focus.

"The cries," she said as the ocean grew colder. "Trinity was

behind the door, but I couldn't help her. I'd failed. And the voice said I belonged here instead. I was so tired of trying to reach her."

"Yes." Richard winced as Trinity's screams grew louder—a child's fear and a little girl's pain and a woman's betrayal.

"I've heard them before . . ." Sarah couldn't stop shivering. "I've been hearing them forever, and I just left her there. I abandoned her. I gave up."

Shame seethed around them. It would have sucked Sarah away, except for Richard's grip still wrapped around her wrist.

"The voice is only a memory," he reminded her. "It can't reach you here. The ocean can't have you. Tell me who was waiting for you at the bottom of the ocean. Who didn't want you to return to the door?"

She pressed her free hand to her temple, feeling his touch there, too, from beyond the memory. The ocean's voice grew more and more familiar, the longer Richard's control was there to help her.

"The wolf!" Sarah clung to the burst of clarity and to Richard. The ocean churned around them. "Tad Ruebens was the ocean's voice. I abandoned Trinity to let the currents take me straight to his wolf. God, what if he's what I've been searching for all along? What if he's the one who called me to Lenox, so he could turn me against you and the rest of the team?"

"Ruebens is dead. He's not real outside the dream."

"But he's still calling me." Even though the consciousness she'd connected with in the house had seemed more familiar than the nightmare's voice, it had been the same darkness calling her. The same destruction.

"The nightmare's matrix is calling you." Richard's logic knifed through her panic, creating a pool of warm, calm water around them. "Whoever's triggering your projections is playing on your fear of Ruebens's symbol. But the wolf is dead."

"I saw him in my vision in my bedroom. I—"

"My men killed him. Believe that whenever he appears in a projection. See only what's really here."

"I can't . . ." The water roared around them. It was inside her again. Filling her. Taking control.

"Focus only on the vision's images, not your fear of them." Richard tucked her head beneath his chin, his gentleness a long-forgotten memory. *"Feel only our connection. You and me, not the dream's hold. You can breathe now, Sarah. Your lungs are clear. We're separate from the memories we're seeing. Show me what the ocean was hiding from you down here in the darkness. What couldn't you see before? Show me the hidden secrets in your dream."*

Sarah didn't want the memories anymore. She didn't want either of them to see. But there it was, reaching for her. What she'd needed to hide from most. What she'd promised never to return to. Her need for Richard—Rick—to find her, comfort her, and never let her go.

And he was there now. Their hearts were beating together. Her hands were locked around his powerful arms. Her breath was mingling with his energy. Her lips were hovering just beneath his.

Every dream and longing and desire she'd given up because she couldn't have him were just inches away. All Richard had to do was say that he wanted her again. That he'd always wanted her. That nothing would ever feel more real than holding her in his arms.

"Sarah . . ." His fingers tangled with her hair. *"You don't want this."*

"No."

She clung to him shamelessly. It was freezing again, the water bitterly cold. Her lips nuzzled his neck no matter how

hard she fought to stop. His warmth, the answering desire rag-
ing through his mind, tempted her to taste him, kiss him, make
him respond even more.

"Please . . . ," she said. "Don't let me go."

And then he was kissing her back and it was everything
she'd dreamed it would be. His mouth opened, and with a
groan he was demanding, devouring, needing the touch and the
feel of her, of them, that they'd never shared. He was encourag-
ing her instead of holding back. Feasting on her. Demanding
that she leave the darkness behind.

At the bottom of the nightmare's ocean, she could have this.
She could have Rick back, and she'd never be alone again. A
part of her knew it wasn't real. But it felt too good, threading
her fingers through his dark hair and arching into his strength.
Wrapping her passion around his and setting them both free.
Until they existed only in this timeless moment where they
were beyond the damage and the betrayal and the guilt. Noth-
ing mattered here but her fantasy to make him hers, and his
answering compulsion to keep her forever.

Richard's hands roamed her body, his fingers clenching on
her bottom with just enough bite to make her want more. He
lifted her until she was plastered against him, his need raging to
bind her to him until being safe and unemotional and in control
would never be possible again.

Her nails scraped down the hard muscles of his chest, then
up again, searing him.

"This is where you've wanted him all along," whispered the
wolf's voice.

Then, suddenly, the sea's currents were caressing her, too.
Encouraging her. Directing her. Outside of her. Terrifying her,
because she couldn't stop herself from responding.

The vision darkened as her compulsion grew to distract the man in her arms, seduce him, lure him closer. She could barely see Richard's face. She framed it with her hands.

"Slowly," the wolf whispered. "Gain his trust slowly."

Sarah shook her head.

She tried to break free of the vision.

Her fingers fumbled with Richard's shirt. She couldn't stop herself from lifting it over his head, revealing his Watcher's Creed branded into his right shoulder.

Specto. Tego. Asservo.

Watch. Defend. Preserve.

"Rick?" She strained to make out his expression. To warn him about the dream's intent. "Help me . . ."

He was fighting, too, she realized. Responding to her fear, trying to push her away. But she could feel him not being able to stop kissing her. Touching her.

The nightmare had taken control.

Richard's fingers feathered along the hem of her sweatshirt. Then he was sliding the material up her body, his mouth claiming the sensitive skin swelling above her bra. Their vision vibrated with the erotic sizzle of his tongue stroking and his teeth biting and his lips promising her ecstasy.

"He's yours now," the voice chanted. "You have him right where you've always wanted him."

And right where the nightmare's ocean had needed him—out of control and primed for the attack Sarah could feel building within her, programmed behavior she wouldn't be able to hold back for long.

Revenge. She could finally have her revenge, the vision was promising. Her nails dug into Richard's thighs. She fought the emotions driving her. Her hatred, and the nightmare's, too. The darkness that had drawn her in with promises of saving

Trinity, then dragged her to her dream's barren floor and the command to—

"*Kill me?*" Richard said, finding his voice. His hungry gaze hardened at the rage building inside Sarah.

Talons closed around her arms. He'd transformed into an avenging raven, staring down at her with death flickering in his midnight eyes.

"*Kill him!*" the ocean screamed. "*Before he destroys you.*"

"*No.*" The still-sane part of Sarah clung to the knowledge that his dream image was there to protect her.

Hesitating sent pain streaking through them both. Trinity's cries sliced through Sarah. She would have collapsed, if the raven weren't holding her. He caught her close, lifting her into the safety of his wings. Sarah gazed into his fierce expression and saw the darkness of her own soul. But there was understanding there, too. Acceptance of the truth they'd come for. She was evil, but he'd never let her go. Just as he'd promised.

Her hands came up.

Her fingers circled his neck.

The compulsion to strangle him grew stronger, but her raven merely watched, trust in his gaze and his thoughts and his relaxed hold.

"*I can't stop,*" she said. "*He wants me to kill you.*"

"*Take him,*" the wolf's voice demanded. "*Take him before he destroys us.*"

"*She won't kill for you here,*" her raven screeched into the roaring ocean. "*She's not your weapon anymore.*"

Then he was suddenly Richard again—Rick—and he was using all his telepathic strength to regain control of the vision. He swallowed against her grip.

"*You won't allow the voice to make you kill,*" he insisted.

"That's why you pushed Maddie away and tried to make her leave. It's why you didn't want her in the dream helping you. Subconsciously, you sensed the danger here. You're not a killer, Sarah."

But she had been. She'd been too weak to save too many precious lives. The ocean was right. The voices had always been right. Darkness, not Trinity's light, was where Sarah belonged. There, at the bottom of an empty ocean, where she'd never hurt anyone again.

"Kill him!" the wolf demanded.

"Let the vision go," Richard insisted. "We've found what we needed. You don't want to kill. It's Dream Weaver programming that we can reverse, now that we know."

Before Sarah could respond, the ocean wrenched them back to the image of a blood-soaked door.

"You're hurting her," the wolf said. "Kill him, so she can be free."

Trinity begged for help behind the door. Richard held Sarah tighter, to keep her from killing herself to get to a child.

"Let me go." Her nails tore at the skin on his arms and face. "I'll kill you if you don't let me go. I have to open the door. I have to—"

"Break the link," he demanded. "You have to break free."

The water surged, dragging them down again.

"Release the memories, Alpha. Let me bring you back. Release!"

His command, calling her Alpha, ripped at the vision, returning Sarah piece by piece to a reality outside the nightmare's warped demands. Until everything in the vision rushed to black, and then she was—

Awake.

Stunned.

Back in the lab's gym.

In Richard's shaking arms.

He was holding her against his chest, both of them sprawled on the gym's mat, his body braced behind her. His broken breathing rumbled beneath her ear. Sarah crawled, stumbled to her feet, then ran across the gym.

Her mind was spinning. She couldn't remember anything clearly except the craving to kill and her willingness to do whatever the nightmare wanted, to stop the screams still ringing through her mind. Revulsion, self-loathing, sent her to her knees. Her muscle control dissolved into convulsions. Richard was beside her. He reached for the pouch of medication he carried with him everywhere, then inserted a needle into her left arm, pushing one of his recovery meds into a vein.

"Let this circulate through your system," he said. "It will take care of the worst of the side effects."

"Get away from me."

She couldn't stop shivering. He held her head while she lost the contents of her stomach.

"I don't—" she started to say.

"You don't want me here." He brushed her hair out of her eyes and studied her pupils. "I know. But I'm all you've got tonight."

He'd made sure they were alone, she remembered. He'd forced her to fight him so she'd lose control. Then both their mental barriers had evaporated in the dream, and they'd given in to the need for one another they'd both been denying. Only it had been the nightmare driving them to that perfect moment.

It had consumed their vision. Her memories of the dream had taken on a life of their own. And they'd wanted Richard dead. Again.

She could still feel her hands around his neck. The command to kill still ruled a part of her that wasn't completely back. Meanwhile, her lips were tingling from his kisses and the passion that had consumed them. Sarah wiped her mouth with the back of her hand. Richard's gaze followed the movement. He closed his eyes. Then he stood and walked to the other side of the gym.

Her breathing and pulse settled as her bloodstream metabolized more of the medication he'd injected. She pushed back until she was sitting. Richard didn't move. His shields were locked back into place. It was unsettling, not being able to sense what he was thinking again after their minds had merged so deeply.

But she didn't have to know.

She could guess what was coming, no matter what he'd promised.

"Just say it." Betrayal hurt even worse the second time around. "You're already halfway out the door. Tell me I'm too fucked-up to risk your position to back me. You were right. Trinity's not real. Her cries and whatever that was I saw in Lenox were just another way for the center to control me until I lured a prime target into the nightmare's trap. Go report to your leaders. Let's get this over with."

Richard crossed the room in a blur. He pulled Sarah to her feet and held her suspended off the ground so they were eye to eye.

She'd wanted to face his desertion with the same defiance that had saved her at the center. But the secret place inside her that his dream touch had warmed was aching now. Bleeding. Sarah was bleeding, tiny drops of emptiness filling the heart his protection and fierce belief in her within the vision had split wide open again.

And now, there he was. *Rick*. Working up the courage to tell her once again that his duty to his brotherhood had always been more important than her.

"You're not getting off that easy," he said instead. "Not until you tell me exactly how long Ruebens's wolf has been in your dream, telling you to kill."

CHAPTER SIXTEEN

"Talk to me." Richard made himself put Sarah down and move away.

Keeping his hands and his emotions to himself after the passion that had just consumed them was impossible. But he'd do it somehow. The tactical significance of their vision had to stay his focus, not the compulsion to drag Sarah back to the exercise mat and make love to her until she was screaming for him, proving that it had been more than her Dream Weaver programming binding her to Richard.

"I just tried to kill you," Sarah said to the empty space over his shoulder, "because a nightmare told me to. Trinity doesn't exist. She never has. What else is there to talk about?"

Her rapid recovery from their vision, even quicker than from the previous two projections, was as shocking as the rest of what had happened. Her psychic stamina was escalating as rapidly as her programming's hold. It wouldn't be long before Richard would lose his ability to guide Sarah's projections. Soon, it would be her choice alone what her legacy became.

"Let's start with what it's going to take to convince

the council that this was a successful exercise rather than a reason to neutralize your legacy."

Her attention snapped back to him. "You . . . you're going to lobby your elders to keep playing with this insanity?"

"*We* are." He could still hear a child's voice calling to Sarah through the lab's psychic buffers. And a man's deep, unintelligible command. He could feel Sarah's mind struggling not to be absorbed by them.

She stiffened, sensing his awareness. "Not trusting you isn't losing my nerve. It's self-preservation."

"Not when I'm your only shot to find Trinity."

"She isn't real." Her eyes filled with the kind of loss that destroyed souls. "I must have realized that when I couldn't open that door in the nightmare. That's why I couldn't connect with whatever we found in my parents' house. Trinity's never been real."

"You won't know for sure until you and your sister and I get back into your nightmare and dig for the truth."

"The elders aren't going to let me go back." She sounded almost relieved. "What if I try to kill someone again?"

Her fear of losing control, her fear of herself, filled their link. There wasn't a flicker of the malice or revenge that the nightmare had triggered.

"Then you'll pull back," he said. "Just like you have twice now. You've developed the control you need to find Trinity. As long as you take the help you need with you, you'll succeed next time."

Her darker impulses would remain a threat, but Richard had sensed the truth in her mind. The vision's homicidal commands weren't a product of her own thoughts—she'd fought them too hard.

She was staring at Richard as if he were the one losing his mind. And maybe he was. Jeff wouldn't understand the risk he was about to insist she take with him.

"The ocean told you to kill me," he pressed, "but I'm still here. Your mind is not the threat the Brotherhood should be worried about. The council needs your nightmare to get to the bottom of whatever the center's doing, as much as you need Watcher support to find Trinity. And if I have my say, it won't be a vision or a lab exercise this time. Once we sell the council on it, your next dream will be a sanctioned reconnaissance mission, just like the trip to Lenox."

Richard was saying "we." He was offering to risk his career, facing the council with Sarah by his side and asking them to take even more risks with her legacy. From the start, meeting her had challenged who he thought he was, everything he believed in. And he'd had no choice from the beginning but to challenge her back, always pushing for just a little more than she thought she could handle. Now he was asking her to trust him to push her even further.

Sarah nodded so tentatively, she barely moved at all.

"Good." He tried to project back confidence.

She crossed her arms and stared daggers.

"Has the ocean told you to kill before?" he asked.

"No." Her tentative smile made him long to see a dozen more. To own more of her kisses, too, and to coax out more of the sighs she'd made as their bodies melded within the vision. "Your raven seems to be what it took to trigger that impulse." Her gaze chilled. His dream symbol flashed through their link. "The voices have been satisfied with stalking just me before now."

"But they focused on me," Richard said, "when I challenged the water's hold on your consciousness." He waited for her to follow his logic. "The same thing happened to Maddie when she tried to pull you out of the nightmare. Then to me, when you woke in your sleeping quarters."

"I . . ." Sarah hugged herself tighter. "No. I was just . . . Maddie was too weak to hold the bridge to the dream. And I'd gone too deep to pull out. The darkness was closing in and she wouldn't leave without me, and the ocean—"

"Would have trapped you both, if you'd stayed any longer." Richard had felt their imminent collapse as soon as his raven dove beneath the nightmare's surface. "The same way the consciousness at the house struck out at me and the other Watchers who were threatening its objective."

"What objective, besides pushing me over the edge?"

"There's a component of your programming designed to protect your dreams from outside tampering. Sleeper programming designed to return your legacy to center control whenever they need you."

Sarah swallowed.

Started to talk.

Swallowed again.

"But why would Maddie be a threat?" she forced out. "The center's wanted her with me from the start, controlling my messed-up powers. We were supposed to be some kind of super weapon together. Protecting my mind from her can't possibly benefit them now."

"Unless you're growing strong enough for the center to manipulate without your sister's emotional control balancing your projections. Maddie's mind focuses you, but she also holds back your darker impulses. If you don't need her to maintain a dreamscape, and if she'll see the center's embedded impulses within your programming as a threat, then—"

"She's in a position to stop whatever the center has planned, just like you." Sarah's gaze shifted to the bruises on his neck.

"We won't know for sure until we can get you back to your nightmare with the support you'll need to control your search for Trinity." It would have to be a council-sanctioned mission, a plan they logically had little to no chance of convincing the elders to implement. But Richard's intuition was already screaming that it was the Brotherhood's best opportunity to counter the center's tactics. "The only other insight we have into what the government's up to is that there's a leak in the Brotherhood."

"Leak?"

"A mole, informing the center on key operations."

"And after my nightmare you thought it was me."

"The council wondered, yes."

"But not you? Not even after a center team was waiting for us at my parents' house?"

"Not since your mind accepted my raven image into the nightmare, no. I've been able to read you ever since. Your focus has always been on saving Trinity, nothing more. There's a darker presence in your projection, but you're not controlling it."

Sarah was staring at the floor between them, seeming smaller and even more fragile by the second. She had to come to the next logical question on her own, and had to give him a chance to help her find the answer. He could feel her thoughts scanning, analyzing, tumbling through the reality she didn't want to face and the inevitability she couldn't avoid.

"What about Trinity?" She finally looked up, still weak, still scared, but still fighting.

"What about her?"

"She's the one calling to me. Finding her is the reason I've fought so hard for the ocean dream. It's why I went with you on that pointless mission. But all of it was just a center ploy. You're talking like we're going back—done deal, no matter how dangerous the dream's matrix is. And Trinity's not even real."

"Isn't she?" Richard could feel her fighting the truth that he could only now accept. "Forget about Lenox for now. You found her in the nightmare." He could see the door again, waiting in her ocean dream. And Sarah's blood seeping into the churning water as she fought with the latch. But Sarah was resisting the symbolism of what they'd just discovered together. She didn't know how to trust the hidden truths she'd freed from her own mind. "I was right there with you in your vision. What were you feeling?"

"I . . ." Sarah's hands clenched. "I couldn't reach her."

"That's right. You couldn't reach *her*. Not *it*. Not a static component of some dream's matrix manipulating your obsession to somebody who isn't real. There's someone there, Sarah, a consciousness you're attached to. Your mind's strong enough to know that. Now look deeper. Feel the complete memory. What's behind the door?"

"The . . ." Sarah stared. "The truth," she whispered, her composure shredding, her fingers clenched as she fought back tears.

Richard took her hands. He couldn't stand to watch her shivering. He turned her palms into his. When she didn't pull away from his touch, he dropped his telepathic shields completely.

"You were terrified." He leaned closer. "So terrified, you let go of the door, no matter how badly you wanted to get through. You were afraid—"

"Of the truth. That's what she said in Lenox. The little girl in my lucid daydream said I didn't want to believe. That I never would."

Her mind was moving with his again, bouncing back and forth between her memories of the nightmare and the lucid dream in her childhood bedroom. Her unspoken trust as she shared it all with him felt like cool spring rain, washing him clean. He sensed the exact moment that Sarah accepted what she'd known all along.

"Trinity was there, in the nightmare," she said, the instincts he needed her to trust finally taking hold. Instincts that had pulled her back from the vision's demand that she kill him. "And I felt her in Lenox, too. I don't know what happened. Why I couldn't get through to her in either place. But . . . she was real."

"She's real." Richard breathed for them both until she caught the rhythm and her lungs began to fill on their own. He held on to the reality of her fully accepting him into her memories for the first time. "I'm not sure what happened in your old bedroom, but we're not going to stop until we find Trinity. Together. Your mind's always known it can trust me. It reached out of the nightmare to me for help. *Me*, Sarah. Your—"

"Raven," her mind projected.

Only this time, the mention of his dream symbol

wasn't followed by a surge of hatred. Her breathing stayed even, flowing in and out in time with his. Something close to acceptance flickered in her gaze as her thoughts followed his, back to the moment when he'd rescued her and Madeline from the nightmare. Then to their debriefing vision and his battle with the wolf's presence, his determination to bring Sarah back. His willingness to die protecting her, the way he and his entire team had put their lives on the line to get her to Lenox and back.

Richard found himself wanting to cradle her head against his shoulder, kiss her and make the intimacy they'd just shared real beyond the dream. He wanted the future he'd told her he never should have offered. He waited instead.

Other things were more important than his selfish need to hold on to the passion and belonging they'd just rediscovered. Like being Sarah's Watcher. Being by her side from now on, fighting for her legacy. Earning more of her trust back even if he never had another chance to feel the rush of desire, the promise of more, that had filled them in their vision. Sarah's mind had accepted him again. Nothing could tempt him to betray that trust.

"Tell me you believe that you don't have to do this alone," he said. "I'm here, Sarah. Your twin and Jarred are behind you one hundred percent. Madeline was furious when she learned I'd taken you on a mission without her. You belong with us no matter what's waiting in your dreaming mind. You can lose yourself in your programming's matrix, and we'll be there to help you control it. We'll have your family with us when we pitch the idea of a dream mission to the council. But you have to stop seeing your own mind as a threat. If the elders sense your fear, it's game over. Do you understand what I'm saying?"

Confusion, doubt, flooded their link. But she nodded slowly, accepting the truce he was offering.

"I'll do whatever it takes," she said, and he could sense her shoving down the destructive instinct to keep hiding. "But I don't know how. I'm not like you. I can't turn my emotions off and turn my confidence on just because it's time to fight. Show me how to convince your council that I can be trusted. That you and Maddie and Jarred and I can help them find Trinity, so the Brotherhood can stop whatever the center's using Dream Weaver to do to us."

"I don't recall inviting your principals to this meeting, Colonel Metting," said one of the holographic images shimmering at the other end of the conference room.

"My sister and I are no one's principals anymore." Sarah stood with Maddie on one side of her, Richard on the other. She felt like a total fraud, relying on their minds to enhance her power and control as she faced the council. "We're done being psychic test cases. The center's or yours."

"Maddie agreed to participate in this circus to protect her sister," Jarred said, standing to Maddie's left. "But continuing to treat the Temple sisters as though they're the Brotherhood's enemies is off the menu."

Neither he nor Maddie knew much about what was going on. But they'd come, regardless. They had Sarah's back just as Richard said they would. Because she belonged to them. Because they were her family. That degree of trust after everything that had happened was insane. Humbling. And Sarah never would have trusted it without Richard's help.

"The center is this meeting's focus," said Jacob, the lead elder. The council's images were being transmitted to the bunker from seven classified locations. "If we didn't perceive the Temple Legacy as valuable to that endeavor, your presence would never have been accepted at our command site."

"Accepted?" Maddie asked. "Is that code for deciding a legacy's fate without consulting the *principals* involved?"

Sarah could feel her twin wondering how this confrontation would get them any closer to finding Trinity. She could feel everyone's thoughts now whenever she didn't consciously use the mental shields Richard was strengthening. Ever since their link deepened within the vision, her powers were expanding even faster. She could hear everyone's questions. Sense their confusion. Their fear.

Jacob's condescending gaze flicked to Sarah, then back to Maddie. "You and your twin still aren't in control of the effect of your legacy on the world around you. If the center were to regain full command of your abilities, the damage done would be our responsibility. Our mission is to—"

"Do the right thing?" Sarah asked. "How about partnering with my family instead of treating us like we're faceless pawns in some war? Because that sounds pretty right to me."

Richard had begun the meeting by filling in the elders

on their discoveries from her debriefing vision, including his personal guarantee that Sarah was not the Brotherhood's mole. The elders had been as unmoved by his assurances as they were by her challenge now.

"Your refusal to accept that my sister and I can be part of the solution to your problem," she said, "not only endangers the people I care about, but your league of Watchers. My dream is a direct link to the people closing in on you. Isn't that enough to make partnering with us a necessity, right or wrong?"

The room slowed around her. Sarah could feel shock in response to her rational, calm delivery. She could read every mind, every heartbeat, every consciousness—including the thoughts of the elders, who weren't aware that she could sense them through the psychic shielding at their locations. She could feel Richard waiting, confident in her control, while he buffered the cries for help still reaching for her from her nightmare.

She could feel him wanting her, too. Needing her. Holding himself in check, so she'd have this chance and however many more chances she needed, without the distraction of dealing with the passion they'd lost themselves to and the question of what they were going to do about it.

"The Temple Legacy has already benefited the psychic realm," Richard said to the old men, whose images were now wavering. "They've assisted us in defending countless other legacies by helping end Tad Ruebens's Dream Weaver plans."

"Have they?" Jacob asked.

"My sister and I are here," Sarah said.

"Are you?" another elder asked—Sebastian, the one

whose hologram was projected closest to Sarah. "Are you fully here with us, or is your consciousness still in thrall to the center's programming?"

His mind fixed on Sarah's.

He frowned when she blocked his attempt to access her thoughts.

Sarah pictured the door barring her from the truth in her ocean dream, centering her thoughts on the light she needed to find on the other side of it. Then she concentrated on Sebastian's consciousness. Welcomed his thoughts into her own. She felt Richard shielding her intent while his own gifts enhanced her range.

Sebastian blinked when he realized she'd locked on to his energy. His mind rejected hers with so much force, Sarah stumbled backward. Richard grabbed her arm, kept her on her feet, then returned her to his side. The rightness of his calm presence beside her, within her mind, could become addictive if she let it.

All seven elders were frowning now. There wasn't a single condescending, tolerant smile amongst them.

"As you can see," Richard said, "Sarah's control has grown enough for the council to consider the next phase of her legacy's union with the Brotherhood."

"What union?" Maddie's fingers tangled with Sarah's. Her anxiety sizzled through them. "We were brought here to deprogram Sarah and to neutralize Tad Ruebens's embedded dreamscapes. So you maniacs could move on to manipulating some other unsuspecting legacy and leave us the hell alone."

"Meanwhile," David, the darker-skinned elder, said, "your sister seems more inclined to merge your legacy with our mission by the day."

"Since when?" Maddie asked.

"Since she and Colonel Metting brought you and your fiancé to this meeting," Jacob said, "to suggest that none of us have a choice in the matter."

Silence filled the conference room. Sarah could sense Maddie waiting for her to set the man straight.

"Trinity is real," Sarah said to David instead. "Whoever she is, the center has her. Colonel Metting has made it clear I won't conquer the next dream projection I follow her into without the support of your Watchers and my family to stabilize the matrix. You need to know how the center plans to use that nightmare, and me, to weaken your organization. We need each other."

"And if the nightmare you're so eager to dive back into gives you another command to kill?" David asked. "And next time you can't stop yourself?"

"Then Colonel Metting will be there"—Sarah had already accepted what would have to happen if her darker impulses grew too strong for her to stop—"to neutralize the damage you've let the center create inside of me, for good."

"No!" Maddie's hand clenched around Sarah's.

Sarah pulled away. Richard grabbed both their arms, his presence calming Maddie's confusion and Sarah's doubts that she could see this through. The desire that had coursed between them during the vision's kiss reached for Sarah, too, the pull of the memory stronger now that they were touching.

"I'll get Sarah through the door this time," he promised. She could sense his awareness of the turn her thoughts had taken, but he kept his warrior's focus on the plan they'd discussed. "We'll progress deeper into the ocean's matrix and—"

"My sister is not going deeper into that damned dream." Maddie confronted the holograms. "You're panting for the chance to silence her mind for good. If things turn ugly, you'll have your excuse. It would be a suicide mission."

"Forcibly subduing your sister's consciousness if necessary would be a condition I'm afraid we'd have to insist on," Jacob said. "However, Colonel Metting wouldn't be commanding the mission. The Watcher in charge would have to be someone we could trust to put our directives first."

"Before my family's well-being, you mean?" Sarah's heart stumbled at the thought of dreaming without Richard protecting her.

The elder's attention shifted to Richard. "Your supervision would be required in the lab, of course, to ensure the safety of the minds joined to the matrix. But another would be responsible for protecting the projection."

"I understand." Richard blocked what he was thinking from Sarah for the first time since her vision.

"Well, I don't." She needed her raven back.

No, not her raven. She needed Richard, her Watcher, still stripping away the rising screams from her ocean dream and her fear of what was happening, so she could continue standing there, confident and calm, while she gambled with her sanity. But he wasn't there. He'd deserted her, just like before, as soon as duty required it.

"I'm not going into that nightmare," she said, "being guided by a mind I don't know, whose sole focus would be to shut mine down if I don't deliver the result you want. The dream's already trying to do that to me and everyone else it touches. I may be insane, but I'm not an idiot."

The holograms shifted, faded, fizzled in and out of focus, as if a wave of electrical interference were zapping the transmissions. Except Richard had said the elders were linked to the conference room through psychic projection, not electronic transfer. It was Sarah's anger and anxiety, she realized, interfering with the energy field sustaining the council's images. Her ability to project emotion across realities was having a temper tantrum.

The elders were right not to trust what she was becoming.

"They didn't trust you," Richard's mind said, his thoughts once again hers to read. *"Because your loyalty had never been tested. Now it has, and they have a front-row seat."*

"You shut your consciousness away to throw me off?" She stared at him.

"To remind you and everyone else that you're no longer powerless to harness your gifts."

Richard turned back to his council.

Sarah wanted to slap him for scaring her so badly.

"The mission won't succeed," he said, "unless Sarah trusts that she has the full support of the Watcher team that accompanies her. For that to happen, she'll need to be designated a Watcher herself."

Jacob sat forward. "You want us to accept her into the order? She's had no formal training. No vetting to determine her limits and stability."

"You expect me to commit to being a Watcher?" Sarah asked. That hadn't been part of their plan.

"You and Madeline have already accepted your calling," he reasoned. "You've been watching out for each other since you were children, preserving and defending your own legacy. Making it official will mean you'll have everyone in the Brotherhood supporting you in the dream, whether I'm there or not."

"One for all, and all for one." She glanced at the council's wavering projections. "I'm supposed to entrust your order with my family and the well-being of a child you wouldn't be searching for if I hadn't forced us all into this confrontation?"

"Trust me," Richard's mind said.

"Your recommendation is entirely out of the question," Jacob countered. "Even your principal knows that."

Sarah's stomach churned. Her programming's darker impulses reached for her, but Richard was there to help absorb the dangerous energy seething inside her. His confidence that she could accept this or anything else she had to do was as rock solid as when they'd sparred in the gym. He'd asked her to give up control then, too. To follow him into danger. And because she had, he was now risking even more to back her up again.

She squared her shoulders and faced the council, reining in her doubts and finally embracing the logic of the plan she and Richard had plotted in the lab.

"Then I suppose you see capitalizing on the opportunity to identify your mole as out of the question, too?" she challenged. "Since my connection to whoever's directing Ruebens's programming is the only shot you have at putting eyes and ears inside the center."

"What are you doing?" Maddie's mind asked.

"Whatever I have to," Sarah projected back.

"Exploring my ocean dream offers you unprecedented insight into the center's strategic intentions," she said to Jacob. "Assuming you have the balls to take advantage of what my legacy can do before the center takes another crack at it. Isn't that what all this is supposed to be about? You people watching and guiding and protecting legacies for the benefit of the psychic realm as a whole?"

Sebastian sat straighter. "Why should we believe you'd be of any practical use to us after last night's disasters?"

"Sarah . . ." Maddie warned as the air around them began to sizzle.

But Sarah was already harnessing their link, needing their shared ability to connect with minds through the collective unconscious that all beings shared.

"This is the only way," she said to her twin. *"Richard's right. We either become legitimate assets to these maniacs, or we're already casualties. They either trust us now, or they never will."*

Sarah stared down the council, reaching for Richard's mind, too. Trusting she'd find it at her disposal. And once again, he was right where she needed him. She wrapped herself in his restraint.

How could it feel as if she'd had him there, guiding her, her entire life? Just as the child's cries she didn't fully understand had always been there. As if every mistake, every failure, and every lesson Sarah had learned had led to this crossroads.

"Trusting my psychic abilities may still be a risk," she said to the council. "But you have no idea who your leak is, or where the center is conducting its latest dream testing. Which makes my legacy your only shot at putting them out of business for good."

Chapter Seventeen

Maddie watched her twin face down the council, sensing a fragile independence in Sarah that hadn't been there before. She could feel her sister pulling away from her. Or maybe it was her twin's determination to move toward something else that Maddie was sensing. Toward Metting and the new mission he was dragging them all into. Sarah was cornered and pissed and terrified of her own mind and fighting mad—but in a controlled way this time. She was handling the showdown with the council with an air of discipline, a confidence, that mirrored the restraint of the warrior now standing behind her.

Maddie sent her thoughts deeper into her sister's. Sarah's emotional and psychic shields were wide-open to the man she'd sworn never to trust again. Her connection with Richard was balancing the wilder impulses Maddie usually helped Sarah restrain. Richard's presence in Sarah's mind felt like an immovable core of strength.

Maddie saw colors, too. Metting's purplish black, which Sarah was no longer cringing away from. Swirling hues that represented Sarah's links to Maddie and Jarred were there, the amethyst and turquoise that Sarah found calming. Maddie sensed Sarah needing each of them to help her control the fear that she couldn't see the ultimatum she'd just given the council through to the end. She felt Sarah's conviction that without the Watchers' help, none of them would return from her nightmare this time.

Maddie took Jarred's hand and was instantly filled with his unquestioning support. As one, they stepped behind Metting. Their new position created a circuit through Metting to Sarah, filling her sister with a swell of unity. Purpose. Strength.

"We're here," she promised her twin. *"Whatever you need, Sarah. We're here."*

She sensed her sister's gratitude, then caught the image of her own and Jarred's colors flickering around Sarah and Metting. Through Richard, they all sensed the council's surprise at the power surge they'd generated. The old men's curiosity. Then something so close to satisfaction, Maddie gritted her teeth.

Metting's Brotherhood finally had the Temple Legacy willingly at their beck and call. Maddie could feel the council's smugness. Sarah could, too, and it was pissing them both off. But her twin was also pushing down the impulse to retaliate, gathering her emotions, drawing on Maddie's and Jarred's power, for a different purpose.

She was pushing outward, relying on Metting's knowledge of the Brotherhood's inner workings to identify the location of each elder. Tampa. Reno. Seattle. San Diego. Denver. Saint Louis. Boston. She touched on every elder's consciousness, scanned their environment, then left as quickly as she'd arrived. But not before Maddie sensed

Sarah tagging each mind with a marker that would allow future tracking and location.

"Impressive," Jacob said. "But ineffective. Now that Colonel Metting has taught you cognitive marking, be assured we'll negate the possibility of your locating us in the future. Adjustments like these are common within the Brotherhood as principals grow into their legacies."

"Moving would be wise." Sarah smiled. "At least from your Seattle and Denver locations. The center's tracking your operations at both sites. Would those be the regions where your two Watcher teams were exposed?"

No response.

"You'll find psychic filtering devices just beyond both locations," Sarah added, "within a two-mile radius. Colonel Metting just helped me identify them. He'll be able to show you where."

Two of the elders gave simultaneous orders to operatives beyond their transmissions.

"We're looking into your recommendations," Jacob said.

"You do that." Sarah's voice stayed strong, confident, even though Maddie could sense her shock at what she'd accomplished. "In the meantime, use me. Use my dream. Get whatever information you need to stop the center from gaining control of another legacy. All I'm asking for in return is a chance to get Trinity away from them before you attack."

"The Brotherhood needs the Temple twins"—Metting kept his gaze pinned to the council—"as partners. I'm suggesting a collaboration where our powers grow in tandem. It's how our order was created to function two centuries ago, when a small group of legacies banded together to help others who were failing. The Temples' powers are growing beyond our ability to limit without eliminating them. But if we accept the twins into our order, guide them as Watchers, we'll have a fighting chance to stop Dream Weaver."

Everyone in the room stilled, waiting for the council's decision.

"So be it," Jacob finally proclaimed. "You have until tomorrow to prepare a mission team, Colonel. Ms. Temple, you have one last chance to access your dream programming. This time with Watchers stabilizing your search, while they reconnoiter your projection's matrix for the exact location and purpose of the center's testing on whomever Trinity turns out to be. The council will be forming an infiltration team to send in as soon as we have a target. Welcome to the Brotherhood, and good luck. You're going to need it."

Welcome to the Brotherhood . . .

Sarah had been sitting motionless on the bunk in her sleeping quarters for hours. She'd all but sprinted from the conference room and the council's decision, and Richard and her family's support, and Maddie's questions. And she hadn't moved since.

Not that she could really hide from any of them. They were still in her mind, their concern and strength challenging the shields she'd slammed back into place so they couldn't touch her emotions. She could feel Richard giving her space. Everyone was waiting for her to pull herself together and step back into the confident persona she'd projected to the elders, so she could face the morning planning meeting for the mission back into her psychotic nightmare.

"Help me . . ." Trinity begged.

"Help her," the wolf's ocean voice agreed. *"You're finally ready to see what we've become . . ."*

"Stop it!"

Sarah pushed off the bed. More than ever, her family's and her legacy's survival depended on her staying lucid and free of the dream's pull. But she could feel herself falling back into it, Trinity's cries blending with the wolf's laughter, the wolf's voice dissolving into a little girl's desperate begging. It was the same swirl of confusion and deranged demands she'd sensed in Lenox, unraveling Sarah's sanity into the same manic state.

It was as if the more powerful she grew, with her and Richard's psychic energies more deeply merged, the less stable her hold on reality became. How was she supposed to wait patiently through the night for the disaster this mission was going to turn into? She was becoming death all over again—exactly what Ruebens had programmed her to be. Why couldn't anyone else see that?

"You're finally ready . . ." her nightmare called to her, in both Trinity's and the wolf's voices.

"Stop it!" Sarah yelled into her silent quarters.

She headed for the door, snagging her jacket as an afterthought, suddenly desperate to disappear into the cold night waiting for her beyond the bunker's walls.

The elevator was just a few feet away. She should call Richard. Or Maddie. She should be leaning on them and accepting the help they'd give her and believing in the unified front they'd just sold the council. She kept moving instead. The council had accepted her as a Watcher. Which gave her unrestricted access to the facilities and its grounds. She could already feel the freezing forest waiting for her outside, and her place in it.

She had to pull herself together before the morning. She had to get her head back to the place where she could face Richard and believe all the things he'd promised. She needed to lose herself for a while in the feel of running away from everything and everyone she could hurt far too easily. She needed the night's darkness, which felt more real to the broken pieces of her than the promises she'd made.

Then somehow she would find the courage to return to the bunker and fight for the light and the truth that were waiting somewhere within her dreams.

CHAPTER EIGHTEEN

"They suspect?" the voice said.

"They know." The entire Brotherhood was in flux, including the relocation of every elder, days earlier than their scheduled rotation, to new more secure locations. "It will be even harder to breach the twins' conditioning from now on. Sarah Temple's been made a Watcher."

"We don't need to break down their condition further, do we?" the voice asked. "They're coming to us this time."

"And you're coming for the Brotherhood." He cursed soundlessly. Years of training blocked his emotional response from being detected by anyone within the bunker, or anyone tracking him on the other end of the transmission. "That wasn't part of the deal."

"Our only deal was your compensation in return for information that secures the Temple Legacy for our purposes," the voice said. "What happens beyond that is none of your concern. Sarah will be allowed access to the dream's matrix again. Her mind will fracture. Our control will be solidified. We'll take things from there."

The Watcher heard his own death in the pronouncement.

He accepted once again the necessity of betraying his brothers, even though the recon team had been attacked and other legacies had been exposed while the center implemented unforeseen facets of the offensive he was helping them wage. He had to stay focused on his own objectives—to negate Metting's misguided recklessness and the center's power play for the Temples' gifts.

Everything was in place for him to help the Brotherhood fulfill its responsibility to stop mercenary entities like the center, which were determined to exploit the psychic realm to create weapons out of peoples' minds.

The council was primed to go on the offensive, something that wouldn't have happened without Sarah Temple's rogue programming and escalating instability. The elders would see to it that no further damage was done through her mind. The Brotherhood would complete its transition into a governing presence, rather than remaining the traditionally passive entity Watchers had always been.

He had to see this through to the end. Just one more day. His plans were unraveling, the center was getting far closer to breaching Brotherhood security than he'd ever intended, but it was just one more day before this was over.

"When does it begin?" the voice asked.

"Tomorrow. Noon," he said, committing the final unforgivable breach of his oath by revealing the precise moment that Sarah Temple's mind would be at its most vulnerable. "Mission prep commences in the morning."

"The details of which you'll be ready to provide should we need them?"

"You won't need them." Which made his role conveniently obsolete.

He could feel his contact smiling.

Biting back another curse, he broke the link and lay back on the bunk in his sparse quarters. Quarters that should be subject to regular communications sweeps by Metting's diagnostic routines.

But his center contact had provided undetectable algorithms, a virus that he'd introduced into the bunker's network that scrambled transmissions he made on a pre-set frequency. It was state-of-the-art covert technology, the mechanics of which he'd detailed in his personal log so the Brotherhood could test for similar breaches, as well as develop their own response. Details an e-mail to Metting would deliver tomorrow after the Temples' minds were silenced.

His betrayal would be over then, every dark bit of it. It would be a warrior's end once his motives became clear to those who would first condemn him.

The inevitability of his actions had been set the moment the Temples' destructive legacy wasn't terminated along with Tad Ruebens. And tomorrow he would honor the oath he'd lived by since he joined the Brotherhood. He would preserve the integrity of the psychic realm. He would stay this deadly course, right up to the moment he could extinguish the minds of Sarah and Madeline and Trinity Temple.

Chapter Nineteen

Richard waited in the night's cold shadows, in the woods whose ragged edges had helped Sarah unknowingly shape his raven image. This had been his nightmare landscape first, long before Ruebens's programming led Sarah to project the specters of Richard's past into her own dreams.

In her early Dream Weaver projections, ripples of his forest memories had become a premonition of the Brotherhood's showdown with the center. While listening to her descriptions of Ruebens's dreamscape, Richard had instantly recognized traces of the most painful period of his life. She'd unknowingly plucked the memories from his mind, more in tune with him from the start than he'd realized. They'd connected deeper than he allowed any other person in his life.

"You don't let anyone see the truth," Sarah had said when he'd confronted her about hiding from her own memories. *"You show people whatever you need them to see, to get what you want."*

But Sarah Temple did know him. She had from the start.

And now he could feel her running to the same woods,

into the heart of his long-ago nightmare, making it part of her reality.

He'd given her space after the conference with the council, but he would be running with her tonight. Because he understood this moment as no one else could. She'd need freedom to work through her doubts and fears. She needed movement. More venting, like their sparring in the gym. It was good that she was rejecting the isolation that would have deepened her confusion. She was searching for answers rather than accepting defeat. And he was going to be there to guide her this time, just as before. He'd be there from now on, for as long as she'd let him.

The last twenty-four hours had left Sarah exhausted. Additional physical exertion would drain her even more. But the risk to tomorrow's mission would be worth it, if he could help her accept the very darkness that was terrifying her, shadows she could use to create more than danger and pain once she learned to harness their power.

A rush of energy reached him.

Sarah's panic.

Her denial.

He'd already disabled the sensors that would have alerted command that the bunker's side entrance was breached. Sarah slipped out, dressed in a black knit shirt and fatigues, the color and the moonlight spotlighting her porcelain complexion and deep auburn curls. She peered through the dimness surrounding her. Richard could sense her need to find something, be something, anything besides the dangerous mind she still believed she couldn't stop.

He could feel her confusion at encountering no challenge to her exit. The anomaly didn't slow her for long. He felt a streak of relief as she raced into the woods that had seemed both familiar and terrifying to her a month ago, when he escorted her through them to the bunker. She wasted no time looking back. The need to keep moving flowed to him from her mind. She focused only on taking the next step, then the next breath. On relishing the night's chill as it stung her already-cold skin. Sarah was lost in the moment and the peace of running from her destiny.

Richard mentally reengaged the bunker's sensors and cloaked both their movements. He followed Sarah, close enough not to lose her, far enough away that she wouldn't hear him. If she slowed down or looked deeply enough within, she'd sense his presence. But she was running from their connection along with everything else.

He increased his pace when she did. He felt her heart race. The heightened level of exertion shouldn't have been possible for her still-recovering body. She wouldn't last much longer. He ran with her, breathed with her, felt the tension and anxiety ease within her. She was mesmerizing, a bright flash of motion flowing through darkness and shadow, blending into the night as the silky flash of her hair flowed behind her.

This was how he'd first found her energy in the emptiness of her coma, flying free of the world that had chained her to madness. She hadn't wanted to return then, either. Waking had meant facing the parts of herself she thought no one could accept. But her gifts were ready for more than hiding now. Everyone around her was demanding more. Her legacy. Her sister and Trinity. Him. The council. And not trusting what she was becoming was ripping her apart. Worse, she was creating a self-fulfilling prophecy that could result in tragic consequences. She was—

—tripping over a tree root.

Sprawling forward and catching herself.

Her feet slipped out from under her. She landed hard on her butt, then slid down a hill beside the natural path she'd been following. He sprinted to the spot where she'd disappeared, then headed into the underbrush toward the body he could barely make out below. He dropped to his knees.

"Sarah?"

She was on her back, her chest rising and falling, her eyes closed as she wheezed. He reached to feel for broken bones but stopped, not wanting his sudden appearance to make it even harder for her to get in air. He rested his arm on his knee instead.

"Take it easy," he said. "Let yourself relax."

"Not . . ." She took another wheezing inhale. "Not likely . . . with you looming over me like a specter swoo . . . swooping down from the . . . treetops."

Richard settled back on his heels. If she could talk without pain, her lungs were okay. Likely no injury to her head or rib cage. It wasn't a surprise that she'd known it was him without looking. Having her this close was filling his own senses, crowding out everything else.

"You about done lazing around, playing for sympathy?" he asked.

Her eyelids flew open, and he could have sworn he saw clouds swirling in her dark gaze. She stopped breathing at the sight of him. Then her chest rose on a long inhale. After she'd taken several deep breaths in rhythm with Richard's, he stood and held out his hand.

"Come on," he said. "You've already come this far. Let's finish it."

She scrambled to her feet unassisted. She bent at the waist and brushed leaves and twigs off her fatigues while she gulped in more oxygen. She straightened and wavered, off-balance. He motioned for her to precede him up the hill to the path they'd left, following closely so he could catch her if she slipped.

Once on level ground, Sarah stood petite and irritated beside him. He was mesmerized all over again by her grit. She'd need that inner strength tomorrow. They all would.

"Finish what?" she asked into the night's fragrant silence.

He raised an eyebrow.

"You said it was time to finish it," she said. "Finish what?"

"Your sprint to freedom." He turned and walked deeper into the forest, increasing his pace when she followed. "Who better to lead you through the night than a specter who knows the way?"

"Where are we?" Sarah had been so absorbed in the rush of being free that paying attention to anything but getting away from the bunker had been impossible. Including, evidently, the fact that Richard had been following her. Now he was leading her even farther away from her showdown with her nightmare.

"We're about a mile and a half from the bunker." His

lean, powerful body and relaxed gait were beautiful to watch. Distracting, as they moved deeper into the dense underbrush.

"I thought . . ." Wind rustled through the leafless branches above, overwhelming her with sounds straight from one of Ruebens's earliest nightmares. Except the crisp night air smelled like freedom, with Richard beside her. The moon showered winter white down on them, instead of a summer storm's vengeance. Miles of welcoming nature felt nurturing. Forgiving.

"You thought this might be your last chance?" Richard asked.

"Last chance to do what?"

"To get out before your nightmare destroys everyone and everything you care about."

She tensed, expecting to sense the brush of his thoughts within her scattered ones. But he kept his psychic distance.

"You're taking quite a risk, leading me so far away from the others," she said. "Especially if you're that sure I'm ready to bail on my promise to work with the Brotherhood."

"There's very little any of us can do now to force you to stay. Whether you're behind the bunker's shields or out here dealing with your doubts, you're growing too strong to control by isolating you. It's time for you and everyone else to accept whatever you decide your legacy's going to be."

He sounded almost . . . proud of her impulses to run into the night.

"So," she asked, "aiding and abetting the escape of the

nutcase whose disappearance will give the elders cause to rethink tomorrow's mission. That's your plan for getting your fellow Watchers to accept me? Isn't my just being out here a security breach?"

Richard lifted his chin, motioning toward a spot in the distance.

"Activity in these woods is monitored around the clock."

"Someone's recording every step we take?"

"No one knows you're out here but me, Sarah. Big Brother won't be listening, as long as I trust you to keep your rebellion within reason. Which I do."

"Naturally."

Instead of being kept on a short leash, she was like one of those outdoor pets with GPS chips. Except her invisible tracking device was Richard's mind. And if she'd learned nothing else since being dragged into the center's and the Brotherhood's battle over the psychic realm, it was that if it felt like a cage and worked like a cage, freedom and power tracked by someone else was merely another form of captivity.

"You're going to be working with a lot of my men when we start mission prep." He walked ahead, his hands buried in the back pockets of his fatigues. "You needed a break."

"Which you took it upon yourself to provide." She tried not to stare at the play of black fabric over his muscular backside. "How gracious of you."

"I'm a manipulative bastard. I wanted you out here, or I'd have stopped you at the bunker's entrance. There are safer ways of escaping from the madness filling your mind than running around in the open like the center isn't searching for you under every rock. I wouldn't advise making this a habit."

Sarah stumbled to a halt. "You wanted me out here for what, exactly?"

Richard kept walking, forcing her to keep up. "To convince you that you're not the enemy any of us are fighting. You don't have anything to prove, or any reason to believe that tomorrow can't be successful. You're one of us, Sarah, and we'll help you every way we can. You were born to be with us. You and your sister both."

"Your council and most of your team would—"

"Our council. Our team"

"There are a lot of Watchers on *our* team who aren't buying a word you're saying, any more than I am."

He stopped walking.

Sarah stumbled into him.

"The council made a decision to trust your legacy," he said, "with all its powers and potential darkness, rather than forcing you and Maddie to become something else, something less, before taking your place in our order. It's a policy shift for handling principals that some Watchers will have a harder time accepting than others. But it's the right stand to take. Except the move the council's making won't be successful, neither will tomorrow's mission, unless you find a way to own the trust they're putting in you."

So now the future direction of the Brotherhood itself hinged on her pulling her act together.

Excellent.

A faraway bird sent out its midnight call. Something small and furry scurried through the bushes to their right. There was a surreal sense of rightness to the breeze curling around them, the isolating freedom of limitless moonlight and sharing it with Richard. A rightness that felt alien, as if it belonged to someone else rather than Sarah.

"Communing with nature is supposed to renew my faith in my destiny how, exactly?" she asked.

She couldn't see his face clearly, but she sensed an underlying sadness to his presence. Deep-seated regret mixing with the forest's relaxed energy.

"My parents loved nature," he revealed, instead of taking another tour of her psyche. "From my earliest memories, they'd bring me into the woods on nights like this. At first, I thought it was because they loved picnics after dark. What they loved was growing my powers where no one else could see what we were capable of. My 'greatness,' they called it. Of course, even then the Watchers were nearby. They were comfortable with the shadows my parents were courting. And if my family had kept their pursuits within reasonable boundaries, the Watchers would have kept their distance."

Sarah didn't know what to say. If this was how Richard had planned to distract her, it was working.

He'd never spoken of his past. His family had been one of the Watcher's high-risk legacies several decades ago. From what little Sarah had heard—overheard, as she'd practiced scanning the minds of the Watchers she came into contact with—she knew his parents were no longer in the picture. But Richard kept the rest of who he was, who he'd been before his blind allegiance to his order took hold, a mystery.

He started walking again. Curiosity had her stepping

over a felled tree and hiking up a steep incline to keep up, until they stopped on a shallow ridge. He looked out over the ravine below. She couldn't read his thoughts. But she had a sense that the vista spreading before them was a familiar friend.

He fit here.

He seemed at ease.

Content.

But the sadness was stronger, too.

The ridge wound a narrow, uneven path through the woods. It was rugged terrain. A brutal, fragrant masterpiece. Stark. Peaceful. She glanced back in the direction they'd traveled and saw only more trees. More undergrowth. More hills to climb. They were totally alone, protected by nature and the strength of Richard's shields.

"This was the last forest my parents brought me to," he said. "This is where they died."

Sarah's attention snapped back to him. Her family's own losses were a still-gaping wound that might never heal.

"How long ago?" she asked, still not quite believing he was sharing his own damaged past with her.

"On the night I agreed to undertake the Watcher training and conditioning that would make the Brotherhood my new family."

"How long were the Watchers involved with your legacy before that?"

"Since my birth. My parents were in full control of what they wanted their destinies to be. What they thought they could make for themselves, through me. It became clear to the Brotherhood early on that the development of my gifts needed watching."

"But I thought you people—" She sighed when his eyebrow shot up. "I thought Watchers only involved themselves when there's a threat to the psychic balance or something."

"We're always monitoring. Tracking potential power spikes or possible sources of exposure. What my parents intended to do with their gifts and mine was an ongoing concern. Eventually, the Watchers assigned to our legacy were ordered to stop them."

The forest chilled even more around them.

"What . . . what did they do to your parents?"

"Nothing." Richard nodded toward a section of the forest cloaked in denser shadow. "Until my parents' practice became a threat to the quiet community they were building here."

"They brought you to live under the Watchers' noses?"

"The bunker was constructed ten years ago." He kicked at the rich earth at his feet. "After I'd risen up the chain of command. We needed a central headquarters that would buffer the kind of metaphysical energy our warriors emanate when we train. I knew this area would meet our needs. It absorbs psychic energy. Nurtures it. Many think the forests in this part of the country were havens for refugee followers of the craft during the witch trials. Locals respect the superstitions and steer clear of the deep woods. It's no coincidence the center's complex is only twenty miles from here. The kind of work being done out here requires isolation. So did my parents' plans."

"The craft?" The witch trials had been the genesis of Sarah's legacy. A distant aunt had uttered their prophecy while being burned at the stake for her ability to sense and predict others' thoughts. "Your parents were Wiccan?"

"In name only."

Richard's gaze was still down. There was a tightness to the slant of his cheekbones, a play of taut muscles stretching across bone as he attempted to hold his emotions away from her.

"It was never about theology for them," he said. "The craft was an affectation to mask our powers. They were gypsies. In their alternative society their gifts could have been used for healing, protecting, foreseeing. But the next score was their priority. Getting ahead. Getting away from whatever latest scheme had backfired. I'd never had a home until they built the commune out here. They collected a group of followers. A permanent kingdom they could rule."

"They used your gifts to make people trust them? The way you can manipulate someone's environment and repel unwanted energy? The way you're stopping your control room from tracking us now?"

The way he'd manipulated Sarah at the center, once he'd reached her mind and won her heart.

"They were very convincing," he said. "It never took them long to persuade a mark that one of their incantations was responsible for his good fortune. Some of it was mind over matter. A placebo effect. But my parents traded on their psychic skills and my growing ones. From the day I was old enough to teach the art of scamming, I became their meal ticket. We were common thieves."

"They were. You had no choice. They used you." The way the center had used Sarah and Maddie and countless others.

Sarah was mesmerized. She'd never heard another legacy's story. It had never dawned on her that Richard's gifts would once have been weak enough that he'd have been under someone else's control. That he could understand the emptiness that filled you, when you knew what you were doing was wrong but you had no choice but to behave as you'd been taught. Trained. Programmed.

"If they made me look sick or hungry or hurt enough," he said, "I could scam an invite into any home. Ferret out the most deeply hidden weakness. Prep a mark for my parents to arrive and close the deal."

"You stole from people?"

"My parents took everything they could get and expected me to do the same—for the family." Richard stared into the woods. Into the past. "For a long time, it was about pleasing them and keeping them from beating me when I failed at whatever task they gave me. I'd catch hell when we were discovered. It was always my fault. I thought it was finally over when we came here. The lying and hating what I was and never being sure where we'd wake up tomorrow. This was going to be my home. Then the others started showing up."

"Other witches?"

"More gypsies. A community of them. And my parents were determined to rule the bunch, controlling a network of miscreant activity up and down the East Coast. Except there's a hierarchy to tribal living. Another family with more standing in the community became the presumptive head of the clan. Which put them in my parents' way."

Wind howled through the leafless branches above them. Sarah pictured a lonely boy, running to this stark place and dreaming of freedom. Family. A future where his conscience could be cleansed of all he'd done.

"Your parents expected you to help them oust the reigning family?"

"I was sixteen. They would have had to kill those people to take their place. That's how gypsy kingdoms are lost and won. My parents had to prove they were powerful enough to lead. By then, I was the strongest weapon in their arsenal."

A weapon of death, just like Sarah had been trained to be. Only it had been Richard's flesh and blood trading on the dangerous gifts of a teenage boy who was ready to grow into a warrior, whose dedication to protecting others ran soul deep. Richard had lived through his own nightmare. His own childhood had been destroyed because of a legacy he hadn't asked to be born into. He'd had to face his own moment of truth about what the rest of his life was going to be about.

"You stopped them, didn't you?" Sarah was as certain of it as she was of her next breath. She was finally seeing, understanding, the real Richard. "Instead of helping your parents hurt that other family, you joined with the Watcher team that stopped them."

CHAPTER TWENTY

"The Brotherhood stopped my parents." Richard felt the dark memories slip closer.

He'd come here to help Sarah understand her own path. But he'd needed her here, too, he accepted. He'd needed the same honesty with his past he'd pushed her into. He needed the warmth and acceptance and understanding Sarah couldn't yet give herself. And maybe, just maybe, they needed each other.

"The council had been fine with the petty theft and minor felonies my parents had committed," he said, "and my father's parents before them. But my folks were about to use our legacy to take a human life, for greed and power. My psychic skills were on the cusp of expanding beyond their control, and they had no use for teaching me restraint or even common decency. Their plans would have irrevocably changed who I was meant to be."

He stared into the starkly beautiful vista spreading out before them. On nights like this, when the past weighed too heavy and there were too many hours before dawn, Richard came to this place to remember the future that he'd won on the same night that he'd lost everything.

"The Watchers confronted your parents?" Sarah moved closer.

There was understanding in her eyes. Compassion Richard had never let anyone close enough to offer him. Because he never would have believed them before now. Before Sarah.

"*I* confronted them." He'd never forget his parents' fury and disapproval. "I was done being their pawn. I didn't want anything to do with their new utopia. I wanted to be free and learn something about the real world. Maybe find a way to go to college and begin a career. I expected them to be angry. I didn't anticipate their threats to disown me, and then when threats didn't work, to stop me however they had to."

"You either did what they told you, or—"

"I would cease to exist. They couldn't afford to have me leave, knowing what I did about them and how they operated." He looked deeper into the forest that had become the backdrop for Sarah's first nightmares. He could almost see his parents' deadly serious expressions when they'd told him he'd pay for his desertion. "I needed to think. I walked for hours, circling the camp and my problems and shutting out the world. That's when the team of Watchers approached me."

"Isn't that forbidden?"

"The council had made a decision to intervene—to get me out. Initial contact is attempted whenever possible before a principal is extracted, in an effort to avoid resistance."

Memory flickered across Sarah's face.

"Like you talked to my mother when you first came to work at the center," she said. "Maddie told me she found your private cell number in the admittance file my mother kept."

"It was essential that she trust me with your well-being in case I needed her help to protect you."

Sarah nodded. He felt her relax, the history between them sitting easier the more he let her see who he'd really been. What had made him who he was now.

"My parents were furious," he said. "But they still trusted me to protect the family or they wouldn't have let me leave camp. When I returned hours later, they were waiting for me, and they were armed."

"The Watcher team let you go back?"

Winter wind carved into Richard's skin, robbing him of the warmth of Sarah's consciousness reaching for his through the emotional shields that could no longer keep her out.

"The team had explained that it was time for me to leave. That the abilities I was just starting to understand needed to be honed, trained, enriched. With my parents, my potential would be perverted. Degraded. The Watchers were prepared to take me, whether I was willing or not."

"But they let you go?"

"To make up my own mind. Taking me against my will would have damaged the Brotherhood's chances of integrating my gifts into the order, just as it has with you and Maddie. I talked them into letting me go until I was sure."

"You were destined to be in charge." Sarah smiled, and it felt as if dawn were breaking over Richard. Inside of him. "Even as a teenager, you were a natural leader. So, when you talked with your parents again, they—"

"They basically told me I'd been an asset they'd cultivated their entire lives, and it was time to pay up."

Sarah flinched.

He could feel her trying to process the darkness that had surged within him in the moment that his father informed him he cared nothing for Richard as a person, as a son. His mother had just stood there by the man's side, staring at Richard as if she couldn't stand the sight of him. He'd felt isolated. Abandoned. Dirty. Furious. But at the same time, there'd been a promise waiting for him in the forest rising around them. There'd been others like him, watching and trusting him no matter how many mistakes he'd made.

He hadn't been alone.

He hadn't been locked into a path that would have destroyed his soul.

"You didn't have to allow your parents' mistakes to define who you could be," Sarah said, following his thoughts. "The choice was finally yours."

"Yes."

Understanding washed through Richard. Sarah's understanding.

"Just like the choices you're facing now," he said, "not to keep running from your past. To learn from your failures without being defined by them. To use the insight your experiences have left you to help a little girl who's just as lost as you once were."

"It's not the same. My family never did anything wrong. My parents tried to protect me. I'm the one who couldn't handle my talents or gifts or whatever the hell you want to call them. Now, they're both dead."

"You did the best you could with what little information you had. You didn't cause the circumstances you were born into any more than I did. Some things are simply larger than we are. Some failures are the result of time and fate, necessity and circumstance. Your experience is more common than you think, when a legacy reaches a crisis point. Not everyone can be saved. Not every person involved can be persuaded to put the needs of others before their own."

Her forehead wrinkled while she searched for her own answers in the jumble of their shared emotions. The sadness and guilt and anger and loss they both still felt were tempting her to run again—from him this time. Then her disgust slammed into both of them.

"How could you join the same people who destroyed your family?" she asked. The self-loathing she felt for making the same choice filled every word.

"My parents' greed for power destroyed them, not the Brotherhood." It was the reality he came back to this place to remember. "The Watchers protected me and the world from what my parents would have created in me. My father intended to kill me that night. I felt his lethal intent when I told them I was leaving, but I was too stunned to defend myself. The Watchers gave him a chance to back down. My father refused. They both did. He and my mother attacked the Watchers with their powers. I would have been next if the team hadn't stopped them. I blamed myself for their deaths for a long time, the same as you. So long that I learned not to feel at all so I could keep going."

Night sounds hummed. The nervous energy of

Richard's memories swayed trees and underbrush. The ravine absorbed the release.

"Legacies like ours destroy everything they touch." Sarah's voice was thready. Fragile. "Good or bad. Darkness or light, power like ours damages things that can't be made whole again. Watchers are simply the hall monitors, trying to control the uncontrollable while things go from bad to worse. Until there's nothing anyone can do to stop the insanity but neutralize it before it's beyond anyone's grasp. And that's what I was born to be? That's what you brought me out here to tell me?"

"I brought you here to see the possibilities beyond your hatred for yourself and the people trying to help you. A new world is waiting for you, Sarah. A reality where all of you fits, with people who understand you. Everything you've learned will make you a better Watcher. Everything you're feeling right now will help you identify with others who are like you, and help you fulfill your oath to guide them—starting with Trinity."

It wasn't easy, accepting the daily conflict of living a psychic legacy's existence. He could still feel his shock and rage at his parents. A part of him still wanted to drown in that memory and take the Watcher team who'd killed them with him. Sarah would be dealing with her own dark past for the rest of her life. But she couldn't let it rob her of what could come next.

"There is a calling waiting for you," he said. "It's what's gotten you this far. It's why you held out against Dream Weaver long enough for your sister and me to pull you back. It's the part of you that was created to save others. There's a purpose beyond the rest of the crap you've had to endure."

"My purpose is to swear undying fidelity to an organization that took everything from me?"

"Stop seeing any of us as inherently evil. You're fighting yourself now, not the Brotherhood. Not the center. And you're going to get people killed if you don't stop. No amount of guilt and regret is going to change what you've become or what you have to do next. Watchers saved my life that night, when they destroyed the damaged world I'd come from. Tomorrow, they'll fight to save yours, if you'll trust them."

"They?"

Richard cupped her cheek in his palm, drawn in all over again by her vulnerability and courage and fire.

"*We're* trying to save you," he said, doing his job as her Watcher, but also accepting that he needed Sarah in this place for himself, becoming part of his memories, part of his truth. He'd need her forever. "No matter how it might seem, we know you're not what's out of control. Your legacy is. This is your time to choose. To join us fully, instead of following the same path that's pushed everyone but your sister away from you. The Brotherhood gave my legacy a chance to mean more than damage and pain. That's what I trusted when I couldn't trust myself or them. Every day I wake up and find myself in charge of the warriors I command, I feel like I'm still conning the world. But I keep waking up, and I keep fighting. And because I do, the powers I inherited have gone on to help countless others. That night, when I chose to live instead of dying with my family, my Watchers saved me so I could find you, Sarah."

She gasped. The full force of the emotions he was grappling with consumed them. His need to belong.

His need for her. The compulsion to lose himself to the homecoming her mind had become to him.

Her cheek nuzzled against his hand, the softness of her skin branding him, the same as it had the night he'd first found her at the center. Then she froze.

"What if I can't make the right choice," she asked, "once the ocean has control and I'm lost in the nightmare?"

"You were born to dream." He listened to the voices of the woods shifting around them. In them, he heard what she couldn't yet—the power and possibility of the life she was meant to live. A life he wanted to share. "You've already chosen, Sarah. You're here with me, instead of still running. You'll dream again tomorrow with the Brotherhood's support, and you won't be lost. I won't let you be. Then if you have to run again, whenever the night and the memories become too real, I'll be right here running with you. Trust that. Trust your team. Trust yourself. And no matter what happens, you won't fail. You never have to be alone with your darkness again."

"That's . . ." Her shy smile was a surprise. "Is that the recruitment speech you Watchers give everybody?"

Richard trailed the backs of his fingers down her cheek. His thumb rubbed across the tantalizing curve of her lips. Then his mouth brushed the same spot. She gasped into his kiss.

Heat.

Desire.

Silky promise flooded them. The winter night caressed their skin with fire. She accepted his need, sending back a flood of her own along with the magic that happened every time their minds brushed. He swept her body closer, where he'd wanted her since he held her in their vision. Where he'd always want her.

An insatiable craving flared to life, for more of her, all of her, everything inside her that he hadn't yet touched. For the reality of Sarah holding him, needing what they could become together. It was all new to him, this touching and wanting and believing beyond his duty. Sarah was teaching him to feel again while she learned the same for herself. She was teaching Richard how to dream.

"This is where the worst nightmare of my life happened." He closed his eyes against the feel of her mouth and her thoughts claiming him. "It's where I wanted to help your nightmares end."

"I . . ." Her gaze was alive with need. It was haunted with doubt. "I don't know how to stop seeing the monster in my nightmare."

"The wolf?"

"No." She shook her head. "The monster he wants me to become."

"For a long time, I saw my father's hatred and my mother's weakness every time I looked in the mirror."

And as his penance, Richard had shut down so he could survive and guide and protect and preserve, taking nothing for himself. Then he'd found Sarah. And even lost to him in a coma, she'd instantly become a future he wanted to fight for.

"The only person keeping the monster you fear alive is you," he said. "You don't have to endure this alone. Others want more for you, Sarah. Accept that you're a

Watcher. Survive the battle you have to fight for your legacy. Believe that you're mine. That I'm yours. Give the life you've made me want with you a chance."

Memories swirled around them. His memories still. Hers, too. All of them shared, released, as the haunting rustle of a raven's wings rode the wind and the clouds and the shadows, freeing them of the demons they'd both clung to.

"The Temple Legacy either lives or dies in my dreams tomorrow." Sarah's tiny, searching kiss at the curve of Richard's neck stole his heart all over again.

"Then so do I." He took her mouth with his, needing to consume her, body and soul.

"I . . ." The moonlight in her eyes shone like forever, winking closer for just a moment before it was swallowed by quicksilver tears. "I don't know how to believe in this. The good things in my life . . . All I've ever done is destroy them."

Richard had asked her to believe once before. Then he'd used his duty and his mission to build a wall between them, because he hadn't believed enough himself to fight for what they'd found.

He rested his forehead against Sarah's and found himself praying. Gods and spirituality were unknown to him, but he was praying to every deity that had ever been worshipped for another chance to protect the magical place within this woman that still dreamed.

"I failed you," he said, "when I didn't stop Tad Ruebens from manipulating your mind. But Dream Weaver is his darkness, not yours. You're everything good and loyal and honorable and beautiful that I've been afraid to want. I'd die before I'd let anything happen to you again. Just like you'd die before you'd hurt the people you love anymore, no matter what your nightmare's programming wants. We'll find a way through this together. Tell me you can believe that. Tell me we have a chance."

CHAPTER TWENTY-ONE

Sarah clung to Richard's honesty and his strength while he asked for her future. Her mind swirled with his gypsy's story and his warrior's logic and the emotional honesty he was finally giving her.

There was no reason to believe he wouldn't hurt her again. But safe or not, she could feel herself falling. Sinking. His memories from his family's tragedy surged around them and rustled through the ravine like thousands of tiny wings fighting to escape the night's darkness, as fearlessly as Richard had survived his own legacy's meltdown.

She nestled deeper into his embrace, exactly where she'd always wanted to belong. She yearned to be as fearless as that sixteen-year-old boy who'd found a way to survive the unthinkable—as fearless as she appeared right now, reflected back from Richard's gaze. She wanted to become whatever she had to, to keep him in her life, in her mind. More than ever, she wanted to conquer the nightmares that threatened this new beginning he made her want to believe she could have.

Richard had been her raven. A villain from her past. But the man before her now was so much more. He'd never left her, despite the duty and oath that had been all he'd known since he was a child. He hadn't abandoned her to her psychotic rantings when she was impossibly damaged. He'd accepted his own role in the unfair price she'd been forced to pay, for the sake of other legacies and the innocents his Dream Weaver mission had spared.

He'd guided her and trained her and waited for her to heal enough to see the bigger war being waged around her. A war he believed she could be valuable in, as long as she kept fighting. Kept believing. Kept trusting.

Sending her consciousness deeper into his, she wrapped her mind in the truth that he'd been waiting for her tonight. Not just for duty, but for himself. She was something he needed. Something he'd always needed. He'd run with her because she filled a hidden place in him that was just as broken as her darkest fears. The dream of them she could feel inside him had been there, within his mind, from the start.

"What are we doing?" she whispered.

"I think we both might be starting to live." Richard kissed her softly. "Tonight, it feels like I'm truly alive for the first time."

"Why?" She couldn't stop herself from inching closer, needing more.

"Because you're not hiding from me here, in this moment." His hands cupped her face. "And you won't be hiding from your team tomorrow, when you'll still be scared and needing to run. And I'll be there, Sarah, feeling you reach for your future instead of the past. It'll be better than anything I've felt in my life—even this."

"Richard . . ." She was shaking her head, the taste of

him at once devastating and utterly perfect. "This is crazy."

His groan took her need deeper. She wanted to lose herself in each caress of his mouth.

"If I've learned one thing since finding you." He smiled. "It's that sanity is highly overrated. Come with me, Sarah. No more control. No more fear. Not here. Fall apart with me. Trust me to be there to bring you back."

The night's velvet softness cooled her feverish skin as her clothes slid away beneath his skilled hands. Sarah longed to feel his body completely open to hers, just as his mind now was. When they were skin to skin, she arched into the feel of him. Layers of muscle and strength attested to his Watcher training. But it was the gentleness in his touch, the longing in his mind, that sucked her deeper into their madness.

"Yes," she gasped as his hands and mouth found her breasts.

Her fingers did their own exploring. His breath hissed. His body responded, growing even harder.

"Yes." He drew her to the ground. "Stay with me forever, Sarah."

He rolled until she straddled him. His erection pressed against her damp center, demanding without forcing, throbbing but under the same control he exerted over the rest of his life.

"You're perfect here," he said, "with my moon and shadows and memories. I've always wanted you right here."

She could feel the strain that holding back was costing him. She could feel all of him, while he cherished her body and kept things slow, easy, because he thought that was what she needed. She kissed and nipped down his chest, using her teeth. She raked her nails against the rough patch of hair trailing down his abs to his belly.

"I could devour you." His fingers clenched in her hair.

She looked up from where her tongue was dabbling with his navel.

"Who's devouring who, Colonel Metting?"

She had a moment to appreciate his answering growl. Then the world shifted. He pinned her under him and slid his hands beneath her bottom, pulling her into the thrust of his body.

Her cry filled the night.

He clutched her close, covering her, shielding her, wrapping her in warmth and safety and the feeling of . . . home.

"Are you all right?" He held himself motionless inside her. "I—"

"Don't stop," she begged. Her whole life. She'd waited for this moment her entire life. Feeling complete. Feeling whole, every part of her exactly what it should be. "Please, Richard . . ."

He dropped his head to her neck, and he began to move. She strained and arched at the incredible sensations filling them, both their experiences combining within their link, sharing, building, driving them closer to a perfection she'd never dreamed possible. His kisses found her breasts again. He rocked in and out of her body, each stroke a bolt of sizzling ecstasy.

"Say it." His voice was strained. Barely recognizable.

"What?"

"My name, from your first dreams with me. Tell me

you know this is me. Not a Watcher. Not your raven. Give me your dreams again, Sarah."

"Rick," she gasped, surrendering herself to trusting him with her secrets and her heart and her future. "Rick . . ."

CHAPTER TWENTY-TWO

Richard stood across the dream lab from Sarah. The strain of their third hour of mission prep was taking its toll on her. Still reeling from the power of what had happened between them, needing her back in his arms, her future back under his protection, he had no choice but to give up even more control over what was about to happen.

Even though she was still leery of the mission, Sarah was working with the team. Trying to, anyway. Jeff, the Watcher lead for the dream mission, wasn't pulling his punches. He couldn't afford to, not if they were going to have any hope of securing her legacy from the center.

"They're just colors," Sarah said. "I'm telling you, the voices are controlling the dream."

"They're not *just* anything." Jeff sat directly in front of her, straddling a chair he'd turned backward, his injured leg stretched out to the side. His arms were folded over the chair's back. He already wore the scrubs everyone would use for the mission. "Any more than it's been just voices crying in your mind since you were a kid. If you had mentioned that detail to someone the moment you started hearing what you thought were Trinity's cries, we might not be in this mess. Something is plugging into your memories and using them to project new realities that threaten everyone around you."

Madeline stiffened beside her sister. She and Jarred sat next to Sarah, at the center of the circle of Watchers filling the lab. Madeline's fingers clenched around Sarah's arm. Jarred squeezed his fiancée's shoulder, completing a circle of support, while Richard kept his distance.

But Sarah was in his mind still. In his heart. She'd touched his soul so deeply, he'd never be able to let her go. The others couldn't know the new depths of their connection. Not yet. But it was there for Sarah, for both of them. Their link would get her through this meeting and the nightmare, and into the future she and her legacy deserved.

She took a steadying breath, absorbing Richard's unspoken conviction that she could handle Jeff and his barrage of questions.

"Why don't you save us all time," she said to Jeff, "and just tell me what you want the colors in my dreams to mean? Then we can move on to discussing the only thing that really matters—saving a little girl whose mind the center's trying to destroy, the same way they did mine."

Silent screams battered the mental control Richard was helping her maintain. He heard them continuously now, the same as Sarah. He'd been hearing them more strongly, more frequently, since walking with her, her mind fully open to him, back to the bunker.

"There is no meaning to any of this without your input." Jeff's tone was clipped, his energy toxic, while he baited her. "You convinced the council you were ready to become an active part of this mission instead of another misfiring variable we have to work around. I suggest you convince yourself you're ready, Ms. Temple. Because these men are about to put their lives on the line to protect your stubborn ass."

"I am ready." Sarah's nightmare screamed. She glared at Jeff. "I'm ready to save Trinity, not to be dissected like some lab experiment."

"Warriors prepare to prepare," Jeff said. "You're being treated like a warrior here, not a specimen. Secrets within a team get people killed. We need your memories, even the ones you don't want to go back to, so the team can build a shared understanding of what each piece of your dream might become once we project together. You need them to help you understand the symbols that will lead you to Trinity."

"You want me to tell you that my mind works rationally." Sarah glanced to Richard, miserable. "You—"

"I want you to tell me the truth you're still running from," Jeff pushed. "Stop protecting yourself from us, like we don't already know what you're capable of. These men are veterans in the fluid work of telepathic missions. We've been trained in Dream Weaver techniques, and we know your history with Ruebens. But no one's as intimately familiar with your mind as you are. We need to know everything you can remember from every dream you've ever had. You're a Watcher now. All hell's about to break loose in your mind. Which means the men on *your* team are quite possibly dead, if you don't stop pouting and get to work."

"Pouting?" Sarah's nails bit into her skin, drops of

blood trickling from the tiny cuts she was making on her hand.

Richard sent his consciousness deeper into hers, discovering cloud images battling her panic, rather than the rage he'd expected. Sarah was fighting for control. She was resisting the impulse to lay into Jeff. She was reaching for the new chance she still couldn't quite believe was waiting for them beyond her nightmare.

He added his own energy to the relaxation routine he'd taught her—his confidence that she could do this. She stared at him only for an instant before her focus returned to the others. But everything they'd shared, everything that connected them, had filled that one endless moment.

"Tell them why the colors are so hard for you to talk about," he projected to her. *"Trust them to understand. Trust yourself to handle remembering."*

Sarah looked down at the damage she'd done to her hand.

Her troubled past shifted closer.

"The colors aren't a threat," she said to the team, wincing as she let her mind drift back. "They've always been there to guide me, not hurt me. For most of my life they were the only things I was sure I belonged to. They were the only things that never went away."

Jeff's powerful body relaxed with her first genuine contribution to the discussion.

"We expect your dream relationship to existing themes and symbols to shift as today's projection plays out," he said. "That's how the center got to you at the house. New variations will no doubt arise in the ocean's shifting matrix. Even with our help stabilizing the matrix and

Colonel Metting anchoring the team's link to you from this lab, you could easily lose your identity to the dream. The center knows which buttons to push. Once they feel your psychic energy searching for Trinity's, they'll come after you in unexpected ways. They'll use something you've grown to trust. Something you've told yourself is harmless. Safe. Nonthreatening."

"So . . ." Sarah reached for her sister's hand. "Nothing's safe now."

"Color's been your safe place your whole life?" Jeff asked.

"They . . ." The past's hold on her escalated. "They've surrounded the people and voices in my visions. All my life, they've told me who's who. Whether there's acceptance or danger. They're why no matter how much everyone was concerned, the ocean dream always felt safe to me before this last nightmare."

"Because in the lab we kept you where the water was shallow," Madeline said. "There was nothing in the shallows but the bright colors that you've always loved. Amethyst. Turquoise. Sapphire. The colors you scribbled all over your wall when you were a little girl."

"My wall?" Sarah asked, the lab suddenly spinning in a dizzying whirl. Her bedroom wall . . . The wall her angry, little-girl image had been staring at in the Lenox daydream. "But . . . there were no colors on it in my vision at the house . . ."

Richard's mind filled with the flash of the vivid hues Madeline described, illuminating the decaying, empty bedroom they'd found in the Temples' crumbling old house. He was seeing a little girl with dark auburn hair sitting on a pink bedspread, staring at a wall consumed by swirls of color and emotion, instead of the black-and-white images Sarah had described from the vision. He was feeling the little girl's fear of what she'd painted, what it meant. Her compulsion to cover every flat surface of the room with the same mania. She needed to drown in the colors, breathe them, until the voices she didn't understand stopped hurting.

He absorbed the memory from long ago, shielding it from everyone but Sarah and Madeline, encouraging the twins to dig deeper. Their minds flowed with his until the truth finally bubbled to the surface.

"Oh, my God. I'd forgotten. The colors on my bedroom walls protected me from the madness." There was shame in Sarah's whisper, but relief, too, as a piece of the past her mind had run from fell back into place. "That's why the daydream seemed so familiar. That's the memory the projection connected with. Mom got so mad when I kept painting the walls, that summer I was six, no matter how many times she covered up the mess I made. It felt like those colors were saving me. They helped me believe that some day all of this would end and it would stop hurting, and I'd stop being something people were afraid of."

The room grew still as the team identified with the loneliness, the isolation, of Sarah's story. None of the Watchers were normal. None of them had been accepted. None of their secrets had been truly safe until they'd found the Brotherhood.

Madeline tilted her head to the side. "Colors were guiding you in the ocean dream, too," she said. "They comforted you at first. They helped you swim deeper, taking you toward Trinity's voice. Then the colors you were following disappeared into the darkness."

"Actually, some of them were still there." Jeff had a laptop balanced on his knee. Each Watcher held a similar compact unit, the devices wirelessly connected to Richard's dream database. Jeff called up a report. "You saw at least one color near the door you said barred you from Trinity's location. Reds. A spectrum of reds. They were—"

"Ugly," the twins said in unison.

"Angry," Sarah added. "Like they were warning me."

"Or they were repelling you." Jeff typed their comments into the computer. "You said you couldn't break through. Did the colors stop you? Or did you just give up because reality didn't turn out as lovely as you'd dreamed it would be in your little-girl fantasies?"

His sarcasm sent a flash of energy sizzling from Sarah. Richard directed it away from Jeff, toward himself. Jeff caught the pain Richard couldn't fully mask. His gaze jerked back to Sarah's. He tried to swallow. The motion caught halfway down his throat. He coughed, not taking a full breath until Sarah glanced an apology toward Richard.

"I don't expect anything to turn out the way I dreamed it anymore." Self-loathing filled her. Fear of the madness that drove her to strike out.

"You've been dreaming of colors and cries for help since you were a child?" Richard asked, buying Jeff time to catch his breath.

"Yes," Madeline answered for her sister.

"Since you were kids?"

"Since my mother told me to stop remembering my dreams," Sarah said. "Because they weren't real, and I'd only make things harder for everyone if I didn't stop talking nonsense all the time."

"Good." Jeff cleared his throat. He turned his chair around, favoring his injured leg, and sat back for the first time since the meeting began.

"Good?" Sarah swiped at the moisture collecting in the corners of her eyes. "I've been a freak my entire life, and it's getting worse now, whether I'm dreaming or not. And that's good?"

"It is, as long as your team knows about it." Jeff's smile offered acceptance, if Sarah would let herself take it. "As long as you trust us while you work through it, instead of fighting and failing alone. And clearly, you're capable of doing that, since I'm still breathing after being an unbearable ass. And you're still in control enough to answer questions after you stopped short of strangling me. I'd call that damn encouraging mission prep."

"You . . ." Sarah sputtered. "You were baiting me? You were pushing me, to see if I could be trusted with your team's lives?"

"No," Richard corrected, "to see if you could trust them with yours. And I assure you, you can."

Jeff had opened the meeting, explaining their three-pronged plan: he'd have Watchers scouting the matrix for whatever could be gleaned of the center's logistics and Trinity's location, streaming their findings back from the dream to Richard's lab; the team would protect the Temples while the twins' minds searched for the little girl, the Watchers added power feeding the matrix and preventing Sarah and Madeline from being absorbed into whatever the center was still doing with Dream Weaver; and the twins would once and for all prove their commitment to work fully, openly, with the Brotherhood.

"You have to accept that we'll have your back," Jeff said, "whatever you do in the dream. Whatever's happened in the past."

Sarah's gaze swept the room.

Richard, too, cataloged every man's reaction to Jeff's challenge. Someone from the Brotherhood was leaking information to the center. Likely a Watcher chosen for this team.

Jeff could be sending a traitor into Sarah's mind equipped with the information he needed to hand the center a final victory. Richard listened to his instincts and tried to feel which of his brothers couldn't be trusted. But he sensed nothing out of the ordinary from any consciousness in the lab.

Jeff inched his chair closer to Sarah's. "What aren't you telling us?" he asked.

"The people I care about most in the world are going back into the nightmare with me," Sarah said. "Do you really think I'd keep something from you that could protect them?"

She sounded sincere enough, but Richard could feel her holding back.

"You can do this," his mind promised her.

"I could lose you if I don't stay in control," she projected back. *"Or Trinity or Maddie. You could all die, just like my parents."*

"We're not going anywhere. No one here is going to let that happen."

"Equip your team to counter whatever the dream will do," Jeff said. "Trust us, even with what you think are the weakest parts of your legacy. You have my promise as a warrior, your team will be there for you when you need us."

"You mean we have your personal assurance?" Jarred asked. "Imagine our relief, since a little over a day ago you were seconds away from shooting Sarah dead. Why should she trust you now?"

"Because every consciousness that follows her into tonight's nightmare will be trapped in that altered state if she can't disengage. We'll all find ourselves at the mercy of her Dream Weaver programming if she doesn't maintain control. We all want the same thing—successful mission execution and extraction of everyone from the nightmare, particularly Sarah."

"And while Sarah's beating the center's psychic ass at its own game," Madeline said, "what exactly will your men be doing?"

"For starters," Richard said, "Jeff will know not to allow the colors that have been guiding Sarah through her ocean imagery to repel her from Trinity's door."

Sarah shivered.

It wasn't the first time during the meeting that the mention of the child's name had spooked her.

"Are you afraid to find Trinity?" Jeff's gaze lifted from the gooseflesh rippling over her arm.

Sarah stared at her hands. Richard could feel the last of the fragile confidence she'd brought into the meeting give way to the guilt that had sent her running last night. Then the truth was there, whispering through their link, smacking him between the eyes like a psychic sledge-hammer.

"The red hues in the nightmare were reacting to your fear of what's behind the door." He grabbed Jeff's laptop and scrolled through his database. "All this time, the colors haven't been merely showing you other people. They've been reacting to your own emotions. In the nightmare, they led you to Trinity, then turned you away from her, changing and flowing based on what you were feeling . . . You didn't fail her, Sarah. You just weren't ready to push through the door."

He brought up the records he'd entered after they emerged from Sarah's vision in the gym, sorting the entries by color.

"When Madeline arrived," he said, "she was trying to talk you into swimming away from the voice at the bottom of the ocean, and you saw a trail of—"

"Color behind her," Sarah finished. "Amethyst leading toward the surface. Maddie's always surrounded by healing colors in my dreams."

"Healing colors?" Jeff asked.

"Bright whites and vivid hues." Sarah smiled at her twin's shock. "They felt wonderful whenever Maddie brought them to the shallow water we worked in. At first it was her colors I followed deeper into the dream. Amethyst, mostly. It was like having her with me, healing me."

"But it was your colors you saw," Jeff corrected, "when you followed them to the door. You were the only one in the nightmare then. It was your own consciousness you were feeling when you turned away, when you couldn't open the latch."

Sarah's forehead wrinkled. Confusion rushed through her and Richard's link. But there were more clouds there now, too, softening the impact of the dream memories. Helping Sarah understand the dream symbols' meanings.

"I was going to save Trinity," she said, finally remembering without fear. "I was so sure the reds and pinks and crimsons I was following would show me how to get to her. That I could finally do something good with my legacy, like Maddie has."

"You're here." Madeline squeezed her twin's hand. "After nearly losing everything, you're here fighting, Sarah. That's good. That's amazing. You're a healer, too. My God, you're a Watcher now. There's no end to what you're going to do with our legacy."

Sarah shook her head. "The colors left me when I let go of the door. All that was left were the horrible voices that wanted me to—"

"Or did you leave them?" Madeline asked. "Richard's right. The dream colors have been yours all along, but you've never learned how to use them. Just like when you were a little girl, and you made yourself forget the things you painted on your wall. In the nightmare, when you didn't think the colors wanted you to open the door, when you couldn't get through without them, that was you letting go, Sarah. Forgetting. Then the ocean could take you wherever it wanted to, because you thought you didn't deserve—"

"The light on the other side," Sarah said. Richard felt the full realization of what he'd been trying to say in the woods hit home. "After everything I've done, I didn't believe I could have what was waiting for me on the other side. But . . . the colors returned when Maddie forced her way into the dream."

After Sarah had seen Richard's raven soaring above her, and after her dream consciousness had called for his help. After she'd let herself believe just a little more.

Richard sent his consciousness deeper, straight to the part of Sarah that knew she could find Trinity. He replayed for her the courage she'd shown the council. The generous spirit that had understood his own shattered childhood and helped heal him. The warrior within Sarah willing to endure Jeff's pressure tactics so she could keep fighting.

"The colors have been yours all along," he promised her. *"They're yours to command now, and so is your nightmare. You're ready to remember your past and use it to understand your legacy's future."*

Sarah was looking at him, recalling the moment she'd accepted him into the nightmare's ocean, even though she'd still been clinging to her hatred. She was clinging to their link now as strongly as she was holding on to her sister's hand and Trinity's cries. She was—

"—ready for more . . ." She sent a kaleidoscope of images to Richard and Madeline of everything she was remembering. *"I need to know more, to get me through to Trinity . . ."*

Madeline turned to Richard, sensing the change in his and Sarah's connection.

"The colors and light in the dream are your mind telling you who it trusts," she said to her twin. "They're your instincts in the nightmare."

"And when you doubt what they're trying to show you . . . ," Jeff began. He and the rest of the team were locked on to the twins and how Richard had moved between them, while Jarred curled an arm around Madeline. "That's when the ocean's voice takes over. The dream's matrix led you to the bottom of the ocean. Not your colors—*not* your own consciousness."

Richard felt his men's excitement grow.

They finally had something to work with.

"The colors are your strength," he said. "They're how you'll control where the dream takes you. Use them to search for Trinity and understand the other symbols you find in the matrix. Find her. Your Watchers will be with you, tracking every aspect of the nightmare. Once we have you all back, we'll use what you've learned to find her in reality."

Jeff shut down his laptop, his attention on the twins. "Trust your ability to control what you dream, and whoever's driving the matrix for the center won't be able to manipulate you."

Sarah looked from Jeff to the rest of the Watchers. She held her sister's hand, accepting Madeline and Jarred's support. She leaned back into Richard's strength, memories of their forest escape flashing through their minds. Then her thoughts were filling with light and colors that forced away the confusion and doubt, until the shields he'd helped build came down and everyone in the lab could hear for the first time Trinity's never-ending pleas for help.

A current of awareness spread through the room. The Watchers leaned forward in their chairs, their minds feeding Sarah's power and control as the twins became fully absorbed onto the team.

Sarah blinked.

She leaned forward.

"Okay," she said. "Tell me again how all of this is going to work."

Sarah watched Richard help Maddie and Jarred settle onto their side-by-side exam tables. He hadn't left her since planning broke off and they began mission count-down. Not even when he'd had one of the team members, Lieutenant Donovan, removed from the team with no explanation to either Sarah or Jeff.

Rick . . .

Her Watcher. Her warrior. Her gypsy, who'd always known her better than anyone, because he'd survived the same kind of lost childhood she had. Her future, because he'd never given up on her. He was wearing scrubs and his lab coat, but he'd never looked so strong. So in command. So everything that Sarah needed to help her believe. How did she go back into her ocean nightmare without him?

"You love him, don't you?" Maddie asked with her mind, following the direction of Sarah's stare.

"We . . ." Love? The word felt right. It felt like home. *"We're the same. I don't know how else to explain it, but—"*

"You don't have to know. You just have to believe—in something besides the disaster our legacy made of your child-hood. If that begins with you loving Metting, I'm in, as long as he keeps you safe through this insanity."

Richard was following their conversation through his and Sarah's link. Maddie's unexpected support made him smile so slightly, no one else noticed. A look of trust passed between them, sealing the deal. He finished hooking her and Jarred up to the confusion of monitors that would track their progress in the dream. Jarred methodically rechecked each of their leads. He turned to Sarah next and eyeballed hers.

"Can't be too careful with little sisters," his mind whispered.

The familiar urge to run battled with Sarah's unexpected impulse to fling herself into her soon-to-be brother-in-law's arms. The two warring compulsions invited Sarah's mania closer. She shifted away from her sister's fiancé and bumped into the solid chest that had cradled her body so perfectly last night. She looked up at Richard.

"I can't do this without you," she said through their link. *"I'll never make it back. I can feel the nightmare's darkness closing in."*

The dream would try to take her away from her family. And this time, she didn't want to go. It had been simpler before, when she'd been running from what they wanted to mean to her. Now they were a reality she needed to come home to.

Richard's palm pressed her head into the nook beneath his chin, staking a public claim. It was mere minutes before she was scheduled to dream. Plans were set. What did it matter now who knew how deeply their relationship had changed?

"Let yourself need the people who love you," his mind said. *"Let that bring you back."*

"I'll destroy them." It was the one fear she couldn't shake. *"I'll destroy all of you."*

"Needing us isn't how you'll let the danger take over. Returning to the isolated place that nearly took you away from us—that's how you'll destroy the people who love you."

"Love?"

His dark gaze sparked with the passion pouring between them, but she could feel him hesitating to say the words. She could feel his fear that she wasn't ready to hear them.

"I . . ." Her mind skittered away, then back. *"I do love you, Richard."*

"Rick," he corrected, and they were both remembering the perfect, unguarded moment in the forest when he'd begged her to be completely his.

"I'm more afraid of losing you," she said, *"than I ever was of Ruebens's wolf or my nightmare ocean. Whatever happens, I do love you."*

"Our link will be with you every step of the way." His promise went soul deep. His hands brushed heat up her arms. *"I love you, too, Sarah. I'm not going to leave you alone with your memories or your dreams."*

It was exactly what she'd needed to hear.

It was also impossible.

"But the council said—"

"That was before."

"Before?"

"Before you became part of me. All of me. I couldn't stay out of your projection any more than Jarred and Madeline can function beyond each other's consciousness. We're one now, Sarah. It's done."

"You'll be betraying your oath if you interfere with the mission."

"If that's what it takes to stop the center from peddling psychic weapons technology from your legacy, then it's my duty as a Watcher to do whatever I have to do. I've played this by the book from the start. It's time to fight dirty. Good thing my

parents trained me like hell for that, a long time before I became a Watcher."

"I won't let you destroy the life you've worked so hard for, just because I can't stop my nightmares from taking over my mind."

"If you don't come back from this whole, there is no life for me. Inside the Brotherhood or out of it."

"Your oath means everything to you." She laid her palm over the Brotherhood insignia she knew was branded on his shoulder, just beneath his shirt. *"You'd never survive—"*

"A reality without you in it. Knowing you, feeling you inside me, has been the first real thing in my life. Sensing you trust me so completely that very first day, and then again last night, after all that's happened. Don't ask me to give that up."

But he'd lose everything if she failed.

"You're not going to fail," he said out loud. "You're a Watcher. You're a dreamer. You were put on this earth to do exactly what you're about to do. And your family has just expanded to include hundreds of obnoxious, protective warriors who'll have your back and augment your power, not just the men in this room. You have everything you need to take full control of your legacy. You'll come back to me. You're ready."

Her family . . . Maddie and Jarred, there in her heart. The amethyst and turquoise of their essences wrapped her in warmth. Richard . . . The irresistible feel of him was a deep river of purple, promising forever. And her Watcher team, accepting her broken places and pushing her to reach for the light. All but one of them.

"One of your—our—obnoxious men wants me dead," she reminded Richard. *"Someone here's working with the cen-*

ter. Is that why you had Donovan removed from the team? Do you think he's the mole?"

Richard's mind infused hers with the bliss of forest sounds. *"Don't worry about the mole. Donovan's too green to be on this mission. I need my top men with me, especially when I suspect one of them is our leak. But all you have to know is that I'll be there to protect you, no matter what happens. No one's going to hurt you tonight, Sarah."*

Wind rustled through their shared thoughts. Memories of midnight breezes and heated skin and making love and being reborn beneath the shelter of centuries-old trees. She could smell the tang of pine merging with the essence of earth and sky. She could feel the safety of Richard's arms wrapped around her as they forged an unbreakable bond. It was a perfect dream that darkness couldn't touch.

"Lean back." Richard eased her to the table's firm pillow. "Once everyone is settled with their minds centered on your projection, we'll begin administering the dream protocol." Drugs that would enhance Sarah's psychic focus and augment her ability to link with the other minds journeying into the projection. Medication that would weaken the shred of control she'd used to hold the nightmare back this long.

Jeff stepped to Richard's side, still balancing on the crutches he needed because he'd protected her during her last vision.

"I'll be the last consciousness to immerse in the dream's matrix," he said, "and the last to leave it. Wait for me inside the ocean projection. My men will take flanking positions, ready to follow you deeper into the dream while they report their observations back to Colonel Metting. When everyone's battle ready, I'll link to the matrix with whatever dream symbol your mind assigns me."

"Let's hope it's not a wolf." Sarah was joking. Mostly.

Neither Richard nor Jeff cracked a smile.

"Each Watcher could arrive with his own unique dream symbol," Jeff said. "Or your mind could assign a generic 'Watcher' image to the entire team. Remember the watchword—*window*. When you hear it, know you're connecting with the Brotherhood. We're your safe passage out of whatever situation you're in. Say it for me."

"Window," Sarah repeated.

"And my personal contact key?"

"Home base."

"I'm your last-resource link to the lab. Your home base in the dream. I'll be your link back to this reality while you deal with whatever obstacles are thrown in your path. Keep your focus on Trinity. Let the rest go, so you can evolve in the matrix. Your brothers will pull you back if you need us."

Sarah nodded, even though it was Richard more than any of the rest of them that she was trusting with her family's safety.

"You'll get us home." Sarah turned her head to where her twin lay on the table beside her. They reached for each other's hands.

Jeff's grip closed around their hold. "You have my word as a Watcher."

Sarah looked from Maddie's nod to the promise swirling in Richard's expression.

"And you have mine," she said while the voices in

her mind howled, kicking her heart rate into a tantrum on the cardiac monitor Richard had her hooked to. It was terrifying, wanting to believe this badly. Wanting to feel an entire room of powerful, valiant minds believing in her.

Jeff moved to a table just beyond where Sarah and Maddie and Jarred were grouped at the center of the team.

Richard's hand was warm on her shoulder.

"Trust me," his mind said to hers. *"Come back to me."*

"I will," she promised. *"I'll see you in my dreams."*

CHAPTER TWENTY-THREE

The ocean felt almost too real this time.

And alarmingly empty.

The familiar pull of water washed over Sarah's skin. Currents tugged. But that was it. There was nothing else to see.

"Maddie?" Sarah turned in the shallow water near the surface. She could feel her twin's hand still holding hers in the lab, but there was no one beside her in the ocean. "Jarred?"

Her voice echoed through the sea's hollow perfection. Shadows lurked nearby. She could sense them just out of sight. And there was a malevolence to the sea's dimness, dangerous intent sliding across her body. The cold, wet feel of it wasn't the charming, beguiling sensation normally waiting for her in the shallows.

Overlaying it all was an unnerving silence. Only when she stopped looking for Maddie did she hear a faint hint of Trinity's call merging with a deeper sound, a roar— the ocean's dawning awareness that she'd come back.

The first whiff of panic struck. Where were the colors she was supposed to control? The cries and voices she needed to follow? The water swelled with her anxiety.

"*Relax,*" Richard's mind said to hers. "*You're just getting started.*"

Their link was allowing him to circumvent the headset covering her ears back in the lab—the communication network that connected her to the rest of the team.

"There's nothing here," she said. No programming painting the nightmare she'd never initiated before. "How much time do we have before the center discovers what I'm doing?"

"*Enough. You'll have enough time. You'll have everything you need. Focus on what's there, not what's missing. Build the matrix from your memories.*"

Bright colors suddenly infused the water, a welcome dazzle of beauty. They burst into a magical swirl, infusing Sarah with their essence. The amethyst streaks were Maddie. The turquoise touches, Jarred. Intertwined, their unbreakable link was a reflection of everything they'd found in each other. Everything they were putting on the line to help Sarah.

Their bodies formed as near-solid images in the mist. Maddie's emotions permeated the ocean dream, syncing with Sarah's. Their connection fired Trinity's screams to cruel life.

The little girl's pain sucked Sarah down, rocketing her into the ocean's depths. Maddie sank with her, leaving Jarred's image at the surface, where his job was to bridge Sarah and Maddie's psychic link, augmenting it and communicating their status back to the lab.

Sarah could feel her twin's fear.

"I can't stop," Maddie said.

"Neither can I." Sarah concentrated on the lure of Trinity's call, growing louder the deeper they went.

She tried to visualize the plan. They were supposed to wait until Jeff arrived and organized the team's descent. But returning the dream to the surface was impossible, no matter how hard she tried to go back.

"We knew plans would change once the dream began," Richard assured her. *"Leave your mind open to your team. They'll track your energy. Focus on your connection with Trinity. See what you have to, to find her."*

"We're falling too fast," Maddie said. "Where are we going?"

"It's okay. I just need . . ."

Sarah closed her eyes and listened. She relaxed into the descent, letting it take her closer to the truth. The ocean's voice was there with Trinity's now, mumbling something Sarah couldn't understand, intensifying the nightmare's hold. It was terrifying, but this was what she'd come for.

"I need to be deeper in the matrix to hear enough of Trinity to find her," she said.

She needed to feel more of the fear that had fed the projection the last time.

"Stop," Maddie insisted. "Jeff wanted us to wait—"

"The team can't do anything until I know where to take them." Sarah grabbed her sister's hand, pulling Maddie along with her. "Where are the colors? Can you see them? They're supposed to be here. They led me to the door before, but I can't see them yet. We have to go deeper."

"Five minutes," Richard said through the team's comm link. "Jeff and the rest of the team are going under now. They know you're on the move. They'll be no more than five minutes behind."

Sarah kicked into the currents that were really shadows, dragging her twin through the sea's darkening blue. They were swimming without really swimming. The way what should be a struggle often feels effortless and surreal within a dream. The deeper they went, the stronger Sarah's panicked memories became—the same emotions that had been her downfall in the last dream.

"You'll never make it," the ocean chanted. *"This is where you belong."*

"Help me . . ." Trinity screamed.

"Who said that?" Maddie asked. "Those voices. Are they—"

"They're the dream." Sarah forced herself to remember that she belonged with her twin, not alone at the bottom of an empty sea. But her fear grew along with the memories of how close she'd come to dying and taking her sister with her last time. "The voices are what I heard coming for me as a little girl. When I was in the coma, too. Then in the nightmare."

"They were telling you that you were alone?" Compassion filled their link. Maddie was reliving each memory with her. "You were screaming for help in the coma before Richard found you. You thought no one would ever hear, and that you deserved it. Sarah . . . I'm so sorry. I never knew. Mom and Dad and I, we never knew."

Her twin's understanding wrapped around Sarah, Maddie's regret and her need to make the past right. Her love lit the bubbling water around them, warming them, shielding Sarah from the desperation of the voices dragging at them. They jerked to a stop, both of them breathing heavily. Sarah basked in the amethyst aura surrounding them and her sister's calming presence. The dream's madness swirled just beyond the light's protective embrace.

"Where are the other colors?" Maddie asked.

"The voices are all I've found so far. I heard them as soon as you arrived."

"The ones that have been telling you to give up since you were a little girl? You can't follow them, Sarah. Not without the colors Richard said you should trust. Not without the Watchers here to help."

"I didn't exactly have a choice." Sarah searched the empty water surrounding them. "Now even the voices have stopped. I don't understand. Why is nothing happening?"

"It's not the same dream as before," Richard said with his mind. *"You're different, and you're initiating the matrix. Something's holding the dream back. You have to dig the nightmare out of your Dream Weaver programming. You have to—"*

"I have to lose control." The dynamic she'd feared most was the answer to starting her search again.

"What?" Maddie asked.

"Like I was when I was a little girl. Like in the coma, when there was no connection to anything. Like in the last nightmare, before you came. I'm closest to Trinity and the ocean's command when there's no one else to anchor me."

"When your emotions are free," Richard agreed. *"Even the destructive ones. Like they were when we sparred in the lab's gym, and when I forced you to confront your bedroom in Lenox."*

Sarah's stomach churned. She glanced at her sister. Maddie had nearly died the last time Sarah let the dream's madness too close. She closed her eyes and reached for the voices swirling beyond her twin's aura.

"Sarah . . ." Maddie said. "What are you doing?"

"Welcome back," the ocean gushed in a tone that was a ghastly combination of the wolf's and Trinity's voices.

Sarah's terror returned. She forced herself to feel it, to embrace the shadowy consciousness she could sense just beyond her grasp. Her mind dug for the madness within her programming until it was itching along her skin, up her spine, worming its way into her crumbling psyche.

"What are you doing?" Maddie demanded.

"I'm remembering. The ocean's voice. The red that I saw when the dream sucked me under."

Sarah opened her eyes to see clouds of crimson and black forming around them.

"Good girl," Richard's mind said.

"How are you doing that?" Maddie asked.

"I was scared then. I'm scared now. The colors are going to take us back to Trinity."

"Okay." Maddie's "okay" sounded as if she were staring down a rabid animal. She eyed the threatening haze churning in the water. "Good. But we need to wait here for Jeff and the team to catch up. They'll know how to use what you're doing safely."

Maddie's healing energy reached for Sarah. Her amethyst aura rolled toward the crimson and black haze, swallowing it and Sarah's fear until they dissipated into the ocean's gloom.

"No!" Sarah grappled for the terrifying emotions that had painted the path she needed.

"We need to wait until the team gets here," her sister insisted.

Sarah shook her head. She shook off Maddie's concern. She closed her eyes and swam several yards away, her mind reaching for the strength she needed from—

"From Metting?" Maddie's image grabbed Sarah's arm. Outside the dream, her hand clenched around Sarah's wrist. "Richard's mind is here with you? Is he telling you to do this? We have no backup yet, Sarah. You're losing control. I can feel it."

"I'm—" Sarah tried to pull free. Maddie wouldn't let go. "I'm doing what I have to."

"You're exhausting yourself. Wait until we're sure what we're dealing with. Wait until the others are here too—"

"I . . ." Sarah yanked away. Grabbed her head.

"Help me!" Trinity and the wolf screamed together as soon as she and Maddie were separated.

"The voices are together now," Sarah said. What did that mean? "The wolf's voice is too close to Trinity. The dream is telling me something. If I could just hear—"

"Stop." Maddie frowned when Sarah swam farther away. "It's not safe."

But the voices were growing louder. The ocean's shadows were feeding Sarah's instability. The answers were reaching for her.

"I can't do this and be safe," she said. "And I don't know how long I can keep the nightmare from overwhelming me again. I have to go while I still can, without anyone holding me back."

"Go where? You're not going anywhere without me."

Maddie's bright, healing aura was fading. The amethyst of her control weakened as the voices grew louder in Sarah's mind. Pockets of crimson-draped black re-formed around them.

"See?" Sarah said. "They're waiting for me to follow. I have to trust what my mind is telling me."

"Is this your idea or Metting's?"

"He knows what he's doing. He knows me."

"And I don't? This is crazy, Sarah."

"This is me. Everything you're seeing. Everything you're hearing. It's all me, remember? It's crazy. I've always been crazy. But I can't retrace my steps to the door we need to find without trusting the unstable emotions driving the colors. The dream's matrix is wired into them."

"And you can't fully connect with any of it"—Maddie stared across the distance Sarah had forced between them—"while I'm protecting you?"

"No." Sarah felt her sister's tears, like tiny knives slicing through her heart. "I love you, Maddie. But I don't think I can."

Crimson red rimmed the coal black shadows that rolled closer, creating a demented, blood-rimmed haze threatening to unleash a violent storm. A storm Sarah would let consume her if that's what it took.

"*Help her do this,*" Richard projected to Maddie, absorbing her into his and Sarah's psychic link. "*Help her get this done so she can come back to us. I'll keep you two connected. We'll protect her and stabilize her dream projection together. But this will only work if you let her become what the dream needs her to be, to lead us to the truth.*"

"And what she has to be is alone?" Maddie demanded.

"No," Sarah stared at the brooding, crimson-soaked

clouds. They were twisting between her and her twin, tumbling downward into the ocean. "I have to be free. I have to follow my instincts, knowing that you'll still be here when I'm done. I'm not running away this time. I'm trying to come back completely. No more nightmares."

"*Open the door,*" Trinity's voice whispered from the haze, "*and see what we've become . . .*"

"What happens if the darkness traps you and I'm not there?" Long-ago pain roughened Maddie's voice. "Just like when we were teenagers, and I lost you for ten years."

"The darkness already has me." Sarah accepted the bone-deep truth of what she was saying. "It's always been a part of me. But I have a chance to break its hold now. I'm going to beat Ruebens's programming. Use what I've learned against the center. Find Trinity and the truth about our legacy. Don't ask me to hide from what has to come next. I'm finally ready to face it."

She could feel Richard's trust flowing to her. Maddie could, too. Her twin could feel the courage Sarah had found in her connection with Richard and the acceptance of so much more than her need for him.

"I love you, Maddie," Sarah said into the dream. "I want you and Jarred and Richard in my life too much to let the madness win again. Please help me do this."

Maddie's amethyst energy began to retract, swirling back to her, allowing the bloated crimson and black cloud to spread.

"Come back to me," Maddie said, repeating Richard's parting words in the lab. "Do whatever you have to, Sarah. I'll be right behind you. Just please, come back to your family."

Then her mind was letting go, and Sarah was falling, her consciousness merging with the menacing clouds she'd called into the matrix. The nightmare's currents swarmed. They battered Sarah with Trinity's brittle cries and the wolf's deep laugh as she raced deeper into the dream.

"Help me . . ." Trinity said from below.

"Help me . . ." The words tumbled from Sarah's mouth as she surrendered her mind to the nightmare's mania.

She could do this. She could accept the fear and keep dreaming. The people she trusted to protect her wouldn't abandon her to the darkness. Her family would—

"We'll be there," Richard promised. *"Focus on finding Trinity's door. I'll make sure your team finds you."*

Richard.

Maddie.

The Watchers.

Her family was coming for her.

Breathing was nearly impossible, Sarah was spiraling so fast. Her sight had dimmed to the point of being useless. Crimson and black were oozing everywhere. Outside her—consuming the water and racing ahead. Inside her—drilling deeper, searching for every weak, lonely place that the nightmare could still feed on. Until Sarah thought she'd go insane with it.

"Make the colors guide you," Richard said. Her Watcher. Her heart. *"What are they telling you? Where is the maze you couldn't solve before? Find it. Make the dream take you past it, to the door that was on the other side."*

"Help me . . ." Trinity begged.

"*Hurry . . .*" the wolf's command said in the child's voice.

Sarah breathed in the sound of them, the colors swirling deeper, faster. She focused, pictured the door. Needed the door. She needed Trinity. She needed to know where the madness of her legacy had started and where it would end.

Suddenly, the tunnel emerged around her, absent of water, absent of light. Except for Trinity's crimson aura, which was barely visible and racing ahead. Sarah ran, her hands trailing along the walls, feeling for the door's scarred surface. But there was nothing around the next turn, while the child's screams poured over her, coming from every direction, sending Sarah to her knees, her hands covering her ears.

"*It's your programming's pain,*" Richard said. "*It's meant to stop you. But you've been here before. You know there's more beyond the tunnel. Find Trinity. Focus on her.*"

"She's in danger." Sarah could sense the black cloud's menace. It was the wolf's energy, she realized. It was consuming more and more of Trinity, who was the crimson. "I can't let him hurt her."

Sarah opened her eyes, feeling what she couldn't see—letting her inner voices drive the dream. Light flickered dimly ahead, casting everything in gray, tempting Sarah to run again. To never stop. Except . . .

"The dream wants me to keep moving." She could feel it. "It wants me crazy exhausted so I'll quit before I find the truth. Just like last time."

"*But you're not quitting.*" Richard's confidence washed through her like oxygen filling her starving lungs.

"No." She wanted his beautiful forest back. She wanted both of them safe there, free of Dream Weaver's hold. "I'm not giving up," she yelled into the empty tunnel. "I won't give up until I find the truth."

It was time to end this.

Searching inside instead of moving deeper into the maze of tunnels, she retraced her steps in the last nightmare. She remembered the rushing water, sucking her down winding corridors that led to nowhere. But why a tunnel? What fear, what memory, was Ruebens manipulating to create a maze she couldn't escape?

"Think," she yelled into the dream as Trinity's pain taunted her to find a door she'd never reach.

She could remember another existence filled with emptiness. Failure. A no-win, endless reality where she had only shadows and loneliness for company. She'd been here before.

"What happens if the darkness traps you and I'm not there?" Maddie had asked her. *"Just like when we were teenagers, and I lost you for ten years."*

"Oh, my God."

Sarah had been trapped in the same sea for ten years, knowing only the self-loathing and guilt and madness. She hadn't saved her father. She hadn't deserved to come back from her coma. It was the same overwhelming failure she'd felt in the last nightmare, when she hadn't made it through the door to Trinity.

Sarah braced herself on her hands and knees. Ruebens had re-created her coma. Her nightmare ocean, this endless maze of corridors—it was the bastard's way of trapping her in the same hopelessness that Richard had first rescued her from at the center. Her programming had been designed to suck Sarah back, to strand her in the darkest place her mind had ever known.

"A place you escaped," Richard reminded her. *"A reality that can no longer control you."*

Sarah looked at the tunnel around her. Really looked, for the first time. It existed only in her mind. It represented a past she was done torturing herself with. She had a future to look forward to instead, where she and Maddie were free to explore their legacy with—

"Trinity . . ." she said into the dream. "Trinity is all that's real here. The rest can't touch me now."

And as she released the last of her coma's memories, the tunnel Ruebens had anchored them to disappeared and miles of harmless ocean stretched before her instead, empty, just like when she'd first reentered the ocean. A child's heart-wrenching scream and the wolf's soulless laugh jerked her around to see an intimidating door covered in crimson and black hanging in the gloom. It was the final barrier separating her from the truth.

The colors were melting into one another on its surface: black consuming crimson, Ruebens's dream wolf consuming Trinity's innocence. What remained was a grotesque stain, the tint of dried blood. This was the moment when she'd given up in the last nightmare. But this time light shone through from the other side, around the edges of the door's scarred surface. It was Trinity's light, she somehow knew, waiting just beyond Sarah's reach. Or maybe she'd find the lost little girl who'd been waiting for Sarah in her rotting, abandoned bedroom, so sure, so angry, that Sarah would never come.

"I'm here!" She rushed forward, pounding on the door, searching for the latch. The razor-sharp steel sliced her fingers, but the lock wouldn't give.

"Help me!" a child screamed over a wolf's growl.

"Your team's almost there," Richard cautioned. *"Hold on."*

"But the wolf is with her."

The new consciousness behind Ruebens's wolf image was in Trinity's mind. Consuming her. Sarah could feel it. She was so close to stopping it. She tugged harder, then pounded the door with her fists. She had to break through.

"Stay away from the door. Madeline's bringing the team to you. You just have to—"

The door's black aura surged around Sarah, drowning Richard's voice, smothering her in Trinity's terror. She couldn't see. She couldn't hear. But she wasn't letting go.

"I'm finding you this time, Trinity. I won't let the wolf have you."

She clawed at the metal beneath her palms. Digging through the dark aura, ignoring the pain, she fought with every ounce of energy she had left. Until a streak of blinding brightness flashed through the cracks in the pitted surface, ripping at the steel beneath her fingers. Reaching for her from the other side of the nightmare. Then Sarah became the light and the cracks and the door itself.

She was the latch flying apart in her hands. She was a lifetime of fear and doubt and guilt and shame, exploding into tiny pieces, ripping at her own skin, peeling away everything but what she needed desperately to find beyond the door. Inside herself. Until there was nothing left but Sarah kneeling, her hands covering her head, crying Trinity's name the way she had in her childhood dreams.

The dreams that were finally a reality.

Richard's consciousness was gone—his love and his gypsy intuition and his warrior's logic that had guided her through the projection. Sarah's link to her sister and the Watcher team was silent. She'd had to leave them all behind to get to this place where she could feel darkness closing in on the blinding brightness just beyond her closed eyes. Anger was still seething. Trinity's cries were still searing her mind. Her ocean dream's darkness was gloating, waiting for it's chance to destroy them both.

"Open your eyes," the wolf said, instead of Trinity, "and see what we've become . . ."

CHAPTER TWENTY-FOUR

"Sarah?" Richard called into their link.

She was gone.

His connection to the nightmare's matrix was gone.

He braced his hands on each side of her body and leaned over her exam table until their faces were inches apart. She lay deathly still while her stats, pressure, pulse, and psychic echoes inched closer to the red zone.

"Talk to me, Sarah. Let me back in."

He reached for the tray beside her bed, for the extraction protocol designed to suppress the brain's dream center, but stopped. He couldn't pull her back yet. He had to give her team a chance to find Trinity.

"Her psychic energy is being shielded from us somehow," the tech closest to Richard said. "We're no longer tracking her mind's feedback from the dream. Her levels are off the charts, but she's no longer streaming information."

Jeff's men were with Madeline now. Their reports were still coming through the group's connection and the psychic audio transmission Richard had custom-designed to allow the lab to communicate within a projection. The dream had grown dark around them. They'd been following Maddie's lead, and she'd been secretly following Richard's instructions to find the door and Sarah. Now they were all stranded in the matrix, and he had nothing. No way to get them moving again in the right direction. Not from the lab.

"Update coming in from the control room," one of his techs reported from the lab's corner workstation. "Two level-one legacy teams are under attack. Their principals are MIA."

Two new Watcher teams with critical principals were in crisis?

Richard joined the seated man, warning signals firing through his mind, his intuition on overload. He kept searching for Sarah's consciousness while another part of his mind analyzed the significance of a new security breach.

"Time of contact reported by each team?" he asked.

The tech pressed indicators on the wall projection in front of them, streaming reports from the compromised satellite locations to the lab.

"Both report first contact from unknown aggressors two minutes ago. Psychic links to their principals ended at the same time."

The same moment that Richard had felt the mind beyond Sarah's door suck her into whatever reality now had her.

A new report blipped to life on the lab's transparent wall.

"Bursts of psychic energy detected at the center complex," the tech said.

Richard pressed his fingers to the display, resizing

the readings and calling up new details, searching for the answers he needed.

"Same time stamp." He pressed the receiver at his ear. "The center's making its move," he said to the lieutenant on call. "Inform the council. Lock down all legacies. All Watchers return to quarters and await further instructions. Escalate mission planning for both initiating center reconnaissance contact and repelling an attack."

Something was wrong. The certainty of it scratched up Richard's spine as he removed the receiver from his ear. He placed the device on the nearest workstation and turned to the team dreaming behind him.

It was as if the nightmare had been waiting for Sarah, no matter how difficult it had been for her to find Trinity's door again. And now Sarah's consciousness was beyond the Brotherhood's control at the exact moment that they recorded the first traceable psychic activity at the center complex since Ruebens's death. The council's logical conclusion would be that Sarah's gifts were fully at the mercy of whatever the center was doing.

"Disengage the dream matrix?" the tech monitoring Sarah's stats asked.

"Not yet." Richard's hand closed over the pouch of meds hooked onto the waistband of his scrubs.

It was entirely possible that what he was about to do would worsen the situation he'd led his brotherhood and the woman he loved into. But he had only moments before the decision would be removed from his control, and he could see no other viable alternative.

He let go of Sarah's recovery medication and returned to the tables at the center of the mission team. Shielding his mind from his lab techs, he mentally disabled the psychic receiver translating the team's sleeping energy into the electronic circuitry that kept the lab informed of their progress and communications.

"We've lost contact with the mission team," someone said. "Biofeedback is off-line."

"Incoming transmission from the council," the tech manning the corner workstation announced.

"Handle it." Richard aligned his fingers with the pressure points that would drive his consciousness to the heart of the minds he could still reach in the dream.

"But it's the council. They—"

"I said handle it!" Richard closed his eyes, harnessing his skill at connecting with and manipulating others' realities and picturing the water and colors and deepening dream shadows that he'd placed beyond his lab's grasp.

A hologram shimmered to life across the lab, an elder arriving to take control of the mission and no doubt shut the projection down regardless of whether it forever stranded Sarah's consciousness within the matrix.

Richard's mind connected with Madeline's at the same instant that his gaze locked with Jacob's. Then, releasing every part of his awareness that wasn't reaching for Sarah's twin, he left his brotherhood behind, his consciousness connecting fully with Sarah's nightmare.

"Where did Sarah go?" Maddie asked.

Her sister's thoughts were gone.

Richard's thoughts were gone.

There was nothing. No more images feeding to Maddie about Sarah's descent to the hideous door she'd finally found. No hint of her sister's or Metting's minds at all. Nothing.

"I can't sense anything."

"We've lost contact with the dream lab." Jeff's image reappeared out of the darkness that had overtaken the dream when Maddie lost track of her twin.

At least the swirl of gray that represented Jeff's dream presence reappeared. So did the rivulets of brown that Sarah's mind had projected for the other Watchers. The murky water around Maddie shimmered with the warriors' aggressive energies. Then the ocean seized, creating a volatile wake, and Richard Metting's image emerged within the bubbling aftermath, looking exactly like himself.

"What the hell is going on?" Jeff's aura demanded. "You were ordered to remain in the lab."

"The Brotherhood's under attack. The center targeted two of our principals at the same instant that Sarah was pulled through her door."

"She's on the other side?" Maddie swam toward Metting. Richard's intensity, his unreadable expression, iced through her, when his consciousness had become a welcome pocket of warmth before. "What's happening?"

"I can't feel her thoughts anymore," he said. "I don't know what's going on, except that this mission has conveniently coincided with a center offensive."

"An offensive they can stage"—Jeff's aura deepened to near black—"because of Brotherhood intel they're accessing through Sarah's mind. And now there's no way for us to stop her from giving them even more."

"I'm your way," Richard said. "I was linked with Sarah when she found the door. I'll take us there."

Richard closed his eyes. The dream swirled around them, pushing, driving, rushing them toward something only he could see.

"You've got a hell of a lot to answer for," Jeff said.

"Shut up and let him concentrate." Maddie didn't care how many Watcher rules were broken as long as Richard took them to her sister.

They jerked to a stop so quickly, nausea rolled through Maddie. The bubbling sea settled, revealing Richard's image and the other Watchers' auras around her in the same positions as before. Only they were now grouped before Sarah's hideous door.

"How . . . ?" Maddie asked.

"Sarah's energy," Richard said. "I'm linked to it now. There were still traces of her within the matrix for me to follow."

"And when, exactly, did you form a link strong enough to sense a glimmer of her essence that her twin couldn't?" Jeff asked. "Did you mate with her? Better yet, how is it that her mission team knew nothing about your connection? Including that you've clearly been in constant communication with Sarah, even before we immersed into the matrix."

"I got us here." Richard shot his lieutenant a warning glance. "When none of the rest of you could have."

"Because you pushed Sarah to find the link to Trinity and the center before the rest of the team arrived?" Jeff's aura advanced until it was only inches away from Metting, his voice filled with contempt Maddie had never seen the lieutenant display toward his friend and leader. "You're why we were a step behind, playing catch-up, aren't you? You're the reason whatever consciousness was waiting for Sarah here had the chance to absorb her without the team's intervention. Now you're here, *leading* us, and I have to wonder what the council's going to think about your interference and whether we should proceed at all."

"I shut down the lab's ties to the dream," Richard said. "We're working on our own until Sarah releases the matrix."

"Because you wanted to stop the elders' intervention into the mess you've created?"

"Because we need time to bring Sarah's consciousness back. Then I'll reengage, and we'll return to sort this out with the council. The elders won't try to pull us back without knowing what's happening within the matrix."

"That's your priority?" Jeff's voice dropped to a menacing tone. "Saving the woman you love, even if it means hijacking a mission?"

"This mission is to reclaim a legacy the council can't afford to lose, especially now. The center's attack is too conveniently timed. The council's obvious next move is to assume Sarah's the leak, then to abandon her consciousness to the center's purposes until a Watcher team can infiltrate the complex."

"There's no other explanation for what you've allowed to happen."

"Except it's a trap. This dream has been a trap from the start. Sarah's not the leak. I would have sensed it. Which means—"

"There's still a Brotherhood mole helping the center drive this farce, and part of his objective is to make Sarah look culpable for the center's latest assault." The black curling at the edges of Jeff's gray aura began to ease off.

Maddie turned to face the door that was covered in the black, forbidding aura that had swallowed her sister's dreaming mind. There was no crimson now. No mottled merging of colors. There was only the soulless black shadow now that hadn't been able to take control when she and Sarah had been together.

"They wanted Sarah's mind to appear aligned with Trinity's all along," she said, following Richard's reasoning. "They're forcing the council to attack by making our legacy appear to be the Brotherhood's primary threat. And if we don't bring Sarah back we'll have no way of convincing the elders that she hasn't been a center asset all along. All of this has been about manipulating the Brotherhood into an ambush."

Richard's image stepped to Maddie's side. "Except they've miscalculated significantly."

"Miscalculated how?" Jeff demanded.

"Sarah's not stranded," Richard said, and Maddie could feel the faith he was projecting toward the door, maybe even through it. Rock-solid belief that Sarah was still fighting, wherever her consciousness had gone, and that they could reach her.

"She's not helpless anymore," he said. "She knows we'll come for her. Whatever's going on beyond that door, Sarah's our conduit inside. We just have to wait for her to open a window and let us in."

CHAPTER TWENTY-FIVE

Sarah opened her eyes to the unexpected silence of a cell-like laboratory identical to the one she'd barely survived at the center. White on white—floors, walls, cabinets. The rest stainless steel. Sterile. It was the landscape of the hell Dream Weaver had become, until she'd escaped into Richard's world of Watchers and new beginnings.

The wolf's deep laugh throbbed through her.

The walls of the laboratory vibrated with the sound, expanding and contracting.

Sarah spun around, but instead of Ruebens, there was a little girl behind her, strapped to an exam table. Its back was raised, propping her in an upright position. Tubes and wires were attached to her face, her arms, her legs. Monitors and other machines whistled and chirped the child's physical and psychic status.

"Trinity?"

Sarah tried to rush to her, but she couldn't move from the door. She tried to call to Richard for help, then to the rest of her Watchers, trying to visualize the window that would connect them to her. But her thoughts were no longer her own. Tears blinding her, she stared into the crystal clear, blue eyes staring back from the six-year-old's solemn face.

"See what we've become . . ." the dream said in Trinity's voice. The child's mouth didn't move.

A menacing crimson shadow grew between them, blocking Sarah's view, cloaking the entire room. It seared Sarah with cries of a little girl's broken innocence, then fury and hatred and determination to make others pay for the emptiness that she'd endured.

"Stop!" Sarah cried. "I don't understand."

But she did understand. Too well. It felt as if her own memories were attacking her. The mania raging inside Trinity was as familiar as Sarah's own heartbeat. She'd endured the same hopelessness of being lost to her strange abilities, abandoned to them, while her mind disintegrated and the peaceful, quiet world she craved slipped further away.

Sarah's life had been a prison long before she lapsed into her coma. No one had ever said to her what she could feel Trinity needed to hear.

"I'm sorry," she told the child, her heart breaking as the haze refused to clear. "I'm so sorry I wasn't there to help you."

She couldn't move closer. She couldn't hold out her hand to Trinity while she tried to help the child understand who she was and what she'd been created for.

"I've known about you my entire life," Sarah said. "Somehow, I've always known. I've heard your cries, but I've never been able to understand."

"You didn't want to understand," the wolf said from somewhere Sarah couldn't see, somewhere too close to

Trinity. "You never wanted the truth that would bring you to this place."

"Whose truth?" Sarah's hatred for the dead man raged. "Yours? You turned me into a monster. You wanted me to kill people."

"I showed you what you were born to be," he said. "But you were useless."

"You almost destroyed me."

"What have I destroyed?" the wolf asked, his voice changing, rising, becoming younger. "Except your ridiculous fantasy that you can become a healer, like your sister. Or what is it you want to be now? A Watcher? A savior, instead of the powerful weapon that your mind has the potential to become? Thankfully, we've taken that decision out of your hands. Your legacy's destiny is now safely back where it belongs."

"We?"

"Of course," he said in the little girl's voice. The crimson hiding Trinity from Sarah's view began to evaporate.

"I won't let them you hurt you anymore," Sarah promised the child. "I'll protect you."

Laughter shrieked through the room, the sound harsher than the screams. The walls, the floor, began to quake. Sarah sprawled to her knees.

"Protect me?" Trinity asked, speaking for the first time. "You hate me. You never wanted me. You never wanted to find me."

She sounded exactly the same as in their vision at the house, but there was something off, as if Sarah wasn't listening to a child at all.

"I don't understand."

"You're too afraid to," Trinity said with her overly mature reasoning. "So you left me with nothing. Now I'm returning the favor."

Trinity held out her hand to a shadow shifting in the corner. The creature lurking there joined her, sitting obediently on the ground at her feet. The little girl threaded her fingers through the gray wolf's coarse hair, taking obvious pleasure from stroking evil. Comforting it. Controlling it.

"Welcome to our nightmare, Mother." Trinity's sunshine-bright smile turned Sarah's stomach. "I thought you'd never come."

CHAPTER TWENTY-SIX

"Mother . . ."

"You're . . ." Sarah couldn't say it. Tears were streaming down her face. She refused to believe it. "You're not . . ."

"Your daughter?" Trinity's sweet smile faded. "Like I wasn't waiting for you at that house? Like you haven't dreamed of me since you were my age? Like you didn't already know the name my father gave me on the day I was born?"

Sarah struggled for clarity. About the past. About all the screams only she'd been able to hear for so long, and all the years that she'd ignored them. It wasn't possible, except—

"You've been with me all my life. You've been—"

"What you painted on your bedroom walls. What's terrified you since my father told you I was alive. What you hated so much, you needed your hit team for backup before you'd find me. I'm you're truth, and you're still not ready to believe."

The words were too mature, Trinity's logic too cynical to belong to a little girl. It was like listening to a brilliant child recite a script. This couldn't be Trinity. It had to be more of Ruebens's programming.

"What hit team?" Sarah asked. "What truth? What did you bring me here to believe?"

Richard and Maddie and the Watcher team were coming. They'd help her reach the real Trinity, whose energy Sarah could still feel beyond the dream's toxic consciousness. The Brotherhood would help her find the little girl outside the nightmare. So—

"So you can kill me?" the child's dream image accused, following Sarah's thoughts.

"No." Sarah had to stay calm and see what was really there. She had to keep the dream under control without Richard and Maddie to balance her. "No one's trying to kill anyone."

"You're so stupid," Trinity's image spat, finally sounding like the child she appeared to be.

Sarah glanced around the room that looked so much like the lab where Ruebens had experimented on her own powers. Trinity's image seemed so at home here. Safe. Calm. A little girl ruled by the logic of a cold-hearted adult.

"This is wrong," Sarah said. "Whatever the center has taught you, however they're manipulating you into doing these things, thinking this way, don't trust them."

"And I should trust you?" Tiny hands clenched in the wolf's fur. "My loving mother?"

"Don't call me that." Bile burned Sarah's throat. Dark waves of it. Memories swelled that she couldn't, wouldn't, believe were true. "I don't know who you are or how you're part of my family. But I'm not your mother. I've never had children."

"That's not what our legacy says."

" '*Twins will be born to the line,*' " the wolf quoted in Ruebens's voice. " '*And with them, great good to commence. Or great evil, should darkness descend. Through them, another will come, to spread light far and wide. Or to cast the ultimate shadow on a lost mankind.*' "

"Yes." Sarah closed her eyes. The prophecy echoed through her mind. "You're the missing piece of what our line was prophesied to be. I'm here to free you from the center's experiments. So I can help you understand that—"

"Understand? Or forget, because you can't face what we've become?"

"I am not—"

"A mother who couldn't accept the abomination she created?" Trinity's stilted accusations were accompanied by an equally adult twist of her lips. "That's precisely what you are."

The wolf rose. He was smiling now, too. It was the same evil expression marring Trinity's beautiful face. Sarah had no doubt it was his words the child kept parroting.

"But my father has always loved me." Trinity's bottom lip quivered as she petted the malicious animal, a little girl's hurt welling in her eyes. She lifted her chin, daring Sarah to contradict her.

My father has always loved me . . .

Sarah saw the wolf's protective posture in a devastating new light.

"Tad Ruebens?" She was going to be sick. "Tad Ruebens was your father?"

"Not by blood. But he loved me from the very start. He *wanted* me, unlike you."

The past flashed through the dream, dizzying Sarah's already-reeling thoughts with images that didn't belong to her . . .

She was lying emotionless on an exam table, in a lab at the center that had nothing yet to do with nightmares or dream programming. Dispassionate hands were manipulating her lower body into stirrups beneath a crisp white sheet. She was asleep. No. She was still in the coma she never would have escaped if Richard's mind hadn't rescued her.

The memory belonged to the man positioned at the foot of the bed, functioning with clinical detachment.

"It's time," Ruebens said in her dream wolf's voice. "The hormone regimen was successful. She's ovulating. Ultrasound indicates multiple eggs, ready for extraction. Let's begin . . ."

The vision swirled to a scene of excruciating pain and innocent beginning.

A faceless woman was bleeding out after giving birth, left to die while Ruebens raised a tiny child to his chest, cradling her as he crooned and calmed her lonely cries.

"I'll protect you, Trinity," he promised the baby. "They will come to take you away from me. They won't understand your destiny. They won't want you, once they realize what you were born to be. But I'll protect you. I'll learn everything I have to, to make sure you're ready. You were born for more than they'll ever understand, even your mother. Especially your mother. She'll be useful, but she's too weak to own the future your mind will rule. You are the Temple Legacy, Trinity, and you're all mine . . ."

Men draped in surgical garb, hidden by masks, pulled a blinding white sheet over the body on the table. The baby continued to cry. Haunting whimpers filled the vision, and Sarah's mind, and the ocean nightmare beyond, then every nightmare she'd ever had.

Ruebens looked up at Sarah—across the damage and death he'd caused during the years that stretched between then and now. He smiled at Sarah and laughed his wolf's laugh, and the vision ripped itself to shreds, taking her sanity along with it . . .

. . . dumping Sarah back into Trinity's lab, where Sarah lay in a boneless heap on the floor, staring into the eyes of the wolf who was no longer by the child's side.

"Congratulations," Ruebens's voice said from the creature's lips. "It's a girl."

Sarah screamed into his laughing face.

It was Ruebens's memories of Trinity's birth she'd seen. She was feeling the demented pleasure he'd taken in manipulating her legacy and an innocent newborn life. Memories he'd programmed within Sarah and Trinity, anticipating a showdown exactly like this one, where the revelation of what he'd done could do the most damage.

"You . . ." She pointed a shaking finger at Ruebens's dream image. "I was defenseless. In a coma. And you . . . stole my child and grew her in another woman's body? All so . . ." Sarah swallowed. ". . . so you could play God with my legacy and create a . . ."

"Monster?" Trinity ripped the words from Sarah's mind. "And now it's time to destroy the monster you never wanted?"

Sarah stared into the darkness, the madness, of her child's anger and accepted that this wasn't merely a dream projection. The six-year-old sitting before her really was Trinity—her consciousness, her energy, her eyes filled with death, all of it programmed by a man who'd stop at nothing to control their powers. Pain stared back at Sarah from her daughter's angelic face. Betrayal that ran so deep, how could Sarah ever break through?

Ruebens had been creating the perfect killing machine all along, only his ultimate focus had never been on Sarah and Maddie. They'd only been test runs on his way to securing Trinity's devotion to his plans.

"Don't trust him," Sarah begged her daughter. "Whatever Ruebens told you about me, whatever he said to drive you to do this, don't believe any of it."

"He said you'd never come," the child said, spouting a dead man's logic, "and you never did. He showed me how you'd kill him, and you did. How you'd hate me, if I came to you like I did at the house. How you'd run the way you did. How you'd bring your Watchers with you into the dream. Like your team's here now, right where he said they'd be. He said to let you think you were losing, then winning, then losing. That you'd keep trying no matter what. That you'd side with them and hate me and keep coming until you helped them kill me."

"No one wants to kill you. I've been trying to find you so I could keep you safe. I'm not running anymore."

But the Watchers did want to take down the mind behind the demanding currents and screams and psychotic ocean's voice and the death and destruction that had been controlling Sarah. They wanted whoever at the center had planted a spy within the Brotherhood. Only, they'd expected it to be another scientist, a replacement for Ruebens. Not an innocent, powerful mind that had been born and bred for darkness.

"Why would you do this?" Sarah asked.

Trinity's gaze lifted, staring over Sarah's shoulder.

Her smile returned.

Her consciousness connected with Sarah's, and together they saw a window form in the horrible door Sarah had confronted, with Maddie and Richard waiting anxiously beyond. It was the window Jeff had said to use to access her team. The vision of it was so vivid. More powerful than anything Sarah had ever experienced in the ocean matrix on her own. She could feel her twin's exhaustion, the Watchers' determination and commitment to complete their mission, Richard's worry for her. His love.

And Trinity was accessing it all so effortlessly.

She was eager for their arrival.

"It's a trap!" Sarah tried to call to them. *"Don't follow me."*

Amusement flickered across Trinity's expression, telling Sarah no one would hear her unless her daughter allowed them to. The child was already more powerful than Maddie and Sarah ever would be.

"Why are you helping them do this?" Sarah demanded. "What did Ruebens promise you?"

Through Trinity's consciousness, Sarah saw Maddie and Richard step toward the window. The lab shimmered within the dream's matrix as Sarah's mind slipped deeper into nightmare.

"You love them." Trinity stroked the fur of Ruebens's dream image. "Not me. And once you're all gone, I'll be free."

"Free from what?"

"My loving family," Trinity said in her creepy adult

cadence. "The only minds strong enough to stand be-tween me and what my father created me to be."

Then she opened her mouth and screamed.

Trinity's scream.

Sarah's scream.

Their pain spilled into the child's hate-filled dream. It was a pitiful, lost sound that tore at Sarah's heart and rushed the minds who'd come to protect her through the nightmare's door.

CHAPTER TWENTY-SEVEN

Sarah felt her team's arrival an instant before Richard and Maddie appeared inside Trinity's lab.

"It's a trap!" she yelled over the sound of a gunshot blasting through the nightmare.

Maddie's hand flew to her chest. Richard caught her, lowering her to the ground. Sarah tried to run to her twin. But she still couldn't move, except for turning to see Trinity holding a pistol.

"You shot her!" Sarah screamed.

"Did I?" In a blink, Trinity's hands were empty.

Sarah stared down at the weapon clutched in her own fist now. The dream forced her to turn back as clouds of color, gray and brown, shimmered to life within the room. Her arm lifted. She sobbed. She couldn't stop herself from aiming the gun at her twin.

"I . . ." She couldn't force her arm down. "God, Maddie, I wouldn't . . . She's drawn us all here. She wanted you to come so she could attack the team. She shot you, not me."

"Lower the weapon," the gray aura demanded. It was Jeff Coleridge. "Lower the pistol, Ms. Temple, before my men are forced to take it from you."

"It's not me." Sarah stared down at her worst nightmare—her sister was dying from the danger that Sarah's mind had lured them into.

The lab shuddered. The nightmare's insanity ripped at the dream's matrix.

"I didn't shoot my sister," she said to Richard. "It's the dream. It's Trinity. She's been controlling this all along. Ruebens taught her to hate me and draw us all in so she could make me pay for abandoning her. The center's using that somehow. They're—"

"They're making a move on the Brotherhood." Richard pressed his hand over Maddie's chest. Her blood seeped through his fingers. "Two more legacies have been exposed. We're under attack—"

"Because of information you've given the center through your dreams," Jeff finished.

"I haven't given anyone anything." Sarah tried to connect with Richard's consciousness. She couldn't project to him, or Maddie, or anyone else.

But Trinity was letting her feel Maddie's very real pain—beyond the dream, where Maddie's chest was ripped open and bleeding in the dream lab.

"Like you didn't just shoot your sister?" Jeff demanded.

"It's the nightmare," Sarah insisted. "It's in control. The center wants us eliminated—that's all this ocean dream has been about. Luring Maddie and me here so they can destroy our part of the Temple Legacy. So there's no one left to stop her from doing whatever they want next."

"Stop who?" Jeff asked.

"Trinity . . ." Blood dripped from the corner of Maddie's mouth. "Did you find her?"

"She shot you." Sarah stared at the silent child who was watching the damage she'd caused with sinister fascination. "She opened the window to bring you through the door. She's controlling the matrix. I think . . . I think she wants me to watch you die."

"You really do love her," Trinity said, the catch in her voice pulling at Sarah no matter how many horrible things the little girl had done.

"A child is doing all this?" Jeff's energy flowed closer. "You want us to believe a child has manipulated your powers, and the Brotherhood, and this dream, all for the chance to torture you with your sister's death? That's the best you can come up with when you're the only one who's holding a weapon?"

"Is she?" Trinity asked.

Jeff's aura shimmered to solid form, his injured leg now whole within the matrix—a powerful man whose furious expression was the opposite of the reassuring Watcher who'd asked for her trust when they planned for this mission. He looked down at the assault rifle in his hands, his expression wary. Then his grip tightened and he pointed the rifle at Sarah.

"He wants you dead, too," Trinity said. "He came for me. But why not kill my mother, too?"

"You're . . ." Jeff stared at Trinity, then Sarah. "You're her mother?"

"Trinity's your daughter?" Richard asked.

"You came to kill her?" Sarah demanded of Jeff. Her arm shook as her mind rejected the dream's newest bombshell. The gun she was pointing at her sister shook. The entire room shook. "You promised—"

"To help me?" Trinity's voice was a clipped, feminine

reflection of Ruebens. "And you believed him. My father said you'd believe all of them. You'd believe anyone but me. Even this one"—her glare shifted to Jeff—"who only cares about finishing the personal *mission* he's been secretly executing for a month."

Jeff swung his rifle toward Trinity, confirming that everything Trinity had said was true. Jeff Coleridge, who'd taken a bullet protecting Sarah in Lenox, who'd always had Richard's back, had been betraying Sarah and his brotherhood since Richard brought Sarah and Maddie to the bunker. Maybe even before that.

"No!" Sarah begged as Jeff refocused his hate-filled stare on Trinity. She still couldn't move. "Don't shoot her. She's a confused little girl. She doesn't know what she's doing."

"Your *little girl* is the darkest part of your legacy's prophecy," Jeff said. "She has to be stopped. You all do."

"Drop your weapon, Lieutenant," Richard warned.

Jeff didn't budge.

"So you can cover for Sarah some more?" he asked Richard. "So you can put protecting this godforsaken legacy before what you know is right? You shouldn't be here, Richard. You weren't supposed to be here for this. But you betrayed your oath. Again. Disobeyed a direct order from the council. Destroyed your career. And for what? To help these people leak classified information that's put every other family we're watching at risk?"

"I did it to ensure this mission's success," Richard said. "To keep the Brotherhood from making a mistake with the Temple Legacy that we can't afford to make."

"Oh, there have been many mistakes," Trinity said. "Haven't there, Lieutenant Coleridge?"

Trinity stepped down from the exam table, the tapes and wires that had been attached to her falling free, then dissolving from sight along with the rest of the equipment in the projection's lab. Until the walls, too, disappeared. Everything was gone but the images of the people she'd maneuvered into the dream. The little girl walked toward Jeff, through the nightmare's nothingness, until the muzzle of his weapon pressed into her forehead.

"Put the gun away." The arm holding Sarah's own weapon swung until it was pointed at Jeff.

Every Watcher on the team materialized into their human reflections, all of them holding automatic rifles trained on Sarah.

"Stand down," Richard ordered from where he was still holding Maddie. "Lower your weapons."

The Watchers obeyed their colonel, all of them but Jeff.

"Now's your chance," Trinity said to him in Tad Ruebens's voice. "The question is, do you have the balls to see your plan through?"

"Shut up." Jeff's gun pressed deeper into Trinity's tender skin. "Shut the hell up. That voice . . . It's—"

"The voice of your contact at the center?" Ruebens's sarcasm dripped from Trinity's rosebud mouth. "The voice of the man you passed key information to about the legacy that was tainting your brotherhood?"

"You were . . ." Jeff shook his head. "I was—"

"Feeding the center information about my work with Sarah?" Richard eased Maddie to the ground and stood. Shock hardened his features into a dangerous, feral mask. "You gave away tracking coordinates for our other legacies?"

"No." Jeff glanced at Richard, then back to Trinity. "I only gave up the Temples."

"Information we never needed." Trinity laughed, her voice filled with the sound of a carefree child's innocence, while her words reeked of the kind of evil it took a lifetime to cultivate. "Regular contact was what we required, regular access to Brotherhood logistics. So we let you think your role was vital to bringing about this dream's resolution. We needed your council to believe that Sarah and Madeline and Colonel Metting could never be trusted again—say, at the exact moment that your Watchers were under imminent attack. *That* my handlers needed inside help to arrange. And we've managed just fine, you and I, haven't we?"

"Shut up!" Sweat ran down Jeff's face. "Who the hell are you? I didn't betray any tactics about other legacies. All I gave my contact were details about Sarah's dream work."

"And it's supposed to be okay that the only people you betrayed were my family?" Sarah said, feeling everything she'd fought so hard to believe about the Brotherhood and her legacy's place in it disintegrate before her eyes. "You badgered me into trusting you. You're supposed to take us home. That's what you said in the lab. You gave us your word as a Watcher."

"Like you were supposed to be learning to control your psychic powers and using them to protect others?" Jeff said. "Meanwhile, you were growing stronger and more out of control and the council did nothing to stop it. And you"—Jeff thrust an almost deranged rush of hatred at Trinity—"You're the most dangerous threat of all."

"You bastard." Richard stepped closer. "Our job is to—"

"*Watch. Defend. Preserve.* I know." Jeff turned his gun on his friend, stopping Richard from advancing. "Just like I knew I'd never make it back from this mission alive. But I betrayed my creed and you, and I came here to protect the Brotherhood anyway. I initiated contact over a scrambled comm link in my quarters, on a dedicated workstation. Nowhere else. I never would have put the viability of other legacies—"

"What contact?" Trinity asked.

Her hands behind her back, she toed the ground with her bare foot, the gesture so coy, so childlike, Sarah closed her eyes. There was so much anger, so much evil, inside her child. How could everything have gone so wrong?

"My communications with my center contact," Jeff said. "I was given an algorithm to use to cloak our connection, but I have every conversation recorded for the council to review once I'm gone."

"Or were those exchanges just a dream?" Trinity's smile held no sympathy for the man she'd helped destroy. "A harmless daydream, except for the secrets our link allowed the center to extract from your mind and your bunker's sophisticated computer network."

Jeff spun back to Trinity, fear twisting his handsome features even worse than his rage had. "I'm going to—"

"Kill me?" Trinity asked. "Imagine my surprise. Except, this is my father's dream projection, and he gave it to me to bring to life any way I chose. Watch closely. You don't want to miss my big finish."

Light shot from Trinity's eyes, striking one Watcher, who dropped to the ground. Then a second. Both mortal wounds that Sarah could feel ripping through the men's bodies back in the lab.

"Stop!" Sarah screamed, the dream's hold on her senses lifting.

The men's agony. Maddie's pain. Trinity's warped drive for revenge. Jeff's shock and regret and hatred. It all sizzled through Sarah, distorting the web of consciousness holding the dream together.

Bodies were writhing.

Hearts were shuddering.

Systems were breaking down both inside and beyond the dream.

Sarah should be able to—she had to—stop this. But she was too weak, her mind too fractured, to even reach for Richard. His consciousness was the only one she couldn't sense now. Just as she couldn't sense her own existence beyond the nightmare's surface.

She was trapped once again, unable to release the dream, with darkness closing in and no way to stop it.

"You bitch!" Jeff spat at Trinity, his face contorted with madness. "This isn't how it was supposed to happen."

"She's just a child," Sarah begged.

A child whose insanity had been hardwired into her mind the same way Ruebens had programmed Sarah.

Sarah's grip tightened on her own weapon. The primal need to protect the daughter she hadn't been able to accept before was obliterating her ties to everything else, including her vow to never again kill because of one of Ruebens's dreams.

"You're dead," Jeff said, his impulse to shoot Trinity slamming into Sarah, giving her only a instant's warning.

She fired the gun, the bullet flying—

—into thin air.

Jeff's body had already dropped to the nightmare's floor.

Richard gazed up from Jeff's dead image, while Sarah felt the lieutenant's heart strike its last beat beyond the nightmare. The rifle Richard had used to kill his friend hung limply at his side. His horrified expression told Sarah exactly how badly she'd failed—how empty their dreams for the future had become.

"See," her daughter said as the projection began to fade, along with the last of Sarah's sanity as she listened to the desolation, the loneliness, in her child's voice. "You're just like me. You've always been just like me. Death follows us everywhere. It's who we were born to be. Can you see it now? Can you see what we've become?"

CHAPTER TWENTY-EIGHT

"Maddie!" Jarred was screaming as Richard emerged from the nightmare.

The doctor was trying to stabilize Madeline's blood loss, while Richard's lab techs worked furiously to save the lives of the two Watchers Trinity had attacked. All three had gaping chest wounds, physical injuries that a dream reality shouldn't have been capable of projecting beyond its matrix.

Richard stood amid the chaos, listening to the unbroken beep signifying the flat line on Jeff's heart monitor. His second, his friend, had been the center's spy from the start, while he'd baited Richard and war gamed with him and maneuvered the Brotherhood into the exact position the center had wanted them in. Richard shook off his shock and sadness and fury at his friend's betrayal while he tried to regain enough of his own senses to search Sarah's mind for a flicker of consciousness.

Her energy was gone, both within and beyond the matrix. Lost to him. She wasn't releasing the dream, even though the rest of the Watchers were slowly coming around. He could sense Madeline's consciousness returning to her body. But Sarah's mind had disappeared into a darkness he couldn't reach, while her stats on the machines tracking her condition were maxed to the red zone.

"Come back to me," Richard begged.

She'd trusted him. She'd done everything he'd asked her to do. She'd given herself to her dream, to her team. She'd even trusted Jeff, just as Richard had taught her to. And none of it had protected her from Ruebens's destruction. The bastard had created the third volatile component of the Temple Legacy and trained her in secret. He'd cultivated and programmed Trinity's gifts into a sociopathic super weapon. Sarah had a child, and her daughter had been the danger barreling toward all of them from her nightmares.

Richard bent over her table, somehow managing to keep himself on his feet as he used the last of his energy to sustain his presence in the lab as well as her projection.

"*Sarah . . .*" His mind said as he swam through the dream's empty, churning sea. "*Let me see you. Wherever you've gone, you have to come back. I need you here to fix this. The Brotherhood needs you, and so does Trinity.*"

Maddie's healing touch wasn't there to help him reach her twin. No recovery team was rushing to Sarah's side. There were too many other critical injuries to contend with. Jeff would never again be at Richard's back, supporting him as brother, as a sworn warrior. Richard's mind alone clung to his faith in Sarah.

"You have to be Trinity's Watcher now," he said. "We have to make the elders see that—"

"Step away, Colonel," a voice said. Mike Donovan stood beside Jacob's hologram. "I have orders to take you both into custody."

Richard faced the armed lieutenant and their elder, his hand remaining wrapped around Sarah's, his mind still searching for hers. A four-man security team backed Donovan up, weapons drawn, all of them Watchers Richard and Jeff had busted their asses to train. Richard couldn't detect any of their thoughts. Which meant their psychic shields were being augmented. He shifted his focus to Jacob.

"I'm not a threat to the Brotherhood," Richard said. "Neither is Sarah, nor her sister."

"All evidence is to the contrary," Jacob said.

"You can't attack the center complex without the Temples' support. The center's waiting for us to make the first move, just as I sensed at the surveillance site."

"I suspect they won't know how we're coming," Jacob said, "if your participation is removed from the planning. Taking you and the Temples out of the equation gives us the tactical advantage."

"You're being manipulated, sir."

"We're very aware, Colonel, of our egregious errors in judgment where you and the Temple Legacy are concerned. One of our top lieutenants is dead. Two other Watchers are in critical condition. Legacies have been exposed. Principals most likely taken by the center. How much more damage would you have us absorb before we decree this legacy too out of control and dangerous to be allowed to continue?"

"You'll have to come with us." Donovan stepped closer.

"Not until I recover Sarah's mind from the nightmare's matrix."

"That's no longer your concern," Jacob said.

"It's my only concern at the moment." Richard looked

around the lab at the dazed Watchers beginning to stir from the mission. At Madeline, whose condition seemed to have stabilized thanks to Jarred Keith's efforts. But she wasn't yet fully back. None of the mission team were conscious enough to help him explain what had happened. He had to buy them more time.

"The matrix shouldn't have been capable of physically harming any of these people," he reasoned to Jacob. "Trinity Temple's powers are beyond anything we've dealt with before. We have to understand—"

"And we will," Jacob said. "Once we debrief the team we sanctioned to guide the dream—at the same time we ordered you not to interfere. Then we'll take care of the center and Trinity before any more damage can be done to our order or the other legacies we protect."

Movement to Richard's right caught his attention a second before a sharp sting pierced his arm. He looked down to see the needle being removed. His brain registered a moment's shock at being caught off guard. Then his psychic barriers were dropping, leaving his mind defenseless, powerless. The security team rushed forward.

Donovan and another lieutenant grabbed Richard's arms. His knees buckled.

"My suppression protocol," he mumbled.

"Yes, sir." Donovan was apologetic, but resigned to his duty.

Richard's hand was dragged away from Sarah's. A scream of denial sliced through her mind, then through him to the security team that he could no longer shield from her thoughts.

"Wait," he begged as they dragged him away. "Did you feel that? She's waking up."

"No," Jacob said, "she's not."

Richard looked back to see the man's hologram directing a lab tech to inject Sarah, then Madeline, with the suppression meds that would trap their realities wherever they were currently anchored—leaving their minds in limbo.

The door to his dream lab whooshed shut, and he was dragged away.

CHAPTER TWENTY-NINE

There was no color in the darkness. No gentle warmth or enticing currents. No healing touch calling Sarah to the surface. Everything had been stripped away by the sound of a gunshot she couldn't quite remember. A child's scream, which had become her scream, then had become a truth that she'd never wanted to know.

It was familiar, the emptiness floating around her.

It was home.

It was beyond the madness she'd run from.

Except . . .

She didn't belong in this lost place. She'd sworn never to come back. She wasn't crazy. She never had been. Forgetting and hiding wasn't who she was anymore. It wasn't who she'd been born to be. It had destroyed too much. There was a future waiting. A truth she'd run from. A duty she could no longer deny.

Specto. Tego. Asservo. The Watcher's Creed. Sarah's creed now. She'd been dreaming of this moment her whole life—the moment when she'd be called to protect her legacy. There were people needing her to wake up. People *she* needed. Maddie, bleeding in Richard's arms. Richard, staring down at his dead friend. Trinity—her daughter—knowing only hate and revenge and destruction, never love. Her little girl's faith dying while she cried into Sarah's dreams for help.

Her daughter . . .

Sarah's memories surged back, conquering the vagueness that had filled the chasm between where her body was being held in a bunker detention cell and where her mind had been stranded when her nightmare's connection with Trinity dissolved. It was excruciating, drowning all over again in her dream's destruction. But Sarah had to feel it. She had to see it. She had to escape the safe nothingness her mind had been banished to. She had to face the reality that was far worse than her dreams had ever been.

She needed her team. She needed to make this right, somehow, before it was too late.

She could sense frantic activity as her consciousness returned to her body. She couldn't move, but she could feel powerful minds nearby prepping for battle. The minds of Watchers.

Debriefing.

Reviewing.

Securing.

Planning to . . . silence a deadly psychic power. A legacy that couldn't be controlled. Sarah's daughter had become the center's ultimate psychic weapon, and the Brotherhood was going to stop her.

Sarah's memory replayed the innocence lurking in Trinity's angry eyes. The pain and the betrayal. The light that Sarah had glimpsed shining behind Trinity's scarred, impenetrable door. Bright white light. The purest of colors, glowing with her daughter's potential for redemption. Light that was trapped within darkness, like the dimness of the bedroom where Trinity had met Sarah.

Trinity had said then that she wasn't supposed to be there, that *they'd* find out. Sarah had assumed she was talking about the Watchers, then the center team who'd attacked them. But now that she'd met her child, or at least the little girl Ruebens had brainwashed Trinity into becoming, she knew better. She'd heard the desolation in her daughter's voice when their nightmare finally ended.

Trinity had felt trapped. She'd become trapped as much as Sarah was, in the deadly evolution of their legacy. And at the Lenox house, Trinity had been afraid that someone at the center would discover her mind reaching beyond them. She'd been afraid that Sarah would never come. That she'd always be alone.

Trinity's whole life had been Ruebens's programming, believing that his evil was all she had. That Ruebens was the only one who loved her. That except for the death he'd raised her to cause, she was nothing. Exactly the way a part of Sarah had once felt, exactly the way she'd been vulnerable to Ruebens's tactics before Richard had shown her a new dream to believe in.

Her daughter had been taught to hate Watchers and to hate her family and to hate all but the darkest parts of her legacy. She'd never learned to balance the explosive dichotomy at the heart of their family's strength, any more than Sarah had before Richard taught her, protected her, and loved her.

But a part of Trinity wanted to be different, Sarah was certain of it. A part of Trinity was still searching, needing to believe Ruebens was wrong. The part that was dying, because no one else had come for her. The part that had haunted a house for five years, running everyone else away while she waited for her mother to come home.

Sarah still didn't trust the Brotherhood she'd been absorbed into. A part of her would always blame the council for what their blindness had allowed Jeff Coleridge to do while they focused their distrust and contempt on Sarah's weakness. But Trinity deserved the same chance she'd been given. She deserved a life beyond the prison of the center's experiments and training where she'd been trapped since birth. A future Sarah alone couldn't give her child.

CHAPTER THIRTY

"Richard?"

Sarah's call fluttered through the silence of their minds, across the distance separating their individual locations at the bunker. Their psychic senses fired to life along with their link. The medication dampening Sarah's ability to project relinquished its hold, the way she'd been able to defeat the potency of Richard's other chemical safeguards. Only now, his strength was augmenting her growing powers, helping her recover even faster.

"I'm here." Richard's thoughts caressed hers, filling her mind with magical sounds: wind, night creatures, a canopy of tree limbs rustling overhead, filtering the moon's silvery glow.

"My sister?" Sarah asked. "Is she—"

"Madeline's stabilized, but her consciousness was sedated like ours."

"Your mind . . ." Sarah pushed deeper. "I can barely feel you."

"Suppression drugs. I couldn't project through them without your help. Now that you're here, I can . . . For now, I'm managing to block the bunker's sensors from picking up our psychic energy."

Energy that flowed from him to Sarah, then back to him,

the circuit never ending. Through their link came the sensation of Richard's lips caressing her cheek, her temple, her mouth. Sarah kissed him back, absorbing his grief and anger over Jeff. His concern for the council's hasty plans to attack the center complex.

"You came back to me." His mind stroked hers. "When I couldn't feel you after the dream matrix dissolved, I thought I'd lost you."

"For a while." The tears Sarah had been holding back flooded their link. "A part of me wanted to stay lost between the dream and here. To hide again."

"I know, love," he said. His understanding and hearing him say "love" healed her as nothing else could. "I'm so sorry I couldn't protect you from——"

"The truth?"

She needed him to tell her it had all been just a horrible nightmare. But she knew he couldn't. And she couldn't let him.

"My child's been taught to kill, just like I was." Sarah's mind sank deeper into the fantasy of her head nestled in the crook of Richard's shoulder.

"But you're not a killer, Sarah." The warmth of his voice, his breath on her cheek, made her long to be lying naked in his arms beneath forest moonlight.

"I was going to kill Jeff," she said, "once he'd made the decision to shoot Trinity."

"He put us all at risk. He lost his perspective on what our order was created to do. He——"

"He was your second-in-command. Your best friend is dead because of me. You killed him to save my daughter."

"Stopping him and the threat he'd become to the psychic realm was my job." Richard's conviction that he'd done the right thing was as real and as heartbreaking as his acceptance of

his parents' deaths. "Your family is the Brotherhood's future, you and other powerful legacies we need to join us. The council may not be able to control you, but they can't stop the center without you. They'll grow to trust you once they know the whole story."

"They've neutralized my mind. At least they tried to. They don't want my help."

"They don't have a choice. Give them time to realize that. Because of you, they know who Trinity is and how she's being used against us."

"Because I failed to control the dream while she attacked our team."

"Watchers aren't perfect. Missions fail. But you're still fighting. You found me. You're unpredictable and flawed and dangerously powerful, just like your daughter. But you've become everything a Watcher should be, Sarah. You're everything I've dreamed of."

His kiss and his confidence feathered through their connection. Desire burst to life. It felt as if the sun had risen just beyond their closed eyes, the light growing brighter by the second, banishing the last remnants of a winter's nightmare. Sarah clung to their link. He was Rick again in their stolen moment, and he would never abandon her.

She was still terrified of losing the amazing feeling of him in her mind. She was still afraid to believe in this kind of perfection when the Brotherhood and the center and even Trinity were doing everything they could to destroy the world Sarah finally wanted to live in. But she'd been right to seek him out, to trust him when she still wasn't sure she could trust anything the council said or what they'd do next. There was nowhere else she wanted to be, she realized, except fighting by Richard's side.

Within their shared consciousness, she inched away, breathing deeply.

"What do we do now?" *She sent her awareness deeper, joining his mind and hers with the Brotherhood.* "I can feel the council preparing for battle. Do they know what happened in the dream? An attack on the center complex may be exactly what Trinity's handlers want. Do they know what she's capable of if I can't reach her again and get her to stop?"

"They'll have debriefed the mission team by now. They'll know the basics of what happened."

"Then why are you still sedated? Jeff was the mole. You—"

"I protected Trinity after she attacked two of my Watchers. To the council, my priorities are clearly too conflicted for me to be trusted."

"If the Brotherhood attacks, the center will—"

"Use Trinity's as a mind-control weapon to deflect the assault."

"We can't let that happen. There's still innocence inside her. I felt it. We have to get her away from the center before it's too late to reach the light I know is still there."

"You will. I'll help you link your consciousness with hers."

"What? No. We need to talk with the council first. Convince them to hold off on—"

"They're not going to stop." *Richard's dream touch was a soothing caress down her cheek.* "They have no reason to trust us. We have to beat them to your daughter."

"But I can't hear her cries now, and our bodies are still sedated. How—"

"Create a new dream reality based on the projections you've shared with Trinity—one you design this time. Your minds are still connected, even though Ruebens's programming has run its course. It's time for you to take control. Madeline and I will help you."

"But . . ." Project into the mind of the little girl Ruebens had raised to attack her? "Trinity hates me, Richard. Enough to try to destroy the Brotherhood along with me. She's been told I abandoned her. That I refused to accept what she was. How do I get her to believe me now?"

"You tell me." Richard's faith and pride filled their link. "I found you when you didn't believe in anything or anyone. I found you again when you'd convinced yourself you hated me, because I knew how to reach the part of your mind that still needed me. Now it's your turn to fight for the person you love. Your daughter needs you, Sarah. Show me where you've dreamed of finding Trinity."

CHAPTER THIRTY-ONE

Sunlight warmed Sarah's eyelids. The decadent sensation became her new dream's beginning. Warmth and beauty and promise waited patiently for her discovery. She tentatively opened her eyes, and there Richard was, his strong body lying beneath hers, cushioning her from the forest's rough floor. Dawn's pink light was just peeping over the horizon, showering their projection with incandescent beauty.

"Richard?"

His lifted his hand. He traced the contours of her face with his fingers.

"You're really here," she said. A dream's illusion had never felt this real.

"And you're magnificent." His touch stroked down her body as if he wanted to memorize the feel of her.

He sat up, bringing Sarah with him. Bits of forest green fell from his hair and from the same fatigues and dark shirt he'd worn when they'd last been in the woods outside the bunker. Sarah was in outdoor clothes, too. Their scrubs and Richard's lab coat were gone.

"Let's see where your mind's taken us." He kissed her fingers and tugged her to her feet.

They gazed out over what should have been the ravine where his parents had lost their confrontation with their Watchers. In its place, an ocean vista spread. So beautiful. So perfect.

"This is from my nightmare." Sarah stepped to the lip of the ravine. "It's what I imagined would be waiting on the other side of Trinity's door, at the bottom of the ocean."

Light, like morning's new promise, sprinkling hope across a diamond-kissed shore . . .

The sea stretched toward the horizon, cradled by silky sand that didn't belong at the base of a Massachusetts forest. But it was a perfect vista. A perfect promise. Complete with the fluffy, welcoming clouds from the meditation routines Richard had helped Sarah fill with her favorite images.

"This is where you should have found your daughter." Richard sounded equally mesmerized. "Your mind was looking for Trinity here, even in Ruebens's matrix."

"We're beyond the nightmare's hold." The wind ran its fingers over the water, rippling the surface in a shiny display. "This is where we were meant to meet. But we lost this place when Ruebens hid Trinity from me."

"You'll bring her back." Richard drew Sarah more securely against his chest. "There's still time."

Salt flavored the air. Surf roared against miles of sugar-fine sand. The richness of this new dream—with the trees behind them and the ocean beyond and the amethyst-tinged clouds merging the sea with the sky— was the destination Sarah hadn't been able to draw, she realized. All those years ago, when a little girl had drowned her bedroom walls with color, this is what she'd been trying to see.

"There's Madeline." Richard pointed toward the shoreline. "What's that beyond her? Is it—"

Sarah raced down into the ravine, her stride kicking up sand when she reached the beach at the bottom. She sprinted to her sister, only to stop a few feet away. The chest of Maddie's surgical gown was covered in blood, the sight made even more grotesque by the enchanting scenery around them.

"Thank God you're okay." Maddie launched herself into Sarah's arms. "Where are we? How did I get here?"

"I'm not sure, except . . ." Sarah hugged her twin, wincing at the nearly insubstantial feel of Maddie's normally strong body. "Except I needed you here, or I couldn't do this. I need my family, Maddie. Promise me you're going to be okay. That you'll be okay when I come back."

"Come back from where?"

Maddie pulled away, leaving a crimson stain down the front of Sarah's fatigues. She turned toward the shoreline as Richard approached and wrapped a strong arm around Sarah's shoulder. The three of them gazed at the massive door sitting at the water's edge, between Sarah and the sea.

It wasn't the hostile portal that had barred her way within Ruebens's dream projection. It wasn't the scarred door of Sarah's childhood bedroom. It was beautiful, shining in a new morning's light, made entirely of crystal clear glass that she couldn't see through. Not yet. But what lay beyond was calling to her.

"I have to go after her," Sarah tried to explain. "I know she hurt you, but—"

"But she's your daughter." Maddie turned back. "No matter what Trinity did in Ruebens's dream projection, no matter who's controlling her at the center, she's as innocent as you were when your dream wolf commanded you to manipulate peoples' minds. And we're running out of time before Dream Weaver owns her forever."

Storm clouds popped over the horizon, rolling toward them, blocking out the morning sun. Shadows fell. One final truth remained to be told, if this enchanted place was to become reality. One final battle had to be waged. Too many years had passed. Too much hadn't been seen.

"It's beautiful." Richard nodded Sarah's attention back to the door. A pinwheel of purples and blues and greens were swirling across its surface.

"You're not coming back without her," Maddie asked, "are you?"

Richard took Sarah's hand.

"I can't leave my daughter there alone," Sarah said. "I know what they're doing to her. What they did to me. And she doesn't expect anyone to come. She believes she's alone. She tried to make sure of it, she hates herself so much."

It was the same empty nightmare Sarah had lived for too long.

"But the council," Maddie said. "They have to be planning a response to her attack. If they find your mind linked with Trinity—"

"They'll target both of us."

"They'll likely detect your psychic projection as soon as your consciousness emerges wherever Trinity's being held at the center complex," Richard said. "I won't be able to project with you. I'm not strong enough yet. There will be no cloak. Your energy will tip the council off."

"They'll know exactly where to find us." Sarah waited for Maddie's warning. Her sister's demand that Sarah stay there, in her beautiful dream projection, where it was safe.

"You want the council to know you're there, don't you?" Maddie eased away. "Do you know enough, remember enough, to stop Trinity this time?"

"I . . ." Sarah wasn't sure how to answer.

"You know she drew Jeff's attention away from you in the nightmare," Richard said, "when you were who he'd aimed his rifle at."

"And you know she needs you, no matter what she said," Maddie insisted, "or she wouldn't have connected with you in your bedroom in Lenox. The center team was in place. They didn't need her there to distract the Watcher team. And Trinity wouldn't be so angry that you didn't believe she existed if she didn't need you. Remember how hurt you were when I found you at the center? You were out of control. You hated me for not protecting you. You know how that feels, and you know how to get through to Trinity. You have to make her understand that—"

"That I love her." Sarah would remember forever the moment Maddie had finally broken through her Dream Weaver–induced mania. "I have to make her believe that I'll never abandon her again."

"Help her see past the lies in Ruebens's program-

ming. Help her want what you were meant to be together." Richard gazed at the perfection around them.

"Make her want this place." More blood seeped from
Maddie's chest wound. "Make her believe that she's part
of our—"

"Family." Sarah followed her sister's gaze to where
the sand met the sea and the sky swooped low to join
them. "Ruebens tried to take this from us. Trinity's the
final piece of our legacy. I have to make her see that this
is where her gifts belong."

"You will." Madeline pressed her hand to her chest.
"I know you will."

Sarah hugged her twin one last time.

"I don't want to leave you here," she said.

"We'll be fine." Maddie stepped to Richard's side.
"We'll be here waiting for you both."

Richard didn't want to let Sarah go. He never wanted
to be anywhere again, where he couldn't feel her mind
connected with his, feeding his consciousness, making
him stronger and better and more alive just because she
was there.

But Sarah had to protect her child from the showdown
brewing between Trinity and the Brotherhood. She'd
become the Watcher he'd known she could be, which
meant he had to let her go long enough to do her job.

"When Brotherhood sensors detect your psychic move
toward Trinity," he said, "the council should come to
me. I'll do everything I can to convince them to work
with you inside the center. Leave your consciousness
open to that. Give them a chance to trust you again. Give
them a chance to accept Trinity."

Sarah nodded.

She took a long look at the healing place she finally believed her legacy could become.

"Dream of me here." She flowed into his arms and kissed him.

"Always," he promised. Sarah would own his dreams forever.

The vibrant colors flowed outward from the door, expanding until they were just beyond their reach. Sarah turned toward them and their swirling center. Her fingers touched the pinwheel of hues, disappearing to the other side as she moved closer.

She looked back, her eyes shot through with the same mixture of amethyst and turquoise and vivid blues. She smiled at Richard. Then her entire body crossed through and vanished beyond the door, taking the colors of her dream world with her.

CHAPTER THIRTY-TWO

Sarah strained to hear, to see, to feel. But there was nothing in her projection. It was worse than the last ocean dream, when the mission had first begun and she'd been alone in the water. There was no programming to follow here. Nothing to build even a backdrop for the dream. There were no voices or cries. No energy to feel her way through.

There was only Sarah and her need to reach her daughter before the center stole Trinity from her for good. Would her daughter's voice sound the same as in the nightmare? The vision in Lenox? Would she still be determined to punish Sarah? Or had all they'd shared before been warped by Ruebens's programming, and the real Trinity's consciousness was still waiting for Sarah to find her?

In the darkness of her sedated mind, beyond the circuit of energy that her sister and the man she loved had created to help her, beyond the dream reflection of the future she wanted for all of them, Sarah was finally fighting for the truth. All of it. She was searching for the missing piece of her legacy's promise, and she knew exactly where to find it.

Memory sizzled through her, sparking a rush of color and transient light through her mind. She was back in her bedroom in her family's first house. Though the vision was cloaked in shadows, she could see her Barbie pink chenille bedspread. Her favorite stuffed animals. What appeared to be her childhood self sitting on the bed, drowning in the vivid colors she couldn't stop herself from painting on her walls.

Sarah moved further into the vision. She approached the bed, realizing the image of herself sitting cross-legged on the spread was wearing scrubs, not pajamas. Crimson paint coated her hands, paint the color of blood, and her eyes were a clear blue. Once again, her memories had led her to her daughter.

The same as before, Trinity was fixated on the images she'd created on the wall. The mural had been crudely drawn, but the disturbing complexity of its content made up for its lack of finesse. There was a dark sea that perfectly depicted the malevolence of their nightmare. An endless tunnel. The horrifying door. There was a forest within the swirling water, too, filled with a flurry of colors that spoke of need and want and running and belonging. Every edge was jagged. Every color too dark. The manic energy of the brushstrokes had been painted by an unsteady mind.

The wolf was still there, a demonic caricature howling into the ocean, overseeing it, stalking the edges of every horrible event of the last year of Sarah's life, waiting for his chance to go in for the kill. But above it all, beyond the madness, was the seascape Sarah had just left. At the top of Trinity's mural, the sun was shining dawn's glory across perfect sand and docile currents, and brilliant colors were curling into the harmless spray each wave made as it found its way to shore. And it was that picturesque scene that Trinity had washed in crimson.

The future that Sarah longed to create had been all but obliterated by the symbolic wash of too much destruction. Too many battles that had been lost to minds that wanted death instead of redemption. Too much promise had been consumed by deceit. Too many dreams had been lost to nightmares, so the wolf could control a legacy that had been born in death.

"They've controlled you from the very start, haven't they?" Sarah asked the hollow-eyed little girl, trying to understand what this vision and all the others were telling her. "They've controlled your mind and believed no one would ever come looking for you outside Ruebens's nightmare. Except you've been trying to break free of the wolf's hold from the start, just like I did. That's how you found me in Lenox—how you found the memory that would bring me to you. It's why you haunted that place and waited for me all those years, even though you were certain I'd never come. It's why you protected me in the ocean projection. Your mind's never been completely theirs. A part of you never gave up on your own dream of being rescued."

Her daughter wouldn't look at her. It was as if Sarah were gazing at the empty shell of her child. She had no sense of the angry, lost energy she'd felt from Trinity before. But there was no hint of Trinity's light, either.

Sarah dropped to her knees.

"Don't give up." She took Trinity's hands. "You have to keep fighting to break your mind away from them. It's not too late. There's still time."

There was no response.

No flicker of emotion.

But the mural began to move. Seething clouds rolled slowly over the wolf's ocean and the forest Trinity had drawn within it—symbolizing, Sarah somehow knew, that the coming battle between the Brotherhood and the center was building. Sarah could sense Trinity's focus anchored on that conflict, beyond the vision. Her center handlers were preparing to stake their claim on the psychic realm, and to destroy the Watchers who'd sworn to stop them. They would use Trinity to do it.

"I can feel the dark things they want you to do." Sarah squeezed Trinity's hands. "I've always felt them, even though I stayed away too long. I'm here now, and you helped me find you. You helped me dream of this place again."

"*I've been waiting for so long,*" Trinity had said in their Lenox vision. "*I knew you couldn't stay away forever. And I had to see if you were really real . . .*"

"I'm real," Sarah insisted. "And I know you don't want to do what the center's trained you to do. Not all your cries for help were the wolf's programming, or you wouldn't still be here waiting for me. You don't have to fight them alone, Trinity. Let me in, and I'll help you."

The shadows cloaking the room shifted. A warning sound, a wounded animal's growl, rumbled from the little girl's throat. Her daughter's crimson cloud continued to ravage the shoreline at the top of the mural, blocking their view of the peaceful shore Sarah had come from.

"*I had to know,*" Trinity had said before, "*if it was true, what he said. How much you'd hate me . . .*"

"I don't hate you," Sarah insisted. "Let me help you

break away from this place. Talk to me, Trinity. I won't let you give up."

The way Richard hadn't let Sarah go, no matter how hard she'd fought him. His unspoken love had been hers, it had saved her, long before she'd let herself want it.

"He said if you found me," Trinity had said, *"all you'd do is run . . ."*

"I'm here to stay," Sarah promised her daughter, remembering Maddie's pledge to do the same, when Sarah had been lost. "I'm never going away again, no matter what happens. Tell the center I'm here. Maybe they already know. Tell them you have me. Deliver me up on a silver platter. I don't care. My mind's not moving from this reality, from this place where you wanted me, until you come with me, Trinity. So if you really do want me dead, then get it over with."

The next sound Trinity made was so soft, so close to a little girl's whimper, Sarah knew for the first time what being a mother was like. Hearing her daughter's pain hurt worse than Trinity's screams ever had.

"Leave me alone," the child on the bed said, still staring at the wall.

Her voice was so soft. So vulnerable. The cynical edge from their nightmare was gone. The brittle hatred that had led Trinity to strike out against Maddie and Richard and the other Watchers she thought Sarah wanted more was fading. Trinity was more shadow than flesh here. More lost.

"You can't be alone anymore," Sarah said. "Like it or not, I'm a part of you."

"You hate him." The wolf in the mural howled, his voice taking on Trinity's growl from earlier.

"Yes," Sarah agreed. "But I love you."

"Shut up!" Trinity scrambled off the bed, moving to the other side. The dimness around them lifted even more, revealing the fear in her blue eyes. "Why are you here?"

"I'm here because I'm stronger than Ruebens thought I'd be. I'm not fighting alone, the way he wanted me to. The center's plan for you, for us, is failing. Look . . ."

The clouds representing the center's assault on the Brotherhood no longer consumed the mural. As they retreated, more of the manic flourish of color and brush strokes beneath were revealed. Crimson still stained Sarah's idealistic shoreline and dream sunrise, but the images beneath the bloodred haze were stronger, too, more vibrant, while the wolf's picture began to fade. He was still growling, but they could no longer hear what he was saying.

The painting was evolving beyond Trinity's control.

"Stop it." The little girl stomped her foot, her fists clenched into tiny balls. "You can't be here. You can't—"

"I am here, right where you've dreamed I'd find you. My memories of this place have been here with you from the start."

Sarah looked back to the bed separating them, her head pounding. An image of herself as a child materialized, her hands covered in all the colors from her dreams. The bright colors that were coming to life in Trinity's mural.

"Stop it!" Tears glittered in her daughter's eyes. "You'll ruin everything."

"No," Sarah said. "We'll fix everything. Together. But some things need to be ruined first, so we can see what's really there."

Sarah was finally connecting with her child, with the secret legacy that she'd run from. And their psychic energies were mingling, beginning to paint the same pictures, even if their emotions were still disconnected. The childhood image of Sarah in the middle of the bed pushed to her knees. She stood, her legs shaking as the mattress sagged. The little girl looked to Sarah, then to Trinity. She lifted her color-soaked hands to the mural.

"No!" Trinity scrambled onto the bed and grabbed the child's hands before Sarah's childhood image could spread more color on the wall. "Go away. Leave me alone. It's all I have left . . ."

"It's not real," Sarah's childhood image said. She strained to reach the mural. "You've never been real. If you stay here, you'll be—"

"Nothing," Sarah said, conquering the last of the paralyzing fear that had controlled her life since she was a child.

Sarah had let herself become nothing in the darkness of her coma. That nothing had primed her to fall under the control of Ruebens's Dream Weaver programming. It had been where she'd connected with her daughter's energy inside Trinity's nightmare. Fear of who they were and the psychic legacy they'd inherited had become a maze still threatening to trap both their minds forever.

The mural was a reflection of each thing Trinity's powers had achieved. Of course Trinity was desperate to protect it. But to the child, none of it had been real beyond her mind. The center had made certain Trinity felt like nothing beyond their commands. She hadn't been allowed to dream beyond her programming. She wasn't supposed to know how to feel anything but what she'd been brainwashed into feeling since she was a baby. But both were happening now, through her growing link to Sarah.

"You don't have to be afraid." Sarah approached the struggling little girls on the bed. "I'm here now. You don't want the darkness you were born into. You never have. And you know I'm the only person outside your world who can get you out. Let me help you."

Sarah climbed onto the bed. Her fingers now dripping in amethyst and greens and a prism of blues, too, she grabbed the children's clasped fists and pressed all their hands to the mural.

A rainbow of colored light shot outward from the point of contact, illuminating the churning sea and its windswept forest, enhancing every image with deeper clarity. The horrible door became the dazzling, transparent portal Sarah had just passed through. The nightmare's tunnel dissolved under the light's attack, disappearing completely. The wolf snarled mutely at the truth bubbling up from the ocean's floor, then he and his hateful sea were gone completely.

"You're ruining it," Trinity cried.

"You called me for help," Sarah and her childhood reflection said in unison. "That makes this my vision, too."

"I don't want you here."

Sarah looked through the shimmering door in the mural. Early-morning sunlight glared from a shoreline she could barely see. Her new dream was waiting, no storm clouds in sight.

"The center doesn't even know I'm here, do they?" she asked. "You're shielding me from your handlers. You're protecting me, just like you did in the dream. Otherwise, someone would have tried to stop us by now."

"I hate you!" Trinity shouted.

"You hate what you've become. That's what you've been trying to tell me. You want to be free of this place."

That darkness of what Ruebens had tried to create in both of them hadn't been able to destroy Sarah's connection with her daughter. There'd always been a new beginning waiting for them here, where Trinity's dreams remained childlike, untouched, and waiting to be saved.

"If you hate me so much," Sarah said, "why is our light changing your mural?"

Sarah continued to press the little hands she held to the painting's shifting face. The illumination from their touch spread toward the sunrise vista at the top of the painting. Trinity's crimson cloud softened to a rosy hue, then closer to a transparent pink, revealing more of the beautiful images beneath.

"Let me go!" Trinity screamed.

"Never," Sarah and her childhood image both said.

"I'm not—"

"You're loved," Sarah insisted. "You're part of the light on the other side of the door. It's a dream that Ruebens never touched. It's the future you wanted, when you called to me for help. And it can be real, Trinity."

"No."

"The rest of the painting is disappearing. None of it matters now, except that it brought me here to be with you."

"You . . ." Trinity stopped fighting. She squeezed her eyes shut. Impossibly large tears leaked from their corners. "You never came."

"I'm here now. And I'm not alone. Neither are you. Not anymore."

"They'll hate me." The hitch in the child's voice begged Sarah to tell her she was wrong. "Your Watchers—"

"They'll help you. They'll help me fix the damage the center's done to your mind."

"They'll never believe me." Trinity slumped against the wall. "I killed—"

"The men you hurt aren't dead. Neither is my sister. In fact, she's waiting for you there in your painting, where the forest meets the sea."

"She's afraid of me."

"She's afraid of me, too." Sarah smiled, because she trusted her twin to stay by her side, regardless. "I'm afraid of what we're all becoming. But that won't stop me from dreaming. Not anymore. I'm going to keep dreaming and fighting for the light and the promise our legacy was created to be. You should see it, Trinity. It's a beautiful place."

"I . . . I can't see it."

The child squeezed her eyes shut. Her crimson stain over the ocean vista wavered. The remainder of the mural blinked out, disappearing completely.

"That's right," Sarah praised. "The nightmares are other peoples' visions. Let them go. Let me show you how to build your own dreams. Let me take you to a place where you won't have to be scared anymore. You won't have to hate what you're becoming."

"I don't want to." But Trinity's body was shaking, her fear escaping her shields and racing into Sarah's thoughts through the connection of their intertwined fingers. "I can't. They'll be there. They'll—"

"They'll love you, too."

Trinity's eyes shot open. Dark currents of hatred replaced the anxiety Sarah had felt rolling off her. Sarah winced. Her skin burned from her daughter's touch.

"They'll kill me!" Trinity's tiny body barreled headfirst into Sarah, shoving her away from the mural. "You're all trying to wake me up, so you can kill me."

"Wake you up?"

Sarah stared down at the tiny body still shoving against her, trying with less and less conviction to push her away.

"You're . . ." Sarah grabbed Trinity's shoulders and shook her until the child stopped fighting. "You're asleep. That's how they control you, by keeping you asleep when they need your powers. Just like Richard first trained me in my coma. If you wake up, they can't use you to attack the Brotherhood's mission to invade the center."

"Leave me alone," the child begged. "It's a trick. I don't want to die. They said if I wake up without them, I'll die. They'll—"

"You're not going to die, Trinity. The Watchers will come for you. They'll protect you. But you have to wake up and stop whatever the center's about to do. You have to tell me how to reach you."

"You can't make me." A new bout of fury blasted them. "You're all trying to make me do things I don't want to, and I won't. I won't do it anymore. Leave me alone! I just want to be alone."

Trinity shoved harder than before, knocking Sarah

off-balance. Off the bed. Sarah clung to her child as they sailed through the air, crashing onto unforgiving tile instead of the fluffy carpet of Sarah's childhood bedroom. Her senses were scrambling, melting. Her ears rang from impact while she blocked the razor-sharp nails of the little girl who'd landed on top of her.

Trinity's fear and desperation and exhaustion clawed at them, ripping at their skin. Colors consumed them, exploding through their minds until nothing was left but dazzling white. Blinding white. Searing light binding them together and filling the link they'd formed with every memory Trinity had pushed away. Each distant sensation and muffled voice and unavoidable demand that had been made on her vulnerable mind. All of them impersonal and remote and unattached, while a lonely child's heart had begged for help.

"I'm here," Sarah said to her daughter. "I'll help you. I'm finally here, and I'll never leave you again. I promise, Trinity. Wake up for me. You don't have to keep sleeping or dreaming about anything you don't want. Never again. I love you, honey. If you can't believe anything else, believe that. Wake up, Trinity."

The seconds that followed while Trinity's struggles grew weaker and weaker stretched on forever until the child finally collapsed, lying limp in Sarah's arms.

"Mommy?" a tiny voice asked, the light of Trinity's nondreaming consciousness stirring to life within the vision.

CHAPTER THIRTY-THREE

"Explain yourself, Colonel," Jacob said the instant Richard's eyes opened.

Richard shook his head, unclogging the memory circuits he'd designed his suppression meds to deaden. Jacob, not the elder's hologram, was standing across Richard's detention cell, his floor-length white robe billowing around him.

"We've already tried that," Richard said. "By now, you've obviously determined that Sarah and her sister and I might still be useful to the Brotherhood. What else do you need to know?"

"How long has Sarah Temple been capable of projecting beyond your chemical protocol?"

"Since the night Trinity's nightmare first consumed her mind. Her legacy's grown far beyond our control."

"And you? Surveillance detected psychic activity emanating from this location, as well as from Madeline and Sarah Temple's cells."

"I'm part of who Sarah's becoming. If you don't trust her and her twin, you have no reason to trust me."

"At the same time, we detected no target for the projection."

"What?" Richard pushed himself up on his bunk, sitting with his head hanging, his eyes closed. Even the cell's recessed lighting was too painful for his hangover to process. "How long . . . When did the bunker's sensors detect Sarah's projection with Trinity?"

"Then she has gone after the child? And your mind isn't still linked with hers."

"How long ago?"

"Half an hour."

"But there was no answering surge at the center?"

"No."

"You have a team in place to infiltrate the complex," Richard reasoned. "But you haven't yet tried to take the center down. Something has you spooked. What aren't you telling me?"

"Can you feel Sarah now?" Jacob asked.

Richard had been trying to since his mind began digging itself out of unconsciousness.

"There's nothing where our link should be," he admitted to his elder. Sweat beaded on his forehead despite the room's chill. "But I trust her to—"

"We've just detected a psychic burst from the center. The energy readings are stronger than anything we've ever encountered, and they don't match Ms. Temple's psychic imprint or the imprint of any other consciousness we've tracked."

"She's found Trinity." Richard smiled. "That's my girl."

"That's our suspicion. The question is, why? Why would there be a flash of activity now, after thirty minutes of psychic silence?"

"It could be a trap, but the center's already baited their hook. They already think they're reeling us in."

"Exactly why I'm contemplating pulling the infiltration team back from the complex. More unknowns are not what we need, when we're targeting an adversary this volatile."

"Something has changed. Something the center wasn't expecting."

"Such as?" Jacob's gaze sharpened. His mind swept the thoughts and emotions Richard kept open as he analyzed the situation.

"Don't call off the team." Richard pushed himself to his feet, ignoring the way the room dipped and spun around them. "Send the team in. Now. But on a recovery mission, not an assault."

"Recovering whom?"

"Trinity. If you can read her energy but not her mother's, she's sending us a signal. The center itself would have no reason to tip its hand and show us Trinity's location. The child's asking to be brought in, before her handlers—"

"You're suggesting I order the extraction of a consciousness that's strong enough to block the psychic projections of a woman whose unstable gifts have already grown beyond our control?"

"I'm suggesting you bring in the Temple Legacy, sir. And the details about center tactics she'll deliver."

"We're already in position to shut the complex down. We have all the information we need."

"Not about the details Trinity extracted from Lieutenant Coleridge about our legacies. Whether the center's research facility itself survives, the organization behind it and the government already have intel on our principals. Trinity knows what they know. She may be able to tell us who they'll hit first. We need to know more about the government's overall plan."

"The strike team can access that intel from the complex."

"Assuming their mission is successful. The center's expecting an assault, not a covert infiltration. Take them off guard, secure information they'll have no way of recovering, and we have an advantage it'll be hard for them to recover from. We'll have Trinity."

"What about the programming they've embedded to control the child's mind, the way they've continued to control her mother's?" Jacob linked his hands together in his robe's front placket.

"Sarah will help me remove the center's latent foot-prints. Both of the twins are ready to do whatever it takes to reclaim Trinity and their legacy."

"You truly can't sense Sarah Temple?" Jacob's mind began peeling away the layers of Richard's conscious-ness until he reached Richard's memories from Sarah's idealized seashore.

"No." Richard slapped his hand to the wall, bracing himself against the strain of accepting Jacob's presence in his mind. "I can't reach her now."

"But you believe she'll bring Trinity's consciousness back to you and her twin."

"Yes."

"You believe," Jacob said, continuing to read Rich-ard's truth, "the child's been a pawn, and that the mother will be able to negate the center's programming. You believe they'll both be assets to the Brotherhood."

"Yes." Sarah had already succeeded. The surge of psychic energy at the center was proof that she'd reached Trinity. Richard refused to consider any other explanation.

Jacob's consciousness retreated.

Richard sagged but managed to stay on his feet.

"How much of your belief," Jacob asked, "is your fear of losing your mate, and how much is your intuition as a Watcher?"

"Both, equally, sir." Richard ignored the migraine pounding behind his eyes. He stayed on his feet by picturing the smile he knew he'd see on Sarah's face once she was holding her child in her arms. "To be everything I can for the psychic realm, I need Sarah in my life. So does the Brotherhood. She and her daughter and her twin are integral to all our paths. To win the war we're facing, we need legacies like the Temples fighting by our side, even if it means sitting out a few battles. We need them, sir, even more than they need us."

CHAPTER THIRTY-FOUR

Sarah's mind woke with her child's in the white-on-white lab from Trinity's nightmare. Her daughter was curled in her arms, quietly crying, clinging, and more real than Sarah had ever dreamed possible.

It was still a projection. Trinity still lay within her center laboratory alone, Sarah in her cell at the bunker. But her mind and Sarah's were linked now. Completely. Trinity finally trusted her.

"It's going to be okay." Within their projection, Sarah stroked Trinity's silky hair. "I know you're afraid. But you're not alone."

"They're coming." Trinity was shaking.

"The Watchers who are coming will help you. But you have to—"

"The doctors. They'll know I'm awake. They'll send me back."

"Shh. . . ."

Sarah noticed for the first time the equipment around her daughter's bed. The tapes and leads and tubes attached to her child, feeding monitors and readings. There was no one else in sight. Her gaze flew to the door. How long did they have before that changed?

"Trinity?" She sat up and pulled her daughter with her, praying she was helping her little girl become more conscious within her real lab. "Honey, I need you to focus on the door. Lock it, Trinity. Do whatever you have to so your doctors can't get in. Then detach the monitors and sensors they're tracking you with."

"But—"

"Please, you have to trust me, so I can help you from where I am. You have to buy yourself time until your Watchers arrive."

Where was the Watcher team?

Sarah reached for Richard's mind but still couldn't sense him. She looked down to find Trinity staring across the lab. The same red haze that had marred Sarah's shoreline in the vision's mural was oozing over the door, until it completely covered it. The tubes and wires attached to Trinity began to fall away, including the IV hooked to the shunt in her chest.

"Good girl," Sarah pulled her daughter closer in their shared dream. She wiped Trinity's tears away and gauged the alertness of her gaze. "Now let me talk to Richard."

"No! He'll—"

"He'll help you. The Watchers are coming to help you. Let me prove it, honey. Let me show you his mind."

"He'll hate me." Trinity buried her head against Sarah's neck. "Everyone will hate me."

The door rattled behind the barrier Trinity had painted. The little girl whimpered.

Sarah saw a brief flash of her daughter's reality. Trinity lay on a bunk, alone in a room with walls of glass, her eyes almost completely closed as she pretended to sleep. The jumble of wires and tubes from the monitors and other equipment were no longer attached to her. A team of scientists stood on the other side of the transparent walls, an elaborate observation suite beyond them. No one could reach the door or the floor-to-ceiling windows protecting Trinity—as if an invisible field were holding them back.

The men were furious. Arguing. Strategizing how to force their way through.

"They'll hate me now, too," Trinity cried in the vision, curling deeper into Sarah's arms. "They said I'd die if I woke up without them."

"The Watchers will get you out before the doctors can reach you. But you have to help them, honey. You have to trust them."

"They're not coming. Not for me."

"They're already here." Sarah pushed her child away until they were looking into each other's eyes, the vision feeling more real by the second. "I'm a Watcher, Trinity. And I came for you. I'm your guide out. You're awake. You've trusted me this far. Now let us help you be free of this horrible place forever."

The anger in Trinity's mind was gone. There wasn't a hint of the hate from Ruebens's programming. There was only shock and confusion and the smallest flicker of hope staring back at Sarah from her child's blue eyes.

"You came for me?" she asked.

"As soon as I knew about you. As soon as I woke from our last nightmare, I started making my way back to you, honey. And I'm never leaving, whether you let the other Watchers help you or not. If you stay, I'll be here. Right here, with you. Whatever the center does next, they'll do it to both of us."

"You . . . you won't make me go back to the night-mares?"

"No more nightmares," she promised her child, "for either of us. No more living for nothing but other peoples' dreams. The Watchers won't let the center take either of us there again. Now let me contact them."

Within their vision, Trinity looked beyond her transparent walls, toward the angry men grouped on the other side. Then her tiny hand reached for Sarah's cheek. Her touch flashed a rainbow of color through their minds as Sarah's senses rushed back.

"Richard?" Sarah called with her mind. *"Trinity's awake. She's been inside a center lab all this time."*

"I'm here." His response was instantaneous. *"We picked up her energy spike. A recovery team's entered the complex undetected. They're on the way to her. Get Trinity ready to move."*

"She's terrified." Sarah's eyes filled with tears. *"There are men everywhere, the men who experimented on her mind and fed her nightmares."*

"Talk her through it. Prepare her, so the team won't sense her as a threat. The Watcher team will take care of the rest. But she has to go willingly. She has to be willing to leave or the elders will call off the recovery."

"It's the raven," gasped the shaking little girl in Sarah's arms.

"His name's Richard," Sarah assured her. "He looked out for me when the center hurt me. Now he wants to help me look out for you."

"Is . . . is he coming?"

"His friends are. They'll be here soon. You have to go with them."

"Watchers?" More tears flowed. More fear.

"Friends. Your family. Leave your mind open to them. They'll make the men on the other side of the wall go away, then they'll get you out. They'll bring you to me."

"And the seashore? From the painting? I don't like the ocean, but I like the pretty sand and the clouds in the sky over the water."

"Then that will be our first dream together."

Sarah clung to their vision, desperate to hold the little girl in real life. To introduce her to her aunt and soon-to-be uncle, and to Richard. To the world opening up for their legacy.

"We'll paint a dream of the shore together, honey, while we get rid of everything these horrible people have done to your mind. You're the light in my dreams. You're the sun just starting to rise above the ocean, making all the beautiful colors in the sky possible. Remember that, when your Watcher friends come. Remember the dream we'll create once they take you away from the center."

Trinity clung to her in their vision, her head nodding as she tried to believe. Beyond her glass walls, there was a flash of light, a strobe of energy as Watchers dressed in black fatigues stormed the observation room. Scientists tried to relay for help. They were stopped instantly. Not with the automatic weapons Ruebens had programmed into Trinity and Sarah's ocean nightmare, but with the expertly trained minds of the warriors the Brotherhood had sent to claim her little girl.

Sarah saw another flash from her daughter's reality: a child's head rolling to the side to watch her rescuers subdue the last of the men who'd tormented her.

"They're here," Sarah projected to Richard.

"They can't push through her control over the lab's door," he said. *"She has to let them in, Sarah. Tell Trinity to drop her shields. There's no time. She has to let them in now."*

"Trinity?" Sarah said in their dream. "Let your new friends in, so you can come dream with me. I'm waiting for you, honey."

Trinity swallowed, her consciousness flooding Sarah's with so many emotions, Sarah closed her eyes to keep her mind from flinching away. Hope. Fear. Betrayal. Fury. All of it strong, just like her little girl. And weak, just as Sarah herself had been when she'd done the unthinkable and allowed herself to trust Richard.

"Come back to me, Trinity." Sarah pressed her cheek to her child's. She'd never been more terrified than she was in that moment, as she waited, helplessly, for the Brotherhood to rescue the secret part of her she'd left behind at the center. The best part of her. "Come see what we've become."

Then suddenly the Watchers were beside Trinity's bed, both in Sarah's dream with her child and in Trinity's reality. One of the warriors lifted Trinity into his arms.

"Mommy?" the little girl cried as she was rushed out the door, her arms reaching behind her to where Sarah still sat by the empty bed in their dream. "Help me!"

"I'm right here, honey." The Watchers disappeared as quickly as they'd arrived. Sarah's link to her daughter blurred to a blinding white. "I'm right here," she promised. "They're bringing you to me. Stay with your Watchers. Stay with them. Trinity? Trinity!"

Chapter Thirty-Five

Her daughter's lab faded.

Trinity's cries faded.

Their dream dissolved until Sarah could no longer feel her child.

She fought to hold on, to be sure that Trinity was safely away from the center. But familiar arms were pulling her close, pulling her back, anchoring her to another reality. She could sense a strong mind, an even stronger heart, that she couldn't deny. Medication flew through her veins, opening her senses to the world beyond her closed eyes.

"Wake up, Sarah." Richard's voice was coming from the other side of sleep instead of through their link.

"Trinity?" she asked, still sensing her child, but there was nothing to see when her mind reached for their link.

"She's safe," Richard said. "They're bringing her straight here."

"Richard?" Sarah clung to the sound of his voice and the solid strength of him leaning close, and the brush of his fingers, his lips, against her face.

"Come back to me, Sarah."

Her eyes flickered open. "Richard?"

"I'm right here." He smiled down to her. "So is

Madeline. She's coming around, too. Jarred's pacing a trench in the floor next to her."

"But . . ." The bunker's lab came into focus around Sarah.

She was wearing the same scrubs she'd had on when they began the dream mission into her nightmare. She was lying on the same table Richard had settled her onto after the planning meeting. It was as if none of the rest had happened. As if her misfiring brain had dreamed up every bit of it.

But that wasn't possible.

It couldn't be possible.

"Trinity." Sarah pushed up until she was sitting. "I know I met her. I found her. Tell me it's real. My daughter's real. Where is she?"

"She's real. You found her. She's only a few minutes away." Richard pressed Sarah back to the table. "The team was able to cloak their movement once they were beyond the complex. They even think . . ."

"What?"

A moan shifted Sarah's attention to her sister, who was waking on the exam table beside her. Jarred hovered over his fiancée. Sarah reached for her twin's hand. She could feel her sister's mind more clearly through the contact. And with Maddie's centering presence, she could feel Trinity's fear drawing closer. She could sense her child's disorientation at being outside, being driven quickly through the night, being surrounded by strangers, being carried again.

"I'm here," Sarah tried to project to her, but there was no response.

"Her extraction team's shielding her mind." Richard

brushed Sarah's bangs from her eyes. "They believe Trinity's strengthening their reach. That she helped them escape the complex without their movements being detected."

"Her Watchers . . . They have to—"

"They're being very careful with her. She's not resisting. I can feel her, too, Sarah. I can feel her through you. She's doing remarkably well."

An innocent mind. A damaged mind that had never known life beyond suppression and control, loneliness and anger, and—

"Mommy?" Trinity called.

"I'm here, honey." Sarah pushed herself up again.

"They're—" Richard said.

"Inside the bunker." Through Trinity, Sarah saw the side entrance from the woods. A rush of images followed: hallway, elevator, strong bodies moving in a protective circle. Each observation swam with a little girl's panic as Trinity was rushed deeper into the ground, inside once more, shut away from a world she'd never seen.

"I have to—" Sarah's legs buckled as soon as her feet hit the ground. Richard caught her against him. "I have to go to her." She tried to step away.

"She's here," Richard said a second before a six-man Watcher team entered the lab.

One of the men—Donovan—walked straight to Sarah, the beautiful dark-haired child in his arms twisting in his grasp, her arms opening.

"Trinity?" Sarah was engulfed in the sweetest, most delicate hug imaginable. Her child was shaking so badly, and they were both so weak, Sarah was able to hold on to Trinity only because Richard wrapped his arms around them both. "What's wrong? What happened?"

She cupped Trinity's head to her shoulder, and her daughter's silent tears soaked into her scrubs. Richard's hand covered hers. She turned and tried to lay Trinity on the exam table.

"No!" The child clung like a vine, arms and legs tightening. She burrowed her head into the crook between Sarah's neck and shoulder. "Don't let go!"

"I've got you." Sarah sat down instead, pulling her daughter deeper into her lap. "I'll never let you go, honey. I'm here."

"Lieutenant Donovan?" Richard asked while he felt for Trinity's pulse at the base of her neck, then looked into her eyes with the device he used to gauge pupil reflexes.

"She's been agitated," the lieutenant said, "but cooperative. We could sense . . . her mind searching ours. There was no malicious intent. She definitely assisted our escape. We got out clean thanks to your intel on the complex's layout and her augmenting our shields."

"Good girl." Sarah kissed her child's cheek, sensing that Trinity wasn't hearing a word.

It was too much activity. Too much stimulation. Too many voices and minds and images after being locked away alone in room full of windows like a prize rat in its maze.

"You did so good, honey," Sarah projected. *"It's going to be okay. We're going to make everything okay."*

"I can't . . ." Trinity's mind sent back. *"Don't make me, Mommy. I can't . . . I don't want to. I never wanted to. Don't make me . . ."*

"No one's going to make you do any of those horrible things

again. We know you didn't want to. You're free now. We'll never let the center have you again."

Clouds, dark with fear, edged with the crimson of Trinity's rage, flowed through Sarah's mind. Agony seared through her already-crippling headache. She glanced to Richard and caught his flinch. Donovan braced himself against the barrage of energy as well. His eyes narrowed. He and the entire team inhaled. Slow. Deep. As one, they exhaled. All of them were using Richard's techniques to help her daughter, because each Watcher understood exactly what Trinity was going through.

"She's losing control," Maddie said.

Jarred helped Sarah's twin sit up on her table. She was pale and shaking. Her chest was heavily bandaged. But Maddie was smiling at the image of Sarah and Richard cuddling Trinity close.

"I need everyone out of here," Sarah said to the room. "I need to be alone with her and my family, so we can calm her down."

Donovan's gaze shifted to Richard.

Richard's nod released him.

The Watcher team turned to go.

"Thank you," Sarah said to the men, her gratitude warring with her lingering resentment toward the Brotherhood. "Thank you so much for protecting my little girl. My legacy. You're all . . ."

"You're welcome." Donovan waited while his team preceded him from the dream lab. He studied the quietly crying child in Sarah's arms, a hint of a smile kicking up the corners of his mouth. "It was our pleasure."

The lab's door slid shut behind him, sealing Sarah's

family within its protective walls. Richard crouched until he was looking up at Sarah.

"The council's given us whatever time we need to stabilize Trinity," he said. "They'll debrief the recovery team first, before they'll need your report."

"How?" she asked, feeling his calm, soothing energy easing her and Trinity's confusion. "How did you talk the elders into all this?"

"Logic," her gypsy answered with a devilish glint in his eyes. He patted Trinity's back, smiling when she didn't cringe at his touch. "Unemotional, unattached, objective logic. It was the most important con of my life, and I failed miserably. Jacob saw right through it. He saw my love for you and the complete conflict of interest our relationship has become. And he still made the right choice for the psychic realm. Because you had gotten through to Trinity enough for her to send us the sign we needed."

Sarah clutched her child tighter.

"We came so close to losing everything," she said.

"But you're here now." Maddie placed her hand over Richard's on Trinity's back.

"We all are." Jarred added his touch to their physical link, all of them merging with Trinity's mind, their energy washing through her panic like cool, healing water.

Trinity sighed, her body relaxing against Sarah's, the storm clouds in her mind receding. One tiny arm slipped up to encircle Sarah's neck. Her thumb popped into her mouth. It might have been an immature coping reflex for a six-year-old who'd seen and done the things this powerful six-year-old had. But in so many ways Trinity was still a baby. An innocent, untouched consciousness waiting to soak up the light and the positive energy she'd been denied for so long.

"She's falling asleep." Richard rubbed away the tears leaking from Sarah's eyes. "She finally feels safe."

Sarah looked around the brotherhood's lab, built by her brilliant warrior not just to help her and Maddie, but to help them all prepare for this exact moment. The war wasn't over. The psychic realm was still in play, and none of them knew for sure how much tactical information the center had acquired through Jeff and Trinity's link.

But another innocent mind, a critical legacy, had been saved. A new bond had been forged. The Brotherhood would live to fight another day, stronger and wiser than before.

"We're finally home." Sarah smiled into her daughter's curls as Richard stood.

"Yes, you are." He kissed her while Trinity's mind drifted into a deep sleep that would be free of nightmares.

"Dream of me," Sarah whispered into Trinity's ear. "I'll be waiting by our seashore, where the sun's just beginning to rise . . ."

INTERACT WITH DORCHESTER ONLINE!

Want to learn more about your favorite books and authors?
Want to talk with other readers that like to read the same books as you?
Want to see up-to-the-minute Dorchester news?

VISIT DORCHESTER AT:
DorchesterPub.com
Twitter.com/DorchesterPub
Facebook.com (Search Pages)

DISCUSS DORCHESTER'S NOVELS AT:
Dorchester Forums at DorchesterPub.com
GoodReads.com
LibraryThing.com
Myspace.com/books
Shelfari.com
WeRead.com

9 781428 511118